W9-ARX-153

THE
SLAYER
CHRONICLES

FIRST
KILL

▼

Kai
Lambert

· HEATHER BREWER ·

THE SLAYER CHRONICLES

FIRST KILL

speak

An Imprint of Penguin Group (USA) Inc.

SPEAK
Published by the Penguin Group
Penguin Group (USA) Inc., 345 Hudson Street, New York, New York 10014, U.S.A.
Penguin Group (Canada), 90 Eglinton Avenue East, Suite 700, Toronto, Ontario, Canada M4P 2Y3
(a division of Pearson Penguin Canada Inc.)
Penguin Books Ltd, 80 Strand, London WC2R 0RL, England
Penguin Ireland, 25 St Stephen's Green, Dublin 2, Ireland (a division of Penguin Books Ltd)
Penguin Group (Australia), 250 Camberwell Road, Camberwell, Victoria 3124, Australia
(a division of Pearson Australia Group Pty Ltd)
Penguin Books India Pvt Ltd, 11 Community Centre, Panchsheel Park, New Delhi – 110 017, India
Penguin Group (NZ), 67 Apollo Drive, Rosedale, Auckland 0632, New Zealand
(a division of Pearson New Zealand Ltd.)
Penguin Books (South Africa) (Pty) Ltd, 24 Sturdee Avenue, Rosebank, Johannesburg 2196, South Africa

Penguin Books Ltd, Registered Offices: 80 Strand, London WC2R 0RL, England

First published in the United States of America by Dial Books,
an imprint of Penguin Group (USA) Inc., 2011
Published by Speak, an imprint of Penguin Group (USA) Inc., 2012

3 5 7 9 10 8 6 4 2

Copyright © Heather Brewer, 2011
All rights reserved

THE LIBRARY OF CONGRESS HAS CATALOGED THE DIAL BOOKS EDITION AS FOLLOWS:
Brewer, Heather.
First kill/by Heather Brewer.—1st ed.
p. cm.—(The Slayer chronicles; 1)
Summary: The summer before ninth grade, when Joss sets off to meet his uncle
and hunt down the beast that murdered his younger sister three years earlier,
he learns he is destined to join the Slayer Society.
ISBN 978-0-8037-3741-9 (hardcover)
[1. Vampires—Fiction. 2. Horror stories.] I. Title. PZ7.B75695Chrv 2011 [Fic]—dc22 2011006061

Speak ISBN 978-0-14-242196-3

Designed by Jason Henry
Set in Meridien

Printed in the United States of America

All rights reserved. No part of this book may be reproduced, scanned, or distributed
in any printed or electronic form without permission. Please do not participate
in or encourage piracy of copyrighted materials in violation of the author's rights.
Purchase only authorized editions.

ALWAYS LEARNING   PEARSON

To my Minion Horde:
Without you, I am nothing.

▶ ACKNOWLEDGMENTS ◀

First and foremost, an incredible amount of gratitude is due to my editor, Liz Waniewski, for her brilliance and saintlike patience. You make me a better writer, Liz, and the world needs more people like you in it.

Much love, respect, and props go to my fabulous agent, Michael Bourret, who keeps me (somewhat) sane and on the road to success, no matter what.

Well-deserved thanks and high-fives to Team Vlad at Penguin Young Readers. You know who you are, and I owe you big-time for your support, your friendship, and your unfailing belief in me and my characters. Without your blood, sweat, and tears, who knows where Vlad (and now Joss) would be?

Hugs and kisses to my incredibly supportive sister, Dawn Vanniman, for being there for me, and for being awesome. And all sorts of love to my Minions, who understand me like I understand them. You get me like nobody else does, Minions, and this book is for you.

Paul, Jacob, and Alexandria—you never fail to amaze me, Brewer Clan. When I am down, you lift me up. When I am sad, you make me laugh. And when I am telling you all about what the voices in my head told me to do, you nod and smile in the way that I need you to. Thank you for being my everything. I couldn't do any of this without you.

CONTENTS

▼ ▼ ▼

THE SLAYER CHRONICLES

FIRST KILL

▼

PROLOGUE

Abraham's heels clicked along the marble floor as he moved the length of the room. His breaths were even, as usual, but there was a tension in his muscles—an imminent dread that was impossible to ignore. The room was dim, the only light pouring in from the arched windows all along its longer side. It was growing dark. The sun was setting behind the building, casting a warm orange glow across the sky. Outside the window, the shadowed London Eye stood watch.

Seated in a tall, ornately carved chair at the end of the room was a man in his eighties, his hair frosty white. His eyes spoke with wisdom beyond anything that Abraham had yet to experience. To the old man's left and right were several smaller, but just as ornate, chairs holding several other people, each of varying age and experience. Abraham knew each of them—some better than others—but no words or expressions of greeting were offered. This was not a social visit. He had been summoned for a distinct and important purpose.

As Abraham approached, he knelt, following the usual pomp and circumstance of a Slayer Society Headquarters meeting. With a nod, the old man gestured for him to stand and respond to his summons. Abraham stood, cleared his throat, and began. "Masters, you have called me here with a question—the question of who will be next in my bloodline worthy of serving our noble cause. I submit to you that I have seen evidence of the Slayer gene in my nephew Greg McMillan, and call upon you for permission to approach the boy with enlightenment."

A murmur passed through the gathered group, one filled with a doubt that troubled Abraham, though he would never admit to it. Once the murmurs had quieted, the elderly man spoke. "You have been called upon to answer that question, yes, Abraham. But what of the child we have asked about? He seems far more likely to wield a stake someday than your nephew Greg. As you know from tracing the bloodline, it has been determined that the next Slayer in your family will likely be a niece or nephew. But it is highly more likely that the child will be fostered by your brother Harold than your brother Michael. The genetic tests that we've run on hair and blood samples collected from both your brothers show that the Slayer gene is in its dormant state within Harold's genes, which means that his offspring are the likely receivers. The odds of this gene skipping generations and miraculously appearing within one of Michael's children is preposterous."

Abraham counted two heartbeats before he spoke again. "Harold has a son and daughter. But neither Joss nor Cecile seems the right fit for the Society's needs. Both are far too emotional, and—"

"They are children, and children are emotional creatures, Abraham." The old man waved his hand dismissively through the air. "Tell us more about your nephew Joss."

Abraham paused. He was never one to openly disagree with the Society's whims, but for a brief moment, he hesitated before answering. "Joss is currently ten years of age. Smart enough, with quick reflexes and adequate speed. But he lacks the drive to further his physical attributes, to better himself in that regard, of his own accord."

"He is not yet training age. Eight more years may awaken that drive within him."

Abraham's chest tightened. "He is also incredibly empathetic."

"He has a scientific mind."

"He is not the next Slayer." Despite his mastery of self-control, Abraham's voice rose, echoing off the walls of the Slayer Society Headquarters. Once he realized it, he dropped his eyes in shame.

The old man leaned forward, his demeanor calm, his expression full of compassion. "We believe that he is, Abraham. The sooner you come to accept that, the sooner you can begin preparations for his training."

Abraham shook his head, his eyes still on the marble floor below. When he spoke, his voice had softened to a near whisper, as if to make up for his previous tone. "Joss is weak. Not just emotionally. Physically. I'm not sure he could survive the training."

The man sighed heavily and sat back in his chair. "Then he will die, Abraham, and your bloodline in the Society will end. But if he *is* the next Slayer in your family, you *will* train him. Of that, you have no choice."

"And if he refuses to train?" Even as the question left his tongue, Abraham reached out for it with all his wanting, but it was too late. He'd asked a query to which he already knew the answer.

The old man met and held his gaze, a look of sadness about him as he replied, "Kill him quickly. Family deserves mercy."

▸ 1 ◂

THE NEXT GREAT ADVENTURE

Hey, brat."

"I'm not a brat. You're a brat." Cecile wrinkled up her little nose, impossibly making herself even more adorable than she already was. Joss smiled. She was right; she wasn't a brat. But he loved teasing her, loved making her cross her arms defiantly in front of herself the way she was doing now. Besides, it wasn't like she really thought he was being mean. He was just playing, as always.

He reached out and gave one of her pigtails a light tug. "You're a way bigger brat than me. Come on. Mom says breakfast is ready. We're having French toast."

"Jossie, will you help me with this first?" She held

up the nude torso of a Barbie doll in one hand and the matted-haired, disembodied head of the doll in the other.

Joss sighed. "Only if you stop calling me Jossie."

It was a lie. He would have fixed it for her no matter what. He'd do anything for Cecile. But it was worth a try. Once he'd popped the poor doll's head back into place, he said, "Want a piggyback ride?"

"Yes!" She'd no sooner said the word than she had leaped up onto Joss's back. They bounded down the stairs to the kitchen. As Joss ran, jiggling her up and down on purpose, Cecile squealed with laughter.

The kitchen, decorated in clean, bright white and sunshine yellow, greeted the siblings with a warm, happy air. It had been home to them for five years, since three days before Cecile had celebrated her first birthday and eight days before Joss had celebrated his fifth. Joss loved this kitchen. He couldn't ever imagine gathering with his family anywhere else to discuss the coming events of the day, or grabbing a snack with his sister in the afternoon once each had returned from school. The kitchen was more than just a room where they cooked their meals and ate their breakfast. It was the soul of their house. It was, more than any other room, home.

Joss turned around and leaned back, dropping his little sister into her chair by the counter. As she landed with a thump, she erupted in laughter once again.

Then Joss took his seat beside her. Their mom was busy dipping slices of bread into a bowl filled with cinnamon-speckled eggs, then delivering them into a sizzling hot pan on the stove. As she flipped each piece, she hummed a happy tune. No one, Joss thought, was as happy as his mom. She always wore a sunny expression and a smile on her face. She was warm and outgoing and more friendly and kind than anyone he had ever met.

Cecile shifted impatiently in her seat. If there was anything more impossible for a young kid to wait for without at least a few complaints, it was French toast. Grabbing a pad of paper from the counter, Joss busied his sister with a quick game of Tic-tac-toe. She won the first one, but set her bottom lip in a pout. "You cheated, Jossie."

Joss shook his head. "I didn't cheat. How could I cheat? You won. Nobody cheats to lose, Cecile."

Folding her arms in front of her, Cecile slanted her eyes at her big brother. "You let me win. Don't let me win. I wanna do it myself."

A smile settled on Joss's lips. She was smarter than he'd given her credit for. The truth was, he had let her win. He hadn't wanted her to feel the upset of losing, so he'd drawn an *X* next to where it would have been a winning move, and silently congratulated himself on being such a good big brother. But Cecile was right. It would be better to have her learn on her own. After all, it wasn't winning that really counted, but the journey to that win. He nodded. "Okay, let's play again. You *X*'s or *O*'s?"

"*O*'s! I love *O*'s!"

"Last game, you two. The French toast is almost done." Mom went immediately back to humming her happy tune.

The second game lasted merely seconds and ended with Cecile pouting. "I hate losing."

Joss tickled her ribs, instigating another fit of laughter. "But did you have fun?"

"Yes!" Cecile shrieked.

As Mom slid his plate in front of him, topped with a stack of French toast, covered in sweet, sticky syrup, Joss smiled at his sister and picked up his fork, ready to dive in. "Then that's all that matters."

Once Joss had finished cleaning his plate and was scooping up every drop of gooey syrup that he could manage with his fork, he glanced at his mother, who was leaning against the counter, sipping her coffee and flipping through the morning paper. "Did Henry call yet? He's supposed to tell me what time they're coming tomorrow night."

She shook her head, looking up from the article she'd been immersed in. "Not yet, but I'm sure he'll call this afternoon. Are you sure you want to spend the *whole* summer with your cousins, Joss? That's a long time to be away from home. You might get homesick."

"I'm sure. It's Henry! We're gonna go camping and build a fort and Greg's even gonna teach us how to play baseball. It's gonna be so much fun. I can't wait to go." As if in an afterthought, he muttered, "I wish school was already over."

From behind him, his dad ruffled his hair. "You only have one more day there, sport. I'm sure you'll survive."

Joss wasn't exactly convinced of that, but he smiled back at his dad before sliding off his stool and carrying his plate and fork to the sink, where he rinsed them clean before placing them in the dishwasher. As he retrieved his lunch sack from beside the microwave on the counter, his mom caught him in a hug, her worried mom eyes meeting his gaze. She smelled like tangerines. And French toast. "You behave for Aunt Matilda and Uncle Mike. And you call if you need anything, even if you just feel homesick, okay?"

Joss gave her a squeeze, resisting the urge to roll his eyes at how she was acting. He could take care of himself, and he was always nice to his aunt and uncle. But his mom was taking a weekend trip to see his ill grandmother this afternoon, so she'd be gone before Joss got home from school today, and couldn't wait until then to say whatever she felt she needed to say. And she wouldn't get back until Sunday afternoon. Tomorrow evening, Joss would be barreling down the road in his uncle's car, playing the alphabet game with his favorite cousin. But right now, it was his job to make sure that his mom felt okay about letting him leave for almost three months.

He gave her another squeeze. "I'll call you, Mom. I promise. Lots."

Slipping from her arms, he picked up his backpack and flung it over his shoulder, planted a peck on Cecile's head, and waved to his dad on his way out the door. The bus was already waiting for him at the stop, so Joss ran.

As he climbed aboard Bus Thirteen, a familiar tension settled into his stomach. Most of the seats were completely occupied, and the ones that weren't were occupied by one person. As he made his way down the aisle, jostling slightly at the rough movement of the bus as it took off down his street, several lone-seat occupants slid their legs into the empty space beside them. One set his backpack in the space, indicating that it, too, was taken. The message was clear: *You're not welcome.*

"Sit down back there." The bus driver's voice was rough and raw, as if he'd been screaming at kids all morning.

The last thing Joss wanted was to be the subject of more screams, so he turned to a pale, freckled boy who was currently sitting in the middle of a green bench seat and said, "Hey, man, let me sit here, okay?"

The kid glanced around, as if seeking the approval

of his peers. Then he sighed heavily and slid in toward the window. Joss thanked him and took his seat. The remainder of the bus ride was quiet and awkward. In other words, it was a typical day so far for Joss McMillan.

When the bus came to a stop in front of Summers Elementary, the boy he'd sat by pushed past him, as if eager to be free of Joss. Joss hung back. He was in no hurry to begin his school day, and had no one waiting for him to step off the bus. Joss was, for the most part, alone. And what's more, he'd convinced himself over the last two years that he actually preferred being alone.

It was a lie that he told himself every day to cover up the pain of being completely friendless. If only his cousin Henry went to the same school he did. Henry was funny, inventive, and never once questioned the things that Joss did. If Joss ran faster than him, Henry gave chase. If Joss caught a ball, Henry slapped him on the back in approval. Henry was the best friend a guy could have.

But he didn't go to Joss's school.

By the time the bus had all but emptied, Joss had summoned up the courage to exit the bus and enter the school. No one really looked at him as he moved up the sidewalk or down the hall. In fact, if Joss hadn't been able to feel the warmth of the sun on his shoulders or the cool of the air-conditioned hallway, he might have thought that he was dreaming. Or a ghost.

Either, he mused, would have been better than being the invisible boy.

He wasn't certain when he'd become invisible, only knew that it had something to do with his ability to outrun everyone in the school, even the kids who were all about sports. Joss could catch a ball like nobody's business, was an excellent thrower, and an amazingly fast runner. His reflexes and strength surpassed even the most gifted athlete his age at Summers Elementary, and for some reason, that made him a target for hatred. He'd tried making friends. But no one—not even the unpopular kids who got wedgies every day—wanted anything to do with Joss. So he floated through school, the invisible boy, getting good grades and waiting for someone to notice him.

He doubted that would ever happen.

The last day of school before summer break began was pretty much useless as far as anything regarding education went. Before Joss realized it the recess bell rang.

He liked recess. Not for the usual reasons, but because recess meant that he could seek out his favorite spot in the hollow of the old oak tree on the far corner of the playground and immerse himself in whatever nonfiction tome he'd discovered recently among the piles of books in his local library—his latest favorite being the study of assassin bugs. He'd begun gathering as many of the creatures as he could find, and placing them in his collection for display. Assassin bugs, it turned out, would lie in wait for other insects and then stab the prey with their beak and inject a toxin that would dissolve the prey's tissue. Then they'd suck up the other bug's insides, like a Slurpee. And sometimes, when other food wasn't available, assassin bugs would even eat each other. The idea fascinated Joss.

The playground at Summers Elementary was small, but filled with everything that a kid could ask for: Three swing sets, a jungle gym, teeter-totters, monkey bars, a merry-go-round, and a giant slide occupied the grass-free area behind the school. Mostly, Joss would escape to his hiding place behind the tree, but every once in a while, like this day, he braved the far set of swings, the ones that were just small enough to make them appear boring to the rest of the kids. He sat on the swing on the end of the set, the one closest to his tree, and swung back and forth quietly, daydreaming about all the fun he and Henry were going to have this summer. Several yards in front of him, a group of kids was playing kick ball. Joss watched with an air of disinterest, despite the fact that he very much wanted to play with them. But he knew, from times past, that his efforts to interact would be met with denial. Still, when a boy he recognized from the lunchroom misjudged his kick, sending the ball flying in Joss's direction, Joss's instincts took over and he leaped from the swing, catching the ball in his hands before his feet had even touched the ground.

The boy who'd kicked the ball dropped his arms to his side, a look of annoyance on his face. Several heads turned Joss's way to see what was causing his upset, and each of their expressions darkened as well. Joss's jaw began to feel very tight.

Holly Whittaker stepped forward, hands on her hips. "Give us the ball back, Joss."

She acted as if it hadn't been kicked toward him, as if he'd invaded their game and had stolen away the ball on purpose. His jaw ached from the tension. "I didn't mean to catch it. It just kind of happened."

Tommy Hart snorted. "Yeah, just like it *kind of happened* that you beat Billy at that race last week, cheater."

Joss turned the ball nervously over in his hands. The truth was, he hadn't cheated. But he had forgotten to pull his speed back so that Billy could win and save Joss the embarrassment of being unusually quick. "I didn't cheat. I'm just fast."

Holly stepped closer, her voice filled with venom. "Everybody knows you're a cheater, Joss. Now give the ball back, *cheater*."

With a clenched jaw, Joss held the red ball up for all to see. "This ball?"

Then, before she could reach for it, Joss dropped

the ball, raising his foot in a kick. The ball went flying. So high that it seemed to be enveloped by the sun. Then it came down, settling atop the roof of the school.

A feeling filled him quickly, then shrank away again, as if hiding in shame. It was joy for having taken revenge. Joss's stomach twisted and turned with guilt. He wasn't proud of his actions. In fact, he was sickened by them. But what was done was done. He blinked at Holly and the others, whose faces wore looks of surprise, anger, and hurt. "I'm sorry."

They didn't believe him. Who would? But Joss *was* sorry. He'd let his anger and desire for revenge get in the way.

Before anyone could give him a richly deserved punch in the eye, the bell rang, signifying the end of recess. Joss tried to apologize again, but each member of the kick ball group simply shook their heads, as if they hadn't expected any better from the likes of him, and gravitated toward the school. Once the playground was empty, Joss followed, hanging his head in shame.

The rest of the day passed, blissfully, without incident.

Once at home again that afternoon, Joss lugged his backpack through the front door and flung it into the hall closet. He hurried into the kitchen and had to resist the urge to jump up and down when he saw the answering machine flashing that there was one message waiting. He pushed the button and held his breath hopefully. "Hey, Joss! Henry here. Dad said to tell you we'd be there at five o'clock tomorrow, so get packed and ready. Oh, and Mom said not to bring any bugs. They gross her out. See ya!"

With happiness moving his feet, Joss ran up the stairs to his bedroom. His suitcase had already been packed by his mother the night before, but Joss wanted to double-check that she hadn't forgotten things like his magnifying glass, or his well-worn paperback copy of *Identifying Insects*. Neither were sitting on his desk where he left them, but Joss made a mental note to check his suitcase as soon as he went downstairs. Parents, even well-meaning parents, just couldn't be trusted with the important things.

Looking over his room, Joss sighed. The truth was, he was really going to miss waking up here every morning for the next few months. He loved his room. Loved the jars on his bookshelves filled with various stick bugs. Loved the framed specimens on his walls. His favorite was, of course, the Black Corsair hanging over his bed—a gift from his grandfather when he was eight.

He remembered that trip vividly. He and his parents had gone to visit his grandparents on the outskirts of Bowling Green, Kentucky, one summer. His grandfather was teaching him how to chop wood for their campfire one night, and as they turned a log over, Joss spied the most magnificent specimen of insect that he'd ever seen. It was in perfect condition, shiny black head and dull black wings. Grandpa told Joss that a Black Corsair was a "nasty little critter," and that *Melanolestes picipes*—as they were known in the scientific world—would run down other insects in their hunt for food. It would chase them and never stop until it caught its prey. They were known to suck the blood of rodents, and even humans. And disturbingly enough, they preferred to go for the eyes and lips.

Luckily this one was dead already. His grandfather took it home and mounted it, and six months later, Joss had opened it as a gift under the Christmas tree. He treasured it. Not just because it was such a rare species. But because it had been a gift from his grandfather, who'd inspired his love of entomology before passing from this life into the Next Great Adventure.

That's what he'd called dying. The Next Great Adventure. Grandpa believed that beyond this life, there was something bigger, something better for us all. The thought gave Joss a smile. He missed his grandfather.

That night, after dinner and some mindless television, Joss lay tucked neatly in his bed, staring up at the frame of the Black Corsair and wondering if his grandfather had been right about death, if it really was an adventure and not something to fear.

With that thought, he drifted off into a deep, dreamless slumber.

• 2 •

CECILE

Nothing had woken Joss.

He was awake, certainly. He lay in his bed, cozy and warm, despite the chill of night. But there had been no sound, no movement that had brought him out of sleep.

There was only the darkness, and a feeling that something wasn't quite right.

As he pulled the covers back, that little voice in his head—the one that'd been enjoying his soft bed and cozy covers—told him to cover up quickly and forget about the unsettling feeling that was poking at the edges of his brain. It was nothing, the voice urged. Probably just the wind.

But Joss couldn't go back to sleep, no matter how tired he was. He had to take a look around and see for certain that nothing had woken him, and that all was well and nothing was lurking under his bed or just inside his closet door.

He paused before swinging his feet over the edge of his bed. He didn't believe in monsters. His dad had explained movie special effects to him at a very young age, and his mom had told him all about the genius of the imagination. But a part of him—a small part—shrank back in fear at the idea of placing his feet on the floor in the dark, not knowing who or what might be lurking underneath his bed at this late hour. What if it had scales or claws or a venom that it might inject into Joss and proceed to slurp out his insides?

Nonsense. Monsters weren't real.

With a determined breath, Joss's feet hit the floor, and the sudden shock of cold sent them back underneath the covers for a moment. Maybe the voice in his head was right. Maybe it was nothing.

But then there was a noise. Soft and familiar. For some reason, it sent a bolt of fear through him as it never had before. Cecile was crying.

Despite his initial resistance to her very existence, Joss adored his baby sister. And he was the only person in their house who was even remotely capable of calming her down after a nightmare. Which meant that despite the nip in the air, he was getting out of bed.

Tiptoeing across the bare wood floor, Joss crept to his bedroom door and put his ear to the wood. Cecile had quieted, but he was sure she'd start up again soon. Her nightmares were never brief. Without reason, she'd been having them since she was a toddler. They'd come on the heels of her night terrors, and could only be calmed by the presence of Joss and his assurance that everything would be all right. He wrapped his fingers around the doorknob and turned, pulling the door until it opened a few inches.

Cecile was silent.

Joss furrowed his brow and looked longingly back at his warm bed. But a noise drew his attention to the hallway. The soft creak of mattress springs.

Curiosity filled Joss, and he crept down the hall toward Cecile's mostly-closed bedroom door. Stopping in front of it, Joss whispered, "Cecile?"

There was no sound. Not from Cecile or anything else. The air was heavy with silence. It was almost too quiet.

Joss leaned forward, pressing his forehead against the wood until the door opened just a crack and he could peer inside. What he saw stopped his heart from beating for several moments.

Joss scrambled back from the door. He backed hard

into the wall behind him, his jaw hanging open in utter horror, his trembling fingers clamping tight over his mouth so that his screams would not escape. He slid to the floor, frozen in absolute fear.

Cecile—small, sweet, six-year-old Cecile—was lying on her bed, pale as snow. A dark, fluid line had been drawn from her neck to her pink ballerina sheets. Blood. Cecile's blood. Her eyes, thankfully, were closed. She wasn't moving. Standing by her bed was a man that wasn't a man. His teeth were razor sharp and pointed. His skin was paler than Cecile's. He was a monster, and looked like every stereotypical vampire that Joss had ever seen in a movie or on television.

Joss couldn't move. Not to check on his sister. Not to force the terrible creature from their home. Not to call for his mom or dad. He couldn't budge. And what's worse, the creature—the monster—had noticed him.

It licked Cecile's blood from its lips and stepped into the hall, crouching before Joss. And when it sighed, Joss almost gagged at the smell of his sister's blood on its tongue. "Little one," it said, as if they were old acquaintances. "You weren't supposed to see this. Or me. So forget my face. It will be easier for both of us."

Then the monster touched his finger lightly to Joss's temple, and Joss screamed.

▸ 3 ◂

THE DEATH OF A FAMILY

The funeral home was packed with people—most of whom Joss either didn't know, or simply had no memory of meeting before. All around the room were bouquets of pink roses. At the far end of the room, at the farthest point from where Joss was seated with his hands folded and head down, was a small white coffin. Inside was Cecile, or what had once been Cecile.

He had silently begged the powers that be that her coffin would be closed, that her body wouldn't be put on display for people to gawk at. But his pleas had fallen on deaf ears, it seemed. So Joss stayed where he was, at the back of the funeral home, and refused every suggestion that he go up and say his good-byes.

He would never say good-bye to his sister. Never.

And he wouldn't cry over her shell until his pain had been relieved, either. No, he would use that pain, tuck it somewhere inside of him until he had the strength to find whatever had killed her and bring it to justice somehow.

He'd told his parents about the monster—that he'd seen a creature looming over his bleeding sister, but could not seem to recall its face, no matter how hard he tried. Whenever the smallest detail of the face would begin to creep into his mind, it was whisked away by a gray fog. But they wouldn't listen. They thought a madman had killed Cecile. Joss had tried explaining to the police what happened that night, but no one would listen to him. They simply exchanged glances that indicated that he was merely a hysterical little boy who'd witnessed the brutal murder of his sister. Of course he saw monsters. What other way could his young mind possibly deal with seeing what he actually had?

Now his parents were standing across the room, near Cecile's coffin, as distant from him physically as they had been emotionally since Cecile had died. It had started the moment the police had left that night. All of a sudden, Joss had become the invisible boy at home, the way he was at school. He hadn't just lost his sister that night. He'd lost his family, too.

His parents had said nothing to him on the drive to the funeral home, and once they'd entered the building, it was as if they had had only one child, and that child was Cecile.

Joss squeezed the photograph in his hand, careful not to wrinkle it. He'd taken it from the refrigerator door this morning, knowing that he wanted to look at Cecile, but also knowing that he couldn't possibly stare at her corpse and convince himself that that was his sister. The object lying in that coffin wasn't Cecile. It was merely bones and tissue, held together by preservatives. His sister was now experiencing the Next Great Adventure. He hoped death was that, anyway, that something lay beyond this life. Otherwise, his sister was a part of nothingness now. The thought brought tears to his eyes.

"There is no shame in shedding tears for Cecile, Joss."

Joss looked up. He hadn't noticed his Uncle Abraham enter the room, or sit down beside him, but there he was, dressed in a black, three-piece suit, his expression appropriately solemn. Abraham reached into his inside jacket pocket and withdrew a cloth handkerchief, holding it out to his nephew. Joss shook his head and willed his tears away, careful to keep his attention focused on Abraham and away from Cecile's coffin. With a nod, Abraham tucked the handkerchief away again. "I've been told you were there when it happened."

Joss nodded. He didn't know his uncle very well, had only encountered him on occasional holidays, at parties held by other distant relatives. He didn't know much about him, really. Only that his uncle was a professor of some sort, and a world traveler. "I was. But no one believes what I saw."

Abraham raised an eyebrow. "And what is it that you saw exactly?"

Joss swallowed hard, clutching Cecile's picture to his chest, the threat of tears overwhelming him. But he wouldn't cry. He wouldn't allow himself that moment of weakness. Not until his sister had been avenged. "I don't remember its face. But I do remember the blood. Cecile's blood."

"An injury?"

"Something like that. I can't remember. My brain is too foggy."

"Where was your sister bleeding from and how much blood was there?" Joss's heart grew heavy. He looked at his uncle and begged him with a glance to cease this line of questioning immediately. Abraham gave his shoulder a squeeze, his eyes full of pity. "A morbid question, nephew, but I must know."

The memory of that night filled his mind. Cecile

in her bed, that liquid line of blood running down her neck to her pink ballerina sheets. Joss's hands gripped the chair he was sitting in without him even being aware of it. "Her neck. She was bleeding from her neck. There wasn't a lot of blood, not as much as you'd think."

Joss had once read that an average human child had 2.3 liters of blood pumping around inside of them, so he was amazed by what little blood had actually been spilled in his sister's murder. He never would have confessed those thoughts to his parents, though. They might have locked him up in a nuthouse if he admitted to thinking such things.

Abraham leaned a bit closer and spoke in a conspiratorial whisper. "Take a deep breath, Joss, clear your thoughts and don't force the memory. The harder you think about it, the more like sand the memory will become, slipping between your fingers until there's nothing left to grasp. Now tell me . . . what was the weapon that cut Cecile?"

Inside the memory of that night, Joss looked up at the man's face, but it was just a gray fog. As his uncle had suggested, he took a deep breath and relaxed. Slowly, the fog began to lift, revealing the man's mouth. And horrible, blood-drenched fangs. Joss gasped and locked his eyes with his uncle's. "Fangs! It had fangs. That man . . ."

He didn't know how he could have forgotten such

a critical detail of the event, but now he knew why he'd considered Cecile's murderer a monster. Not just because the man had killed a child, but because the man wasn't really a man at all. He was a monster, a creature, a thing. Joss's heart raced in terror. What if it came back? What if it wanted to finish Joss off, too?

Abraham sat there in quiet contemplation for a moment, before giving Joss's back a gentle pat. After another moment of silence, he stood and moved down the aisle to the coffin. He'd come here to pay his respects and had somehow gotten wrapped up in his nephew's newly bloomed madness. Clearly, he wanted to get out of here as soon as possible. Joss didn't blame him.

But to Joss's surprise, moments later, his uncle had returned to his seat beside Joss. Abraham nodded. "It seems you are correct, Joss. Some*thing*, not some*one*, did take young Cecile's life. I suspect the guilty party is a vampire."

Joss looked at his uncle, trying to gauge whether or not Abraham was playing some sick joke on him at his sister's funeral. All he saw was complete honesty and understanding. But his mind couldn't shut out the questions it begged. "How can vampires possibly be real? And how could we not know about them all this time?"

Abraham's eyes were on the mourners as they

passed by Cecile's coffin. Joss should have been up there, too, but he just couldn't bear it. Maybe Abraham understood that. Or maybe he was just waiting until they finished their conversation to see if Joss would go. "Do you know how big snakes get? Or how many grains of sand are in the deserts? Or exactly what lurks on the bottoms of the oceans' floors?"

Joss thought about each query. He dug deep into the recesses of his mind, but came up empty. "No."

"Well, if you can't answer those simple scientific queries, then what makes you think that mankind is smart enough to discover vampirekind's existence?" Abraham raised an eyebrow at his nephew then. He'd made a valid point.

Who was to say that humans knew all that there was to know about our planet? Joss thought about the so-called scientific evidence behind vampirism that he had read about in the books at the library. So much paranoia, so many graves dug up, all because corpses would bloat, making their bellies look full, while gums shrank, making their incisors appear as fangs? Joss hardly thought so. It sounded like a lame attempt at an explanation to him.

So maybe his uncle was right. Maybe vampires really existed. Maybe one had killed his sister.

"I have connections to that world, if you want justice, Joss." Abraham's chin was strong, his jaw set, as if he very much wanted justice for Cecile as well. "All you need to do is swear on it. Swear on your dedication to taking those monsters down, and I will give you every tool you require to do so."

Joss looked down at the picture in his hand before allowing his eyes to trace along the room to the white coffin at the other end for the first time. He swallowed hard and said, "I swear."

Abraham leaned closer, his voice just above a whisper. "We are called the Slayer Society, and you now belong to us. We'll train you. We'll protect you. We'll be closer to you than any family could. I can't begin training you yet—the rules dictate that you must first be eighteen years old before that can happen. But in the meantime, you should start honing your natural skills."

"But I don't have any natural skills." Joss shook his head adamantly. He was just a boy. Just an ordinary person.

"Of course you do. You have incredible agility and speed, amazing reflexes." Abraham spoke without question, and Joss couldn't help but wonder how he could know these things about his nephew. The nephew he'd only rarely seen or spent time with. "Use the next few years to practice running, archery, wrestling, anything that you can to become the best. Then, after you turn eighteen, I'll send for you. When you see a red wax seal on a letter, hide away and read it alone. It's a secret. As is everything to do with the Society."

Joss nodded, taking this all in. "Can I tell Henry?"

"No. You can tell no one. Nor can you discuss anything pertaining to the Society with anyone but those within the Society." Abraham stood and reached into one of his outer pockets. What he withdrew, he placed into Joss's hand. "This was your grandfather's. He would have wanted you to have it. He was a Slayer as well."

Joss squeezed the pocket watch in his hand. Grandpa had been a Slayer, too. No wonder he'd looked on death as an adventure. Death, after all, was just a continuation of life to Grandpa, and it seemed his life had been a series of secret adventures. Death was just the next one. Grandpa was a Slayer. And now Joss was, too.

As Abraham moved through the crowd, saying his good-byes, Joss looked down at his grandfather's pocket watch. Setting the watch in his lap, he tore the photograph of Cecile, until he'd made a circle around her face, then placed it inside his grandfather's watch. It was a reminder to himself to never forget, and to always, always remember those that you care about. He slid the pocket watch inside his front pants pocket and sat back in his chair, musing over exactly what the Slayer Society was, and exactly how they were going to help him take down the monster that had killed Cecile.

"Hey."

Joss looked up to find his cousin Henry, wearing a suit that was too big on him, and looking like he felt very, very awkward. Normally Henry was a really funny guy, but even he, it seemed, knew when an occasion called for a more somber approach. "Hey, Henry."

"I'm sorry you're not coming to spend the summer with me after all." Henry's eyes went wide, as if he'd just said the dumbest thing ever. "And about Cecile. She was a nice kid."

Joss nodded, trying hard to keep his thoughts away from his sister and the body lying in the coffin at the other end of the room. "Maybe next summer."

"Yeah. Maybe." Henry hung his head. He didn't speak anymore, just stood there awkwardly, likely wishing that he had some words of comfort to offer his cousin, but Joss knew that there was nothing Henry or anyone else could say. This pain ran deep, and only by erasing the cause of this pain would it ever go away.

The man with fangs had caused this pain, and he would pay dearly for it.

A preacher stood and said words that Joss couldn't bear to listen to. After he was finished, everyone began filing out. Henry, who was sitting beside Joss, looked perplexed. "Where's everybody going?"

"To the dinner." Joss furrowed his perplexed brow for a moment. "Isn't it weird how people feel the need to eat after funerals?"

Henry nodded. Then his mood brightened some. "Do you think they'll have cake?"

▸ 4 ◂

INTRODUCTIONS

Joss slipped his pen inside one of the small pockets of his backpack and turned his attention back to the leather-bound journal on his lap. It had taken three years—three long, tormented years—for him to put pen to page and fully describe what had happened the night he'd lost Cecile. It was as if the pain of her death had somehow sealed the descriptive abilities within him and receiving his Uncle Abraham's letter last week had finally set his pen free.

He hadn't told his parents about the Slayer Society. His uncle had strictly forbidden it. They wouldn't have believed him anyway. Who could blame them?

If he'd rambled on about some secret club that would help him hunt down the horrible vampire who drank his sister's blood and touched his temple, erasing the memory of its face from Joss's young mind, they would have put him away in some asylum somewhere. In the nuthouse, as his father was fond of saying. Joss's aunt Margaret was put in the nuthouse ten years ago. From what his father had said, having to put her there had almost made Abraham crazy enough to go to the nuthouse, too. But then something made Abraham's sanity snap firmly back into place. Time had passed, Cecile had died, and last week, Abraham had sent Joss a train ticket. All that had accompanied it was a letter explaining to Joss's parents that he wanted Joss to spend the summer with him, teaching him survival skills, out at a cabin in the woods.

The letter was a lie.

"I swear," Joss whispered in remembrance of the day he had vowed to hunt down his sister's killer and those like him. He closed the journal and slid it inside the largest pocket of his backpack. He was ready for whatever his uncle had in store for him. Even though he had no idea at all what that might be.

He had trained for three years, running as far and as fast as he could manage, perfecting his archery, building up his senses in the wilds of the woods near his house—all things that Abraham had written to him about and instructed him to do. And in the three years since Cecile's death, Joss had come to understand that he wasn't just looking to erase the vampire who'd killed Cecile simply to ease his pain. He wanted the beast to suffer for what he did. Joss wanted justice.

The train jostled and bumped along the tracks. He'd been on trains for four days, traveling the long road from Santa Carla, California, to Rhinecliff, New York. A plane would have been faster, and probably cheaper, but still, his uncle had sent only the train ticket, and the simple note. He trusted that there was a reason for this choice. After all, his uncle seemed a reasonable man. So who was he to argue?

Joss had smiled a false smile at his parents—who'd waved the invisible boy away, still locked tightly in their grief—and packed clothing for a summer vacation that would never happen. This summer, after all, wasn't about camping or hiking or learning about the ways of nature. It was about a new beginning. It was about vengeance. Even though his uncle hadn't precisely said those words, Joss knew he'd meant them. It was time for Joss to begin his search for the monster that had killed Cecile.

He had wondered why Abraham had sent for him now, and hadn't waited until Joss turned eighteen, but he was sure his uncle had his reasons, and would explain them once he reached the cabin. His knee bounced in anticipation of the train stop. He was anxious, anxious to begin his official training and start his life anew.

"Rhinecliff! Next stop, Rhinecliff!" The conductor's voice boomed through the car, jolting Joss from his thoughts. There was something old-world about it, and Joss couldn't shake the feeling that he was going back in time. To a place where people traveled by trains and were shouted at by conductors. The part of him that had watched every episode of *The Twilight Zone* wondered briefly if, when he stepped off the train, it would be into his time, or another; his world, or another. The thought worried him, unsettling his stomach a bit, so he pushed it down deep and gathered up his belongings, waiting for the train to slow.

Once the train jerked to a stop, Joss descended the narrow stairs, luggage in hand, and stepped for the first time onto the platform of the Amtrak station in Rhinecliff, New York.

His eyes swept across the platform, but he didn't see his uncle anywhere. After a moment, he followed the ebbing crowd—which consisted of merely six people—up the long staircase and through the hangar-like room into the train station itself. Once again, he looked around, and once again, he didn't see his uncle. Suddenly nervous, Joss wheeled his suitcase over to one of the wooden benches and took a seat. There was little he could do now but wait, and hope like hell that his uncle hadn't forgotten about him.

Rapid footfalls drew his attention to the door that led to the section of building that resembled a hangar. Someone was running, their shoes slapping against the floor in a hurried pace, one that suggested they meant business. Behind them was another set of footfalls. Joss watched the open door, waiting to see the runner.

A girl burst through the door, her eyes wide and frightened. Joss hadn't noticed her on the platform before, but she was here now, running from where the train had been, looking scared out of her mind. Behind her was a man, dressed in black and gaining ground. The girl whipped past Joss and out the front door of the station. Just as the man passed him, Joss reacted instinctively and put his foot out. He didn't know what made him do it, only knew that the man was chasing that girl, and she'd looked so scared. He had to stop it, whatever it was, from happening.

The man stumbled over Joss's ankle and went down hard, but before he hit the floor, he caught himself, somehow, without touching anything at all that Joss could see, and stood back up. Slowly, he turned his head to face Joss, his eyes piercing and dark. His face was very pale. He searched Joss's face for a moment, as if something about him seemed familiar. Joss straightened his shoulders and opened his mouth to speak—even though he was half convinced that all that would come out would be a squeak. He was surprised how confident his voice sounded, and how steady his words were, despite the fact that he was shaking. "Leave her alone."

The man smiled then, again slowly, and it occurred to Joss that the man before him had to focus to do anything slowly at all. Because he was used to being unnaturally quick. This thought both surfaced and descended back into the recesses of Joss's mind very quickly, almost unnoticeably.

Then the man's smile grew into a maddening grin, revealing two sharp fangs within his mouth. Joss jumped backward at the sight, his heart racing. Broken images of the monster who'd killed Cecile filled his thoughts—images of fangs and blood, but no face. The man—the thing, the vampire—in front of him laughed. "I don't know who Cecile is, but I'm afraid I haven't had the pleasure. Now, why don't you have a seat and mind your own business, Slayer. This girl is of no consequence to you."

Slayer. The monster had called him a Slayer. What did that mean? How did this thing know about the Slayer Society and Cecile? Joss shook his head, shaking all images of Cecile's face from the forefront of his mind. He thought of the girl who'd run outside, how frightened she'd seemed. He could only imagine how scared Cecile had been the night she'd died. Joss tightened his jaw. "Like hell she isn't."

The creature glared at him and for a moment, Joss

was certain it was going to lunge forward and rip his throat out. Joss briefly glanced around the station, but it seemed no one else had noticed the fangs.

"Do we have a problem, gentlemen?"

Joss flicked his eyes over to the man who'd interrupted their tension. Young, mid-thirties, slate gray eyes, and dirty blond hair, sheared into a short military cut. He was lean, but Joss could tell by the way the fabric of his shirt lay on his frame that he was also muscular. And he was hoping that muscular meant strong, because he was going to need every ounce of help he could get if this thing came to blows. The man raised an eyebrow at the vampire, setting his jaw, as if he were very much aware of what kind of monster he was dealing with. "Is there something the boy or I can help you with?"

The vampire emitted a low, guttural growl. It came off as a territorial warning, but Joss wasn't entirely sure why. "Sirus."

The corner of the man's mouth twitched slightly. His hand slowly moved to the leather satchel on his hip. He dropped his tone so that no one else in the station would hear. "The boy is one of ours. And if you're informed enough to know my name, you must know the girl is mine. I'm willing to turn the other cheek this time, but if you make a move, I'm authorized and fully capable of taking you down, despite the complication of exposure. So think about your next move before you make it—think long and hard—and then do it. But do it knowing that I'll take great pleasure in killing you."

The vampire seemed to weigh Sirus's seriousness for a moment. Then, judging him to be an honest man, it nodded and moved out the door. Sirus shook his head and turned back to Joss. "Good to have you aboard, Slayer. I wouldn't have wanted to face him myself, truth be told. Not in a public place. It could have gotten messy, and judging by his calculated movements, he's accustomed to moving among vampires more than humans, which means he'd be strong. Maybe too strong for the likes of me. But the two of us. We probably could have taken him."

Joss blinked in mild confusion. "Taken him? You mean taken him down? But he's a . . . vampire."

The word fell off his tongue and tumbled to the floor in a whisper. It felt strange. It felt surreal.

Sirus nodded. "And we are Slayers."

"I'm not a Slayer. I'm not even sure I know what that is, but I assume it means someone who kills vampires. And I'm not that." But even as he uttered the words, he knew them not to be true. After all, wasn't that why he'd come here? To avenge his sister's death? Surely that would involve a little killing on his part. Joss swallowed, but his throat was parched.

Sirus seemed to size him up for a bit before speaking again. "But you are a Slayer, Joss. You swore an oath three years ago, and every day since then has been preparing you for this day."

At the back of his mind, Joss heard his ten-year-old self responding to his uncle with a determined voice. *"I swear."*

Sirus kept his voice even, as if he possessed an immeasurable amount of patience. "Yes, you did. And the next day your father was hired by a new company. A company that unbeknownst to your family is owned and run by the Slayer Society. A company that moved you to how many different places in just three years, Joss?"

"Too many."

"And each of those cities was chosen for a reason. Some of the most talented Slayers in the Society are stationed in those places. You were being moved around so that each of those Slayers, highly respected members of the Society, could size you up, and confirm that you are as we are, a Slayer." He reached a hand forward as if to give Joss's shoulder a comforting squeeze, then thought better of it and dropped his hand to his side. "After they'd analyzed you, it was time for you to come here, to be trained in the art of slaying and eventually, indoctrinated into the Society. And to be honest, I was hoping that Abraham would be the one to explain it all to you."

Joss shook his head. Not in utter disbelief, but in shock that he had somehow missed the exquisite detail of the Society's plans. At the time it had seemed like just a bit of luck when his father scored a well-paying position at a seemingly reputable company. It had been a bit strange that the company was willing—no, eager, Joss recalled his dad saying—to move his family along with him. And Joss had faced each move with grave determination, knowing that it would be just another house, and never home. Straining now, he couldn't seem to recall anyone who'd obviously been a Slayer. But then, he supposed, they had just been incredibly good at their job and blended in. He wished, much like Sirus, that his uncle had told him that he was being reviewed by the Slayer Society.

He took a breath and let it out slowly before meeting Sirus's eyes. "When do I see my uncle?"

"The great Abraham McMillan? Most highly regarded Slayer of our time?" Sirus smiled, and then nodded slowly, as if making a decision about Joss—a decision he would not put voice to. "Depends on traffic. The cabin is about an hour's drive from here, when nobody's on the road. The girl you saw is my daughter. She knows nothing of the Society and I plan to keep it that way. Secrecy is our biggest ally. So watch what you say while she's around, okay?"

"Don't worry. I'll be careful with what I say." He reached for his suitcase, but Sirus grabbed it first and led him out the station door. With every step, Joss felt more excited the farther away he got from the life that he had known. He was leaving it all behind; all for the love of his sister and his determination to locate the monster that had killed her and right a wrong that never should have been.

Joss stepped out into the bright summer sun and squinted until a large, puffy cloud did him a favor and crossed over the sun, blessing him with brief shade. In front of him, Sirus had approached a beat-up pick-up truck that had been red in its glory days, but was now closer to brown. After placing Joss's suitcase in the back, he pulled a set of keys from his pocket and glanced around briefly. Before he could slide the key into the lock, the girl who'd run from the station—Sirus's daughter—burst from behind the truck and ran into his arms. She was about Joss's age, with hair so many colors—among them purple, blue, and pink—that Joss could barely count them all. The shorts and tank top she wore revealed bronze tan skin. She might have been a teenager, but at the moment, she was acting very much like a scared child. "Dad, I'm sorry. I was going to look for your friend, but there was this man, and he was acting really bizarre. It scared me. He—"

Sirus smiled and gestured his eyes to Joss, who stood at the front of the truck, feeling unbelievably awkward. "Don't worry. I found my friend. And you did the right thing to run. There have been some dangerous people lurking about lately."

Joss shifted his feet uncomfortably. He'd never been the best at lying, and had only really begun to withhold the truth from anyone since the night Cecile had been murdered. His parents had assumed it was some madman who'd killed their little girl. Joss had merely gone along with their assumption, but supporting their incorrect belief was just as bad as lying. He had a feeling he'd be telling a lot of lies from now on. The idea didn't sit particularly well in the pit of his stomach. It felt sour and achy and not at all like the cool, familiar comfort of truth. But he would do what he had to do for justice.

The girl's eyes said she was both relieved and comforted by her father's presence. She looked at Joss and offered a warm smile. "I'm Kat. What's your name?"

"Joss." He cleared his throat. "What grade are you in?"

"I'm starting ninth this fall." She smiled then, and a peculiar, welcoming sparkle entered her eyes.

"Me too." He felt the threat of a smile edging up onto his lips, but it stopped when Sirus caught his eye. "Nice to meet you, Kat."

Sirus opened the driver's-side door of his truck and shook his head, chuckling a bit before getting in. "Come on, you two. Abraham will be expecting us for dinner."

Kat walked around and got in through the passenger door, sliding to the middle and patting the seat next to her as Joss approached. After taking a deep breath, Joss climbed in and closed the door, leaving what he had known as his life behind forever.

▸ 5 ◂

ECHOES OF THE NIGHT

Joss laid in his bed, his pillow wadded into a ball underneath his head. Moonlight poured in through the window, but apart from the dresser and the floor, he couldn't see much of his room. A strange darkness surrounded him, one so thick and black that it seemed almost like ink. His covers felt heavy on top of him, so heavy that he was having a difficult time breathing. The cotton fabric felt stiff and thick, and Joss was certain that if he didn't get out from under his blanket soon, he'd suffocate.

A sound caught his attention and he turned his head to look at the door, at where the noise was coming from. It was soft and steady, like a snake hissing quietly. Throwing his stifling covers off, Joss stood and moved to his bedroom door. He pressed his ear against the wood and listened. For a moment, the hissing stopped.

A slight breeze blew in from the crack at the bottom of the door. The skin on Joss's feet cooled quickly and relief flooded through him. The room was just so hot he could barely stand it. He was debating opening the door to fill his room with cool air when the hissing started up again. Slowly, the sound changed from a low hiss—like someone releasing air from a balloon— to a whimpering cry.

Joss opened the door and stepped out into the hall. He'd hoped for a burst of cool air on his face, but the hallway was actually hotter than his room. A bead of sweat trickled down his forehead and dripped off the end of his nose, but Joss paid it no attention. He was too focused on the sound of someone crying, and the fact that it was coming from the door just down the hall from his bedroom. The cries sounded familiar, and Joss's heartbeat picked up its pace and joined the chorus of sounds around him.

He shuffled quietly down the hall. By the time his hand closed over the doorknob, Joss knew who was behind that door, and who was responsible for the echoes of sadness that were reaching his ears. "Cecile? Are you okay?"

But Cecile wasn't okay. She was dead. She couldn't

be here in her room, crying for him to save her. She was dead.

With a deep breath, he turned the knob and pushed the door open. Cecile was lying on her bed, her eyes closed. A line of blood traced down her cheek to her pink ballerina sheets. Only something was different this time. Her chest was rising and falling, and Joss could still hear her whimpers. Cecile was breathing. Cecile was alive.

He crossed the room, stretching a hand out to brush her bangs from her eyes and comfort her. When his fingertips touched her soft hair, he relaxed. She was real. And she really was alive. He patted her head and knelt beside her bed, keeping his eyes away from the bloody line that ran from her mouth. "It's okay, Cecile. Shhh. Everything's okay."

Big, round tears spilled from her still-closed eyes and ran down her cheeks. Her voice was soft and sad. "No, it's not, Jossie. It's not okay."

Wiping away her tears with his fingers, he leaned close, lowering his voice to as comforting a whisper as he could. "Of course it is. Why would you say that?"

Suddenly, Cecile's eyes opened wide. Her sockets were empty black holes. Soulless tunnels that went on forever, into the deep, into the dark. For some reason, they reminded Joss of that thick blackness that had encompassed his bedroom. Her voice dropped into a deep, gruff tone, as if she hadn't used her vocal cords in ages. "Because I'm dead. And it's all your fault."

Joss moved back, terrified. He screamed, but even as he did, he knew that no one would ever hear him. Cecile lunged forward, her tiny fingernails sharpened into claws. Inside her open mouth, Joss saw white, glistening fangs.

▸ 6 ◂

A SENSE OF DUTY

Joss sat bolt upright on his seat in the truck, alarmed by something he'd seen in his dreams. He wasn't sure what it had been, but he wasn't surprised. Ever since Cecile's death, his nights had been plagued by nightmares—nightmares that he was grateful that he could not always recall.

Sirus and Kat were looking at him, concern filling their collective gaze. It was Sirus who broke the silence. "Everything okay, Joss? You dozed off for a bit."

"Yeah. Everything's fine." He smiled weakly and realized the truck had stopped. "Just a bad dream. Is this it?"

Sirus seemed to gauge him for a moment before

speaking again. "The cabin's just around the bushes and up the hill a bit. If you can manage your bags, Kat and I will carry the groceries."

Joss scratched his head and yawned, shaking off his bad dream. He nodded. "No problem. Sorry I dozed off."

As Kat slid out the passenger door, Sirus leaned back inside and lowered his voice. "It's okay. You'll need all the sleep you can get before training begins."

Joss sat up, excitement filling him. He was ready for this, and anxious to get started. "When will it begin, anyway?"

Sirus held his gaze for a moment, his eyes full of concern—a concern that Joss didn't understand. "Probably sooner than you're ready for."

"When's that?"

"Well." Sirus sighed, as if doing the math in his head. "It'll take us about three minutes to gather this stuff and get to the cabin, and another two or three for Abraham to realize you're here. So I'd say you have about seven more minutes of freedom left."

Joss eyed Sirus for a moment, uncertain what to say. Sirus was acting like Joss was heading for his funeral instead of beginning his Slayer training. He couldn't quite wrap his head around why.

Sirus laughed and patted Joss roughly on the shoulder. "Maybe ten."

Kat grabbed the grocery bags from the back of the

truck and Joss moved around the side, lifting his suitcase from the rear and following Kat's confident stride around a large group of bushes. "Is this it?"

"Yeah, follow me." Kat lead the way, following what looked like something that had once been regarded as a driveway of sorts. Joss got his first look at the so-called cabin.

It wasn't at all what he'd been expecting. Cabins, after all, are small, square, wooden simplicity, nestled in the too-wild woods, with no electricity and not a single modern convenience. At least, that's what Joss's impression had been up until he'd seen the house. What he was faced with was something that threw him completely for a loop. It wasn't so much a cabin as it was a large, pale yellow Victorian-style house, with a wraparound porch. To its left stood a smaller blue house. Both were old. Neither was what he'd refer to as a cabin. Maybe it was the fancy carved wood accents on the outside, but Joss had a difficult time thinking of either place as home to a group of Slayers.

Kat and Sirus carried the bags up the path, crossing the porch of the Victorian with a familiar comfort. Joss wheeled his suitcase up to the steps, then lifted it and set it down just as Sirus was turning the knob and pushing the door open.

After he carried his bags over the threshold, Joss moved into the foyer, but didn't follow Kat into the kitchen. He was waiting in anticipation, waiting for a man he hadn't seen since the day of his sister's funeral. He listened, but the house was silent, as if it stood empty. Even the sound of Sirus breathing beside him fell into the background as Joss listened for the sound of his uncle coming to greet him with open arms. Then, at last, Joss heard the slight creak of floorboards as someone descended the stairs. He looked up, but the face he saw belonged to a stranger—one with dark eyes and a scraggly beard. The man smiled at him and then nodded to Sirus, who responded, "Where is he, Malek?"

Malek jerked his head toward the direction Kat had moved. "Out back. But be forewarned. He's in a mood."

Sirus chuckled. "When isn't he?"

Malek smirked and brushed past Sirus and out the front door. After he'd gone, Sirus turned to Joss. "Leave your suitcase and backpack here. I'll show you to your room in a minute. But first, your uncle will want to see you."

Joss glanced anxiously in the direction Malek had gestured before nodding and setting his bags on the floor. Sirus nodded, too, as if agreeing with some unspoken thing between them, and then strode down the hall, past what looked like an old sitting room on the left of the foyer, a formal dining room on the right at the end of the hall, and a small bedroom adjacent to that. Beyond that, they moved through the door that lead them to the kitchen, where Kat was putting groceries away inside tall, dark cabinets. Sirus set the bags he was carrying on the counter and nodded toward the back door. "Please close the door on your way out. It'll keep the bugs out and give you some privacy. And Joss . . ."

Something dark and heavy crossed Sirus's eyes then. Something that hinted at a warning. "Be careful."

There was a moment when Joss hesitated. It probably only lasted a few seconds, enough for an eye to blink twice or a heart to beat once. But inside that moment, there was so much significance that Joss felt as if he couldn't breathe. This was it. This signified the beginning of change in his life. It was a moment that would shape him, and bring him ever closer to finding justice for Cecile. He was ready, and so excited about beginning his training that he could hardly breathe.

He looked at the door and nodded to himself, ready as he'd ever be. Crossing the room, Joss's footfalls sounded heavy in his ears. He turned the knob and opened the door, then stepped outside. Sitting at the small table there on the back porch was Abraham, a newspaper in his hands, a pipe clenched between his teeth. Without looking at Joss, he removed the pipe and pointed wordlessly to the chair across from him. Joss took his seat and waited. For what, he did not know.

Abraham was dressed in earth tones. Despite the

fact that it was blazing hot, he wore slacks with boots, a button-down shirt and vest. He looked like a cool, young Indiana Jones, trapped in time. Instead of a whip, he carried a stake—a stake that was now held in a leather holster at his hip. And instead of hunting for treasure, he hunted vampires. Joss was mystified. Not a single wrinkle marred the fabric of his shirt, nor was a single hair out of place. Abraham was a perfectionist. In fact, his only flaw was the scar on his clean-shaven cheek—a four-inch-wide crescent shape.

Abraham returned his pipe to his mouth and finished reading whatever article had held his attention, then folded the paper carefully and set it on the tabletop. It was only then that he looked at his nephew. Silently, he went about emptying his pipe into a coffee can on the porch. After he was finished and had placed his pipe in its rightful place inside a leather pouch, he spoke. "Well, you've arrived in one piece. I suppose that's something."

Joss bit the inside of his cheek and dropped his eyes to the ground, uncertain what to say exactly. He'd never spoken much to his uncle. In fact, prior to the funeral, he'd had the vaguest idea that Abraham preferred anyone's company to his. But still, they were family. There was something to be said for that. And there was something to be said for the fact that of all their family members, he'd chosen Joss to train as the next Slayer. He'd seen something special in Joss, and Joss wasn't about to let him down. "I've been working hard nonstop to develop my skills, Uncle. And I'm ready to begin my training now. I'm ready for whatever you have in store for me."

Abraham sighed and folded his arms in front of him. Joss raised his chin again, meeting his uncle's eyes. For the briefest of moments, he'd expected Abraham to utter some words of praise to a boy who'd not only witnessed the death of his sister three years ago at the hand of a monster, but had worked hard to ready himself for training and had achieved a skill level that made him ready five full years early. But all Abraham said was, "They all think they're ready. New Slayers come to us at eighteen years of age, full of bravado, full of pride, and none of them are truly prepared for the tasks that await them. How arrogant of you to think that at thirteen, you're even moderately close to prepared. You're a boy, Joss. And it takes a man to fully train as a Slayer."

Abraham was right. Joss wasn't a man yet. McMillan men were sturdy, strong, reliable. They did not falter. They did not cry. His own father had reminded him of that many times. Joss had argued that Uncle Mike—father to Joss's cousin Henry—was nothing at all like that. Uncle Mike was kind and generous. He cried at sad parts of movies and had told Joss one summer that it was perfectly natural to be afraid sometimes. But there was no getting his dad to listen to reason. As far as he was concerned, McMillan men were one way and Uncle Mike was decidedly another, which made him less of a McMillan somehow, less of a man. And though Joss wasn't exactly certain he agreed with those assessments, he wanted to be capable and strong and reliable for those he loved. He wanted the strength to avenge Cecile's death. Maybe that would make his father notice him again.

A sinking feeling pulled at Joss's insides. "I thought you sent for me because I was ready to train."

Abraham slanted his eyes. "I sent for you because the vampire hive in this area has gotten out of control, and we have need of another Slayer. And since you're the oldest new recruit on our roster, you're it. That's all. You're not ready for anything. You're not special. You were simply born before the rest."

A lump formed in Joss's throat then, one that was difficult to swallow. He wasn't special. He was merely conveniently aged. One step above being the invisible boy.

Abraham picked up the newspaper from the table and opened it, snapping the creases from its pages and dismissing his nephew. "Don't make me regret bring-ing you here."

With a short, simple, manlike nod, Joss turned and

moved back inside the house. Wordlessly, he walked down the hallway, retrieved his suitcase and backpack, and headed upstairs. He wasn't sure where he was going. He was only sure that boys wait to be told where to go. Men find their own way, and Joss was going to prove he had what it takes.

The stairs creaked beneath his feet as he ascended, one hand running along the worn wooden banister. At the top of the stairs was a door on the right with two single beds. Past that, another room, this one with a daybed. Both rooms looked occupied, as both had personal effects here and there. Across from the daybed room was a small bathroom, and past that, back toward the stairs, were two more rooms, one with a queen bed and the other a king, both also occupied. At the end of the hall was another bedroom and a second staircase. Joss peered up the stairs, debating whether or not he should go up. A hand closed over his shoulder and Joss flinched. He turned to find Kat smiling at him. "I wouldn't if I were you."

He hadn't been all that intrigued about the space at the top of the stairs, guarded by a small wooden door, but now he was. There was something to be said about the enticement of all things forbidden, but there was also something to be said about the comfort of following the rules. "Why? What's up there?"

Kat shrugged. "A meeting room or something. All I

know is I was polishing the wood railing one day and got too close to the door and Abraham almost ripped my arm out of its socket."

Joss peered up the stairs curiously at the small door. "How close is too close?"

Kat chuckled and tugged his sleeve toward the small bedroom at the foot of the stairs. "C'mon. Your room is this way."

The room was small, painted green, and was covered in what looked like someone else's dirty laundry. Joss set his suitcase down and looked around, a little befuddled. Then Kat walked across the room and opened another door. She looked back at him and gestured inside the door with a nod. "This one's yours. You have to walk through Malek's to get to it, but it's a nice room."

Picking up his bag again, Joss moved past Kat into a larger room with an old full-size bed and equally old furnishings to match. The patchwork quilt on the bed reminded Joss of something that his grandmother would have decorated with, and the flowing lace curtains only helped to solidify that image in his imagination. This wasn't a place for a man. It was somewhere an old lady would sleep.

Kat flopped on the bed on her stomach and looked up at him. "Sirus tells me you're Abraham's nephew, and that you'll be here all summer to help out."

Joss set his suitcase down beside the dresser slowly,

trying to think of the proper response. He wasn't exactly sure what Sirus had said to Kat about him. He only knew that Sirus had pleaded with him not to reveal to Kat the fact that they were vampire Slayers. "That's why I'm here."

Kat darted her eyes to the door before dropping her voice to a whisper. "Aren't you scared?"

Joss swallowed hard. He was scared. He was utterly terrified of the idea that for who knows how long, actual, real live vampires had been roaming the earth, right under mankind's nose. And now he was going to learn how to kill them. To face down those horrible monsters and extinguish their life. The very idea set his hands shaking. But he couldn't reveal any of that to Kat. Besides, she wasn't talking about vampires. Joss got the feeling she had no idea that they even existed. "Scared? Why would I be scared?"

"Of the wolves, silly! If I were going to hunt wild wolves, I'd be scared out of my mind. Why would you want to do that, anyway? Those things can be dangerous, y'know. And you're kinda young to be killing things, don't ya think?" She shook her head and her bangs flopped briefly over her eyes before she drew them back with a finger and tucked them thoughtlessly behind one ear, not waiting for him to respond—which was good, because Joss had no idea what to say. "Sirus says wolves are a real problem here. That's why the state of New York hires him to come every summer with your uncle and the rest of the guys. Because if he didn't, the wolf population would go spiraling out of control. But anyway, are you hungry? Sirus is cooking enough to feed the entire population of Timbuktu."

Joss shrugged casually, despite the fact that his stomach was rumbling loudly. "I could eat, I guess."

"Cool." Kat slid off the bed and headed for the door. "I'll tell Sirus he can count on Timbuktu plus one for dinner."

"Hey, Kat?" Joss cocked a curious eyebrow at her. He'd been wondering about something since he'd first heard Kat speak, but had only now summoned the courage to ask about it. "Why do you call him Sirus? Isn't he your dad?"

"Yeah, but he's also Sirus." She smiled brightly. "Besides, I like his name."

He nodded, not really understanding. "Thanks for showing me my room."

"No problem. See you downstairs."

Once Kat had gone, Joss opened his suitcase and began unpacking, organizing his belongings in the way he supposed Uncle Abraham would, and taking more time than was needed to do it. The first thing he unpacked was a small silver frame. Inside the frame was a photo of Cecile. She was smiling, her eyes bright and happy. Joss placed her photograph on his dresser and turned back to his open suitcase with a sigh. The truth was, he was nervous now about being here, nervous and excited about beginning his training, and beyond nervous about being away from his mom and dad for the summer—despite the fact that he was now the invisible boy to them. He reached into his pocket and pulled out his cell phone, but frowned at the lack of bars indicating no signal. He was in the mountains, and his dad had warned him that getting a signal might be a problem. He made a mental note to call home later and returned to the task at hand.

Though organizing and reorganizing his dresser contents wasn't going to alleviate any of his stress, it did take his mind off of it for a while. From the small zippered pouch inside his suitcase, he withdrew his grandfather's pocket watch. Sitting on the grandma-style bed, he turned the watch over and over again in his hand. His grandfather had never uttered a word to him about the Slayer Society. He couldn't help but wonder how long his grandfather had been slaying. Was he still killing vampires when Joss had seen him last, just months before his funeral? And if he was here now, would he approve of the way that Abraham had just spoken to Joss? Maybe, if that's how Slayers were supposed to act. Regardless, Joss missed his grandfather dearly. Almost as much as Cecile.

When the last shirt was folded and placed in a drawer and the last pocket of his bag had been zipped closed, Joss was left only with the smell of dinner wafting up the stairs from the kitchen, and the knowledge that avoiding leaving his room was no way to honor his sister.

With a deep breath, Joss walked out the door and headed downstairs, his footfalls strong and sure—even though he wasn't.

When he reached the table, he found one woman and seven men, including Sirus and his uncle. Kat was nowhere in sight. Sirus was standing near the head of the table. "In case you're wondering, I sent Kat next door for a while so that we can make proper introductions. Joss, I'd like to introduce you to our team. We're a family, though a bit more on the dysfunctional side than most, I'd wager. Each of us possesses a particular skill and we'll each be training you in our specialty over the course of the summer, so you'll spend quite a bit of time getting to know us. But why don't we begin with names. The vision to your far left, we call Paty."

The brunette woman he'd referred to stood, and though she was very attractive, the expression on her face said that she took Sirus's compliment as a dig. Her hair was pulled back in a bun, and her skin seemed dry, and devoid of all makeup. Joss wondered if she was trying to erase her feminine side in order to earn the respect of her male Slayer peers. It couldn't be easy to be the only woman in a group of Slayers—especially when she was so pretty. With a stern nod, she looked at him with chocolate brown eyes and said, "My specialty is stealth."

She elbowed the man next to her, the one with shaggy blond hair and sun-kissed skin, his eyes a deep, intense blue. He looked a bit like a surfer. He smiled casually, easily, in Joss's direction. "Hey, little brother, I'm Chazz. In charge of Tac Ops. Tactical Operations, which basically means I'm the man with the plan."

The man next to him—the first person Joss had encountered when he'd entered the cabin—snorted behind cupped hands. When Chazz raised an eyebrow at him, the man acted as if he'd just been innocently stroking his short, black beard. After a moment, he turned to Joss, extending his hand and shaking Joss's. "Name's Malek. I'm the tracking specialist."

"Ash." A young-looking man, maybe in his mid-twenties, stood and shook Joss's hand. "Weapons specialist. I transport, clean, create, distribute, and invent more weapons than you can even imagine."

Across the table from Ash, another man—one with pale skin, bright green eyes, and red hair—raised his hand. "Munitions. If it calls for explosives, you call me. I'm Morgan."

Next to him, a thin man with a quiet demeanor spoke up. "Cratian. I can teach you a few things about reflexes and speed. Physical training is my focus."

That just left Sirus and Joss's uncle. Sirus smiled at Joss. "Your uncle's specialty is hand-to-hand combat, and my gift is in survival. Seeking out food, sticking it out in less than desirable conditions. Think of those survivalist television shows, but without the cameras, and with the worry of vampires."

Joss nodded, uncertain what he should say or do. He felt like maybe he should introduce himself, but he didn't have any idea what to say, apart from the fact that he was bursting with excitement to get started already. Fidgeting some, he said, "So . . . which of these skills will I be learning?"

"All of them." Abraham plucked an apple from the bowl at the center of the table and tossed it to Joss, who caught it with ease. "That's your dinner. You can enjoy your feast outside until Malek is ready to take you to the guard post."

Malek shot Abraham a look—one that was met with a commanding glare.

For a moment, Joss was ready to hang his head and move out the door, ready to wait patiently for Malek to take him wherever he was taking him. But the rumble in his stomach, and the keen irritation at being talked to like he was just a child mingled together within him in a strange cloud that lifted him from where he was standing and moved his feet toward the pot of stew simmering on the stove. He picked up a bowl and started spooning into it the delectable smelling mixture of beef, potatoes, and big chunks of carrots. The room had fallen silent behind him.

A hand closed over his wrist and jerked it back, flinging the bowl from his grip into the wall beside the stove. Stew splattered the counter, the wall, the floor. Joss turned his eyes to his uncle and waited for him to speak.

Abraham kept his tone even but stern as he released Joss's wrist. "I said get outside. And you can forget the apple. Your purification will start tonight. I see no reason to wait a day. You clearly lack both discipline and humility."

Cratian stood. "Not exactly following protocol, are we, Abraham? Let the boy eat. He'll need his strength for the trials he's about to begin. Without proper protein, his muscles won't be able to handle the strain."

"Besides," Malek whined. "I'm hungry. Why should *I* be punished for *his* purification?"

Several Slayers shot Malek a look that said that he'd be wise to shut his mouth. Abraham stood in front of Joss, his chest heaving in anger.

Abraham's gaze was heavy on Joss, weighing him down. "Outside."

Joss looked at his uncle. He was tired of this already, tired of being made to feel like he didn't belong, like he was a burden rather than here to help out. He hadn't been told precisely what training would entail, and so far, had only experienced his uncle's insults. And he'd had quite enough of that. Maybe he was just a kid, but even a kid deserved some answers. "What is this, Abraham? Why am I here? What exactly do you want from me?"

He thought for a second, and then tacked on a burning question. "And what's purification?"

None of the other Slayers moved. Even Sirus stood gravely still. The only sound for several seconds was that of the bubbling stew. After a moment, Abraham returned to his chair, and shoved an empty seat toward Joss with his foot. Joss wanted answers, but he really didn't want to sit down. He paused, but finally relented, too curious and too hungry not to oblige. Abraham sat back in his seat and sighed. "The world you knew before young Cecile was murdered is not the world you know now, boy. Things have changed for you. But they have not changed. Not really. The world remains the same as it has always been. You just didn't know any better before. Just as you seem to be ignorant of the importance of following orders and protocol."

Joss became very still, but he could feel a strange tightening in his chest. Abraham held his gaze. "Vampires exist. Slayers exist as well. We do the honorable work of defending mankind against their bloodthirsty desires. We eradicate them to protect the innocent. We kill them. Before they can kill us."

By "us" Joss was fairly certain that his uncle was referring to people—all people—and not just Slayers. He swallowed hard, trying desperately not to picture Cecile lying in her bed, so still, and failing miserably.

Abraham tightened his jaw. "I have seen things

that would make your worst nightmares seem like the sweetest daydreams. I have witnessed monsters devouring children, mothers, the elderly. And I was there the day your grandfather—my father—stood in the face of a vampire as it ripped out his throat."

Joss's heart raced. Grandpa. Killed by a vampire. Darkness closed in around him—a gloom that he couldn't escape. First Cecile, now his grandfather. His family had been partially erased because of the fanged creatures that lurked in the night.

Something in Abraham's eyes pulled back then, steering him away from the emotions that memory had stirred. His tone became all business. "Only a Slayer can recognize another Slayer, and it's always somewhere in the family line, one Slayer per generation. We see it in their agility, in their strength, in their unusual gifts. I first noticed your gifts when you were five. You could outrun any child in your neighborhood. You could outrun your own parents. And you never tired. Then when you were eight, I saw it again when you took an archery class. You hit the center more than any child of that age should be capable. I knew, then, you were a Slayer, even though I wished many times that you weren't.

"Your cousin Greg. Now, he would have made an excellent Slayer. Hell, even his younger brother, Henry. But you . . . you're . . ." Abraham shook his head slowly, mulling over his choice of words. "You're a disappointment, Joss. Full of too much emotion. You'll feel every kill, likely empathize with the monsters we're hunting, and endanger your fellow Slayers. I don't want you here, even with your advanced physical skills. Those are not enough. But the Society insists that we take down the hive in this area. So I have to train you to fight and teach you how to survive. There's simply no one else available to assist us. Your name, to put it plainly, was next on the list."

Joss folded his arms in front of him, feeling every eye in the room weighing heavily on him. So much for his uncle's empathy. "What if I don't want to be here? What if I don't want to train? What if I'd rather just go home and forget about all of this vampire stuff?"

Several Slayers exchanged glances, as if they knew something that Joss didn't, but should. It was unnerving.

Abraham leaned forward, a dark dare gleaming in his eyes. "Go, if that's what you want. But you'll never have vengeance for Cecile, and by allowing that monster to live, you will condemn others to her fate. Plus, if you tell anyone about any of this, and upset the delicate balance of silence that we have maintained for over two hundred years, the Slayer Society will be on your heels. Keeping the knowledge of the existence of vampires to ourselves protects mankind, and we will protect that silence with our lives, and with yours, if necessary."

Joss gulped.

Abraham nodded. "Besides, Elysia already knows about you. I guarantee it. Once you leave the training grounds, they'll view you as a threat. Your life will be forfeit—creatures like that have no morals against killing a child. That, you should know already."

Oh, he knew. Joss knew all about what vampires were capable of. "What's Elysia?"

After a moment of silence, Sirus chimed in. "It's what they call themselves. Vampirekind. Collectively, they're known as Elysia."

Joss sat in silence for several minutes, taking this all in. It was a whirlwind of information, and he wasn't exactly sure he was up for the job of vampire killer extraordinaire. After all, he'd only seen death once. Would he be capable of bringing death onto another living thing? And if he wasn't, would he be killed? The idea sent a frightened shiver up his spine. Calming that shiver was the promise he'd made to Cecile. He would avenge her death, no matter what. Even if it killed him. "What's purification?" he asked again.

Abraham sat back in his seat, seemingly content that the matter of Joss leaving had been settled in favor of him staying. "We bring certain ideas with us into the Society—ideas that must be removed before training can begin. The ideas that comfort is a necessity, kindness is deserved, and that generosity is to be expected. The world is a harsh, cruel place. You must learn this so that you may face our enemies with strength, independence, and certainty."

Sirus sat forward, his tone reassuring. "The purification part of your training is about tearing you down so that we can build you up renewed. It'll be hard. At times it will feel an insurmountable task. But we've all been through it. You can do this, Joss, if you set your mind to it. Survival begins inside the mind, inside your spirit. It takes commitment."

Abraham continued, as if Sirus had never interrupted. "For three days, you'll be given nothing but water, twice a day. No food. You'll also be on watch for that duration of time. No sleep. You'll be exposed to the elements the entire time, and to any vampires who may find you. No shelter, no weapons. If you survive, you can begin training. Or leave. The choice is yours. If you don't survive, I'll inform your parents that you wandered too deep into the woods, became lost, and perished. The Slayer Society has made all the arrangements to back up my story, as is custom."

Joss's jaw almost hit the floor. How could one organization be that powerful, and how could his own uncle expect so much out of him, especially to join a group he didn't know enough about yet? If it weren't for Cecile, he wouldn't have gotten on that train in the first place. But he *had* gotten on the train. He *had* made a choice to do whatever he could to avenge his baby sister's untimely death. There was no going back now.

Paty shook her head. "Is that really necessary, Abraham? He's just a boy. Do we really need to threaten him with what will come if he dies during training?"

Abraham shot her a look that said yes, that Joss needed to know every grisly detail. Then he leaned forward, meeting his nephew's eyes. "You may wonder why the Society would risk losing a Slayer in such difficult training measures when there are so few of us. The truth is, we used to lose more just by sending them out on missions. By putting a Slayer to the test, we actually save lives. You may die, or you may live—that's up to you."

Joss swallowed again, his throat feeling tight, and said, "When does my purification begin?"

Abraham smiled, but it was not the smile of an uncle to his nephew, or even the smile of a decent human being to a stranger. It was a smile of superiority, full of knowledge beyond anything that Joss could currently understand. "It begins now."

▸ 7 ◂

THE PURIFICATION BEGINS

The woods were thick and Joss found himself breathing heavily as he tromped his way up the millionth hill, following Malek deeper and deeper into the forest, higher and higher up the mountain. If nothing else, he was grateful that it wasn't Abraham leading him to the watch point. His uncle had insisted it be Malek, and Joss wasn't about to argue or question Abraham's authority. He'd save his questions for when it was really important. He wasn't sure when that would be, but he knew the time would come.

As he followed Malek over the crest of the hill, the terrain evened out some and Malek came to a halt at long last. Malek was barely breathing heavily—it was as if the trek was well known to him, and such physical feats were nothing. Meanwhile, Joss was scratching his head, trying to figure out why he could run away from anyone without having to stop to catch his breath, but trekking up a mountain after Malek was tiring. Then he realized it was because Malek was a Slayer and had special skills, too. He also supposed that was because when he was running, it was something he wanted to do. And this—this wasn't exactly on his wish list of ways to spend his summer vacation. He wanted to avenge his sister, yes, but he wasn't looking forward to three days without food, shelter, or protection. The woods scared him. The possibility of vampires in the woods scared him even more.

"This is it," Malek grumbled, his eyes sweeping over the small, overgrown clearing. "If you look down the mountain, you can see the cabin. Our job is to keep watch, make certain no vampires approach. We can't have them discovering one of the training facilities. If we see one, we kill it. So if the time comes, you'd better man up, boy."

The hairs on the back of Joss's neck stood on end as hot anger flushed over him. Malek had no right to judge him. Malek didn't even know him.

Malek shook his head and laughed, slapping Joss on the shoulder. Through a grin, he said, "My best impersonation of your uncle. You hungry?"

Joss paused a moment, not certain he exactly understood Malek's humor, but he was relieved it had just been a joke of some type. "Starved."

The smile slipped from Malek's face, morphing into a pout. "Me too. But technically, you can't eat. So . . . what are we gonna do about that, kid?"

Joss very much wanted to say "feed me," but he held his tongue and looked around the clearing.

Malek shoved his thumbs into his pockets and looked around, too, sighing. "Well, I guess I can show you a little about tracking, get your mind off of food. Mine too. That stew smelled amazing."

"Sorry you couldn't eat before we left, Malek." The guilt weighed on him.

Malek's smile returned. "Don't worry about it, kid. You just worry about getting through today. And tomorrow, you worry about getting through that, and so on, and so forth. We can't all be your superstar uncle. Some of us need practice. Okay?"

Joss's chest felt a bit lighter. He nodded to Malek, who didn't seem like such a bad guy after all. "Okay."

Malek slapped his hands together, their clap echoing into the woods around them. "So. Tracking. The first thing you need to know is that tracking is about using all of your senses to learn about and locate your prey. Look around you and you might notice broken branches, footsteps in the dirt, blood from a recent injury. Inhale through your nose and you might smell a recent campfire, or maybe freshly spilled blood."

Malek paused. "Sorry. It's always blood with these things. You get really tired of seeing it and smelling it."

"What does blood smell like?"

"Rotten and metallic, kid. Rotten and metallic. And when you smell enough of it, you can taste it, too." The Slayer shook his head, as if willing that thought away. Joss couldn't help but wonder what horrors Malek had seen. The blood seemed to haunt him. "Touch things like tree trunks and you might feel a lingering cool. And listen. That's the most important sense you can use when tracking vampires. Keep your ears open and your wits about you at all times."

A sliver of fear wedged itself into Joss's brain then. It slipped in through the base of his skull with an icy tingle.

Malek led him down the trail some, and crouched where they saw a pile of deer scat. "It's very important that you remain observant and pay attention to detail. For instance, in order to learn everything we can about this deer, we place a hand over its scat and feel that it's still warm, which means the deer isn't far from here. We can see some pine needles, so we know where it's been by what it's been eating."

Then, much to Joss's horror, Malek picked up a pebble of scat and popped it into his mouth, gesturing for Joss to do the same. Joss looked up and down the trail, hoping he could spot the stupid deer and end their lesson already, but the trail was empty, except for the two of them. Holding his breath, Joss plucked a tiny bit of deer scat from the pile and placed it on his tongue.

He immediately spit it out. It was all he could do not to vomit.

Malek wore a smirk on his face. "What have you learned from this? What's it taste like?"

Joss spat into the grass several more times. "It tastes like crap!"

With a chuckle, Malek spit a pebble into his palm. It wasn't scat at all. It was a small stone that had apparently been lying next to the scat. Joss hadn't been watching closely enough. "My young friend, this is a lesson that you will never forget. Attention to detail is everything."

Lesson learned. Joss spat into the grass again. "Can I have some water?"

Malek patted him on the back and handed him a bottle of cool water. Joss rinsed his mouth repeatedly until the bottle was empty.

"I'll be here between meals and while the sun's up. You're on your own the rest of the time. And so help you if you fall asleep." Malek's mouth closed into a tight, white line. "Not only will Abraham be royally ticked off, but it could jeopardize your training and our lives, kid. Don't let it. And don't think we won't know. A person has a look about them if they haven't been sleeping. I'll see it on your face if you sneak so much as a catnap, and I'll be forced to tell your uncle. Even though I'd rather share a nice steak with you and send you off to bed. The Society comes first, though, and we can't forget why you're here. Okay?"

Joss slowly released his breath, and when he spoke, his voice came out eerily calm. "Whether or not you believe it, Malek, whether or not any of you believes it, I'm up for this. I can handle anything that comes my way."

Malek chuckled and dropped his gear at the base of a large elm tree. "We'll see, kid. We'll see."

Joss hadn't been given any gear at all—no rope, no tent, no tools. After all, this was to be a spiritual journey for him. It was meant to prove that he had what it took to be a Slayer, that he was loyal to their cause. And it was meant to purify his soul, in some weird way. He was supposed to unlearn everything that life had taught him about empathy and learn a new way of thinking. He wasn't sure how starving in the woods was supposed to teach him any of that, but he was willing to go through the motions to get to the real training.

But then . . . wasn't he training already? Maybe it wasn't hand-to-hand combat, but Joss had already learned some things from Malek. Valuable things that he was sure he'd carry into the field with him in the future. He was in training, despite what Abraham had said. And this was only the beginning.

Once Malek dug into his bag and proceeded to set up a small tent meant to protect him from any potential rainfall, Joss took a seat at the opposite side of the clearing and watched the so-called cabin below. A bird flew from a tree not far from the cabin, breaking up the monotony of Joss's vision, but after he'd been sitting there for about an hour, Joss's butt had lost most of its feeling and complete boredom had set in. He hadn't been tired until there was nothing to do but sit and stare down the mountain. Now he was exhausted and fighting off a yawn. He couldn't let Malek know his resolve was weakening already. It had only been an hour. What kind of Slayer would he make if he couldn't even last an hour in the woods without dozing off?

One hour turned into two. Two turned into six, and by the time Joss's stomach started grumbling loudly, demanding to be fed, he was well into his twentieth yawn. He'd gotten up and walked around the clearing to stay awake, but it wasn't really helping. The woods, while pretty and peaceful, were also incredibly boring. He was almost wishing a vampire would show up so that he'd have something to do, other than watching the cabin, and watching Malek watching the cabin, his thoughts perhaps drifting off to memories involving blood. Neither of them spoke, which was probably a good thing, but Joss was quickly tiring of the silence between them. Just as he was about to try his hand at conversation, Malek sighed and took to his feet. "Time for me to turn in, kid. Sit tight. I should be back before the sun rises. Maybe I'll bring a deck of cards or something."

Joss's heartbeat picked up. "What do I do if a vampire comes?"

"Kill it."

Joss furrowed his brow, completely enveloped by the enormity of the potential situation his imagination had dreamed up. "How?"

Malek grinned. "Any way you can, kid."

He began his descent down the mountain, but turned back suddenly. Joss was sure he was going to give him some clue, some hint at just how to deal with a monstrous fanged creature. But he was wrong. Malek said, "Hey, kid. You need help, you scream, okay? I mean it."

Then Malek was gone, and Joss was left in the woods. In the dark. Alone.

It surprised Joss how quickly the temperature dropped once the sun's rays were no longer filtering through the trees. His skin prickled with goose bumps, and after some time, he began to shiver. He hadn't thought to bring a jacket with him. After all, he was spending his summer in upstate New York. He hadn't exactly gotten the impression that it was jacket weather up here in June. But in the mountains, exposed to the elements, without an ounce of food warming his belly, Joss could believe it. His head ached from not having eaten. He felt nauseous. And tired, oh so tired. His eyes drooped as he leaned against a tree, and it wasn't long before Joss had to force himself to walk the clearing's perimeter in order to stay awake.

Several hours passed before Malek returned, rested, with a full belly and bottle of water for Joss. He tossed the small plastic bottle to Joss and pulled a deck of cards from his pocket, shuffling them as he sat. Joss chugged the water and, though his stomach ached from drinking the cool liquid so fast, his parched throat and dry tongue thanked him profusely. They played several hands of rummy before the sun came up. As Joss was gathering the loose cards back into a deck, he said, "Can I ask you something?"

"Sure, kid."

"If vampires are such a huge problem, why doesn't anyone on the outside know about them? I mean, there are movies and books and stuff, but no one really believes in them. Why don't we just tell people about them? Warn them, ya know?"

Malek smiled and took the deck from Joss's hands.

"People need to be protected, kid. And the sad fact is that most people aren't smart enough to be trusted with the facts. Most people would panic at the knowledge that vampires are real. Then we'd not only have vampires to deal with, but crazy mobs of people, too. It's just easier to do our job by keeping them in the dark."

Joss mulled this over for a bit before responding. "I guess that makes sense. But what if a few people did know? Seems like we could make some money that way. I mean, the Society must need funding, right? Wouldn't that be an easy way to raise funds?"

"I like the way you think, kid. But we're not allowed to take private jobs." Malek grinned and slapped him on the back. "Anyway, it's time for you to return to your post and keep watch. We're not out here playing around. This is an important part of your training on the road to becoming a better Slayer. Less chitchat. More eyes on those woods. And more importantly, what's lurking within them."

They didn't speak for the rest of the long day, and Joss walked the perimeter of the clearing more times than he could count. Then, as the sun had begun its descent once again, Malek gathered up his gear. As he was doing so, Joss dared to ask him a question that had been burning on the edges of his curiosity since they'd climbed the mountain. "Hey, Malek. What was your purification like?"

Malek shook his head, laughing it off. "Let's just say you don't want to know, kid."

"No, really. What was it like?"

Pausing, a momentary serious expression came over playful Malek. "It was pretty rough. I had to be pulled from the mountain and purified the old-fashioned way, with a whip. I don't recommend it."

Joss tried to imagine being whipped by another human being, but couldn't. That wasn't something that happened to real people. It was the stuff of movies, the stuff of books. Not real.

Without another word, Malek retreated down the mountainside, leaving Joss to fend for himself for a second night.

In the dark wilderness, it didn't take long for paranoia to set in. Every cricket's chirp was a vampire. Every breeze through the trees was a vampire. Joss slumped against a tree, his heart beating softly inside his chest, his tongue so dry inside his mouth, his stomach ripe with hunger pains. There had been no vampires—not even a single little sign of the creatures—since his purification had begun. He was beginning to think he'd imagined Cecile's murder, as well as the vampire he'd stopped from killing Kat. Maybe he was crazy, and all of this was simply a part of his imaginary world. Maybe everyone—all the Slayers, even—were part of his imagination, too. This thought crept into his hungry, exhausted mind, and disappeared again like a whisper. Vampires were real, he knew that much. It was just his lack of food and sleep that was making him wonder such ridiculous things.

He watched the sun setting behind the trees, and it wasn't long before darkness took him over.

▸ 8 ◂

PICKING FLOWERS

In the distance, Joss could hear someone humming. The sound was soft and sweet and reminded him of home. Though he was certain it had been night just a moment before, daylight filled the clearing now, illuminating every inch of the forest as far as he could see. Standing, Joss followed the lyrical sound of the humming until he came upon a field of wildflowers. A young girl was crouched in the middle of the field, plucking purple flowers from the ground and placing them in the bunch grasped tightly in her left hand. Her blond curls were pulled up in a ponytail that just barely brushed against her tan skin. She was wearing a yellow sundress that reminded him of the color of his mom's kitchen.

He knew the girl, but feared speaking her name out loud. Because something was wrong with this scene, but Joss couldn't quite put his finger on what it was. "Cecile, what are you doing out here?"

She turned her head to the side at the sound of his voice, but didn't speak. Joss wasn't certain why, but he was relieved to see her cheek clean and tan. When she went back to picking flowers, he crossed the field, daisies bouncing against his ankles as he moved closer to his sister. "Cecile, what are you doing here? Mom wouldn't want you out here, you know."

"I'm picking flowers, Jossie." She turned her head to the side again to glimpse her brother.

Joss's heart skipped a beat. Something was on Cecile's cheek. A dark line. It looked like blood.

Then he remembered. Cecile was dead. She was dead and it was all his fault.

He slowed his steps, stopping just a few feet behind her. His fingers were trembling. "Why are you picking flowers, Cecile?"

"To take them with me." She turned around then. Once again, her eye sockets were black, soulless tunnels. Deep within those dark tunnels, Joss could see flames. When she opened her mouth to speak again, a large centipede crawled out. "There are no flowers in hell, Jossie."

Joss shoved his sister away. He felt terrible for doing so, but he was so frightened, he could hardly breathe.

His chest tightened in panicked breaths and he backed away. "You're not in hell, Cecile! You're not!"

Cecile crawled after him in a twitching hurry, her mouth oozing all sorts of insects, her eyes devoid of all life. She clutched his ankle, crying. "Oh, yes I am. And you put me there, Jossie. You did this to me."

Her tears disappeared quickly as her mouth contorted into a grin. Inside her mouth were fangs. Fangs covered in blood.

▸ 9 ◂

A SIMPLE MISTAKE

Joss woke with a start. Warmth, glorious wonderful warmth covered his cheek, and he sighed in relief that he was no longer in that field of flowers. But his relief didn't last.

Joss sat up and whipped his head around in a panicked frenzy, his mind focused on one thought— a thought that echoed through his head repeatedly. *Abraham's going to kill me!*

His heart raced. He'd fallen asleep. Somehow, despite walking around for hours, despite promising himself that he wouldn't even doze, he'd fallen asleep and it was now morning. Sun filtered through the trees above. The clearing was alive with the energy of daytime . . . and empty, but for Joss, and Malek's unused tent.

He moved quickly, searching the clearing with his eyes, then physically walking it until it was clear that Malek wasn't there. Then he moved outside the circle, searching carefully, all the while wondering if Malek had returned to the house to tell Abraham of his failure. Or maybe worse. Maybe the Slayers had left him here in the mountains alone. He turned toward the trail that led down the mountain and just as he was about to begin his descent, he noticed something on the trail.

Something moist. Something red.

Joss's steps slowed, but he still moved forward, as if he was naturally drawn to the substance on the ground. He crouched beside it, disbelief filling him until he felt as if he couldn't breathe. As he stretched his hand out to touch it, the voice in the back of his head, his reason, his good sense, screamed not to, but still Joss stretched his fingers forth, stopping only when they met with the moist ground. Moist with blood.

It smelled metallic. And slightly rotten.

As if he hadn't been suspecting all along that the substance had been blood, Joss jerked his fingers back, shaking them. His eyes never left the blood. Was it Malek's? Or maybe a vampire that Malek had taken out while he'd been dozing? He hoped for the latter, but couldn't be sure until he saw a body. He also couldn't shake the urge to follow the trail and confirm that it wasn't merely animal blood. Standing, he traced the blood trail into the undergrowth, over a fallen tree trunk, and behind a large boulder . . . where he encountered an arm. Joss froze, terrified, his heart racing, his bladder threatening to release the little liquid it contained at any second.

The arm was pale and looked as if it had been ripped away from the torso it belonged to. It wasn't attached to a body—not anymore—and there was no sign of a body anywhere around. At first, he didn't see any other sign of the owner of the arm. But then, hidden in the bushes to his left, he saw something that sent a scream tearing through him. A scream that he wasn't certain made any actual sound, but ripped through every cell of his body with fear and understanding.

Malek's head was lying in the bushes, its dead eyes staring wide, right at Joss.

Strong hands shook Joss from his maybe-silent scream. "What happened? My god, man, what happened to Malek?"

It was Ash, the Slayer with the kind smile. Only he wasn't smiling now. Joss shook his head, his eyes locked on the gruesome scene. "I . . . I fell asleep."

Ash's eyes moistened with anger. He turned abruptly and hurried down the hill to the cabin below. Joss's thoughts filled with questions. Had a vampire really snuck by him late at night and managed to silently tear Malek limb from limb? Had he actually slept through the attack? What would happen now? The police would have to be involved, that was for certain. Vampires or not, a man had been brutally murdered and the authorities would most certainly have to be told. And if the police were involved . . . would Joss be in danger of going to jail? After all, he was the only person around when Malek was killed. They might think he did it. But would they really believe a young teenager could be capable of such a horrible, brutal attack? Joss nervously touched his face with a trembling hand, Malek's blood smearing across his cheek. Yes, he thought. Police might suspect just about anybody when a man has been torn to pieces.

Soon—Joss had no idea how soon as time became twisted into a vortex of shock—the sound of many footfalls filled the woods as the remaining members of the group hurried up the hill to where Joss now stood. Their eyes moved from this bloody horror to that, but all came to rest on Joss, who was standing there in utter shock, his entire body trembling now, uncertain what to say or do. Abraham stepped forward and barked orders to the rest. "Clean it up. Now. I'll notify Headquarters so they can get a fitting explanation to Malek's family. And Joss . . ." Joss looked up at his uncle, Joss's lip shaking more than he ever deemed possible. He was hoping to hear words of support, of encouragement even, but he knew that would never happen. All Abraham said was, "Come with me."

His uncle led him down the hill, but instead of turning toward the house, he turned away from it, leading Joss to another clearing, this one occupied by a large fallen oak tree and a small wooden shack that had once been painted blue. When they got to the new clearing, Abraham turned to face him. "I didn't want to say this in front of the others, but it needs to be said, and you need to hear it."

Joss swallowed hard. His skin felt prickly, and he was having a difficult time standing still. He blamed it on nerves. Would Abraham suspect he was involved in Malek's death in some way? Was the murderer still lurking somewhere nearby? And why were they here in this clearing? Shouldn't they be tracking whoever, whatever, did this to Malek?

Abraham set his jaw. He didn't raise his voice, but when he spoke, Joss could hear the dark sincerity in his tone. "The fact is that you fell asleep on the job, Joss. And because of that, a man is dead. So I'm going to do you a favor."

"What's that, Uncle?" He blinked and shuffled his feet awkwardly, afraid to ask for clarification and wondering just exactly what they were doing in this clearing with a shack and not in the house with a phone, calling the police. And what exactly had he meant when he told the others to "clean it up," anyway? Clean up the body? The evidence? That didn't sit right at all in Joss's stomach. In fact, it sat like a hard lead ball of wrongness right at the center of his being.

"Get out. Walk away. Leave your training behind. You aren't cut out for this kind of life. So go."

Joss let his uncle's words settle into his mind for a moment before shaking his head. "No. I'm not going anywhere. I screwed up. Because of me, Malek is dead. I have to stay. I have to help find his killer. I have to complete my training."

Abraham sighed heavily. "Your purification was a complete failure. How are you supposed to be purified now?"

Joss didn't know, but he did know that if he walked away from this, he might never sleep a dreamless sleep ever again. An image flashed in his mind then—the image of a large centipede crawling out of Cecile's mouth. She would never let him rest. Not until vengeance was had.

His uncle paused then, his eyes moving to the small shed. "Of course . . . there is another way."

Shuddering, Joss said, "I'll do whatever it takes."

With a nod, Abraham opened the shack's door and said, "Remove your shirt."

Joss blinked. He couldn't possibly have heard his uncle right. Remove his shirt? Why?

Abraham reached inside the shed and pulled out something long and coiled. He put his arm through the center and looped it over his shoulder. It resembled a very thin snake. Joss recognized the item from an old Indiana Jones movie he saw once with his dad. It was a whip.

Abraham's tone remained emotionless as he rolled up his sleeves. White cotton against tan skin. "Remove your shirt, Joss."

Inside Joss's chest, his heart raged. Did his uncle really mean to hit him with that thing? He shook his head, his eyes locked on the weapon, his thoughts scrambling around the notion that Abraham had almost ended up in the nuthouse not so long ago, after his aunt Margaret had been committed. His reply came out in a terrified whisper. "No."

Abraham's voice softened some. Just enough for Joss to know that he hadn't gone completely insane. "You said you'd do whatever it takes. Well, this is what it takes. Either you face the whip, or you walk away from your training. This will hurt, yes. But we have to complete your purification. Believe me, nephew, I'd rather have you go without sleep and come about your purification with moderate ease than face the whip, but Malek is dead, and Headquarters won't allow us to take you on without purification. We're down a Slayer, Joss, and we need you. Now tell me . . . can you man up and get through this so we can catch the beast, or should I send you packing like a boy?"

Joss looked from his uncle to the whip on his shoulder and swallowed hard. He thought of Cecile and how he'd never avenge her death if he couldn't put up with a little pain. Besides, how much pain had she experienced, all because he hadn't been there to protect her, to save her? A little pain was the least he deserved. "How many?"

"Ten more hours left until the day is done, marking your third day out. So, ten licks. That's nothing. You can do this. Malek did it, and he faced down twenty-seven licks without as much as a yelp. You just have to focus on something and breathe slow and deep."

Ten. That wasn't so bad. If Malek, who now lay in pieces on the side of a mountain, could do twenty-seven, Joss could do ten. Couldn't he? The whip looked so simple, just a braid of coils in a long strand. But the idea of being hit with it repeatedly sent a shock of fear through him. He'd never been hit by anything before. Not so much as a single fistfight or one event of paddling. What would it feel like to be whipped? The closest he'd come to that was being hit in the eye with a swing, and that had been a pain beyond any he'd experienced. It had been accidental, and this would very much be on purpose. Purposeful pain, he imagined, would hurt more somehow. Much more. But this was for Cecile, and for Malek now, too.

After considering his options for a moment—face it like a man or turn tail and run—he nodded at his uncle and pulled his T-shirt over his head, his fingers trembling. Then he turned around, his heart racing in panic. He hoped his uncle would be fast, but mostly he hoped he'd say something before the first lash struck.

Joss took in a breath, deep and slow, just the way his uncle had told him to, and just as he was about to let it out, the first lash of the whip cracked across his back. Brilliant pain ripped through Joss's body and for a moment, his vision wavered. It was far worse than the swing. Far worse than anything he had ever felt before. And just as his back had lit up with a terrible heat, another lash came. The pain was intense, but Joss counted the strikes again his bare skin. One lash. Two. Then a third.

His thoughts came in hot flashes of craziness. He wondered what his uncle was feeling or thinking as he brought the whip down again and again. Did he feel guilty? Was he enjoying it? How many people had Abraham whipped before? He thought about Malek and how awful it must have been to die that way. Had it hurt more than being whipped? He imagined it was far worse, but that didn't ease any of his pain. And what had Cecile's pain been like as that monster drank from her, stopping her heart before Joss could rescue her? He deserved this pain. He deserved every lick of it and more. But it was horrible, and at one point, he was certain that he would lose his mind entirely.

He wanted very much to beg his uncle to stop, but he couldn't. He couldn't form words, and even if he could, there was no way he could leave his training unfinished. This was the only way to right the wrong he'd done to his little sister. The only way out was through.

And suddenly, Joss began to see the light. The pain all but faded to the background of his mind as a strange euphoria filled him, as did the realization that he was destined for something greater, that he was special. That he was meant to be a vampire Slayer.

He could hear Abraham's voice, but it sounded so far away and garbled. It sounded like he said something that resembled, "One more, Joss." But he couldn't be sure. The next thing he knew, he was falling, maybe flying, and he swore he could hear the happy laughter of Cecile.

▸ 10 ◂

A BRIEF REPRIEVE

Pain ripped through Joss's back as something—it felt like flesh, but must have been a bandage—was torn from him in one quick tear. He scrambled to get to his knees, but calming hands stopped him, pressing him back on the mattress that he'd been lying facedown on. He couldn't remember how he'd gotten to the bed. His last memory was of the shadow of laughter that sounded so like Cecile.

"Stay still, Joss. The worst is over. This ought to help ease the pain a bit." Sirus sounded calm, but concerned. Then his fingers gently applied something cool and moist to Joss's back and Joss nearly melted into the sheets. The cool mixture instantly quieted his pain, and for that he was so grateful. He would have hugged Sirus . . . if it weren't for the fact that even the slightest movement made him want to scream.

"Thank you, Sirus." He glanced at the clock on the bedside table. Noon. He'd been out all day and all night. "I don't even remember passing out."

Sirus finished applying the salve, then gently replaced Joss's bandages with clean ones. Once he was finished, he said, "It's been three days, Joss. Your uncle brought you in after your purification and told me to take care of you. Within half a day you developed a fever from infection, and for a while, we weren't certain you'd wake up at all. It's not easy for a grown man to experience a whipping, let alone a young boy."

Joss pushed himself up, his back burning once again. He clenched his jaw against the pain and reached for his T-shirt on the nightstand. "I'm not that young."

Sirus eyed him for a moment as if he was about to say something to negate that fact, but then he shook his head instead and picked up the jar of salve from the bedside stand. After he stood, he said, "You might want to stay shirtless for now. It'll sting like hell to lift your arms. Are you hungry? We've been feeding you soup on occasion, but I bet you could use something heavier by now."

Joss's stomach rumbled in agreement.

Sirus's brow seemed permanently creased with

worry. "Abraham was wrong to whip you. I'll report him to Headquarters later today."

"Don't." Joss's voice sounded foreign, even to him. "It was my fault that Malek was killed. I deserved this, at the very least. Besides, it was only way to purify me so that I can continue my training."

"Malek was a tracking specialist. He likely saw his enemy coming before you could even turn your head. If he chose to face off without the aid of nearby Slayers, that was his choice to make. As for Abraham, he had no right to whip you without the prior consent of Headquarters, so that *will* be reported. Whipping *is* a method of purification, but it is an ancient one not used anymore without permission." Sirus folded his arms in front of his chest. "As for what you deserve, Joss, you deserve a little respect and kindness. That's the least of it. It's a miracle you didn't share Malek's fate. Food's waiting for you downstairs. If you don't make it down in five minutes, I'll bring some up for you."

"Sirus, . . ."

Sirus paused when Joss said his name, and looked back to him from the door. Joss shifted ever so gently in bed and met his gaze, his heart heavy. "Will there be a funeral for Malek?"

"We buried him two days ago, up on the hill, in that clearing you were camped in." He nodded, his eyes misting, and walked out the door.

Joss looked down at the shirt in his hands before

laying it on the bed next to him. Malek was gone, murdered in the most inhuman way possible. And even though Joss hardly knew him, he felt like he had lost a dear friend. With a wince, he managed to stand and move slowly—very slowly—toward the door. He wasn't about to eat in bed like some kid at home with the sniffles. He was a Slayer. He'd eat at the table with the other Slayers.

By the time he'd shuffled down the hall, his head was swimming from the pain and he all but collapsed in a dining chair that Sirus had pulled out for him. He leaned back in exhaustion and instantly regretted it. After a moment, Sirus placed a bowl of steaming beef stew in front of him. Sirus had only just set a spoon down beside the bowl when Joss grabbed it and quickly began to eat. He couldn't remember ever having been so hungry in his life.

Sirus took a seat beside him and watched him eat, then refilled his bowl and watched him for a few moments longer before speaking. "You didn't have to face the whip. That's an ages-old policy that most of the Society frowns on."

Joss hesitated before bringing another spoonful of the delicious homemade stew to his mouth. He didn't dare show Sirus the questioning glance he was holding in. After all, he didn't want to question his uncle's motives for such a brutal step in his process to becoming a Slayer. After all, if whipping was the punishment for doing things the right way, Joss didn't want to know what happened to Slayers who questioned the rules.

Sirus's voice dropped to a near whisper. "Purifying you faster won't make you a Slayer any quicker—you still have to go through training and that takes time. And now, being injured, it will take you even longer, so he's done the Society no favors. We can't go after Malek's killer any sooner, just because your uncle hit you with a whip, Joss. And don't you let him make you believe it."

Joss dropped the spoon in his bowl rather forcibly. With Cecile's trusting face locked in the forefront of his imagination, he turned to Sirus with a glare. "You don't understand."

Sirus set his jaw. "Yes, I do. I understand that you lost your sister three years ago, and I understand that you seem to think that punishing yourself will in some way put her soul to rest. But this . . . none of this will do that, Joss. You don't have to do any of this. You don't have to move around, not getting emotionally attached to people, never settling down, always changing schools, homes, never making friends. You can go home, live out your life in peace, walk away from all the fighting and pain and heartache that Slayers are destined to endure. Get out before it's too late for you . . . the way it's too late for me."

The back door swung open and Abraham stepped inside. His eyebrows rose in momentary surprise as his gaze fell on Joss. "You're up. And eating. That's good. You'll need your strength today."

Sirus shook his head. "No, Abraham. He needs his rest."

Abraham set his jaw. He didn't even glance in Sirus's general direction before speaking again. "Your training officially begins today, Joss. I'll meet you outside in ten minutes."

Sirus slammed his fist on the table. "I said no, Abraham!"

A silence fell over them then and Joss had to fight the urge to slide down in his chair to escape the unpleasantness. He hated the ugly energy that had settled into the room. Pushing his bowl away, Joss began to stand, but Sirus gently stopped him, his eyes on Abraham. "My job as caretaker gives me control in a situation when someone is ill or injured, does it not?"

Abraham took a breath, as if he were about to speak, but Sirus continued before he could say anything. "Joss is injured. Therefore, I'm ordering two days of rest before his training can begin. Enough time for his wounds to heal to the point that it won't affect his mobility. Do you understand?"

The color of Abraham's face had flushed from a pleasant, healthy tan to an angry pink. "If we were in the field, he might not have time to baby his wounds, Sirus."

Sirus held up a hand, silencing Abraham. When

Sirus spoke again, his words were clipped, matter-of-fact, and no-nonsense. "Do you understand?"

With a glance at Joss, Abraham turned and walked back outside, slamming the door behind him. Joss immediately felt a hot ball of tension building up inside his gut. Maybe Sirus thought he was doing Joss a favor, but he was wrong. Joss was going to pay for Sirus's actions. Maybe not now, but soon. Likely in two days' time.

Now, not only wasn't he hungry anymore, he was feeling a little sick to his stomach. "You shouldn't have done that."

"Part of being a man is admitting defeat. You need your rest. Besides, you can barely move."

"I can move just fine."

Sirus watched him for a moment before speaking. "Prove it. Catch."

The apple flew through the air so fast that Joss just barely realized that Sirus had been holding it. Instinctively, he grabbed for it, but pain tore through his back and he cried out. The apple fell to the floor with a thump, then rolled across the wooden planks until it came to rest against the toe of a purple Converse sneaker. Kat bent to retrieve the apple, and rubbed it against her T-shirt until it shone. She bit down on the fruit and, with juice dribbling down her chin, cocked her head toward Joss. "What's his problem, anyway?"

Sirus merely smiled. "I'm afraid our friend here just

isn't getting along with the local wildlife. He'll need a few days to recuperate. Would you mind keeping him company while I work?"

Kat took another bite and chewed it thoughtfully. "That depends. Was it something vicious like a bear, or something stupid like a rabid squirrel? Because I just can't respect somebody who's been mauled by a little fuzzy thing, foaming at the mouth or not."

Joss shot Sirus a pleading look—he had no idea what kind of wildlife was lurking in the woods around here. Except for vampires, that is. Without missing a beat, Sirus stood, turned back to the pot on the stove, and said, "It was a mountain lion. And I'm sure Joss will want to tell you all about it."

Joss could hear the smile in his tone, and really, really wished he knew anything at all about mountain lions. Especially when Kat plopped down in the chair next to him and said, "Now, a mountain lion. That I can respect. What happened?"

He swallowed hard and shrugged to buy some time, but Kat was leaning closer with great interest at whatever he was about to say. So he shrugged once more and said, "Oh, you know. It thought I was a rabbit or something and jumped on me. Or something."

Kat frowned in disappointment. Apparently she'd been hoping for all of the gruesome details of a wildlife attack. She'd probably watched too many dangerous animal shows on Discovery. But it didn't matter—she wasn't about to hear him regaling her with some false tale of When Giant Cats Attack Teenage Boys.

After a moment, she spoke again, but this time to her father. "Mind if we play cards? Or will Abraham get all snotty about me being over here?"

Sirus turned back to them, his eyes sparkling warmly at his daughter. For a brief moment, Joss was seized by jealousy. His own parents had only barely looked at him at all since Cecile's passing. And they certainly hadn't looked at him in a loving or admiring way. The moment passed, though, and Joss realized something that he hadn't until then. He liked Sirus. And he really admired the way that Sirus had stood up for him. Even if it did mean he was going to pay the price for it.

Sirus smiled. "I think you could squeeze in a quick game of spades before Abraham notices you. Or better yet, maybe we should set Joss up for some recuperation over at our cabin. Might be wise to stay out of Abraham's way until his temper settles a bit."

Joss mulled the idea over for a moment before offering a nod. "Yeah. I think that's probably a smart move."

Sirus nodded as well. "Make up the spare room, please, Kat. We'll be over in a bit to get Joss situated."

Once Kat had bounded out the door, Sirus turned back to Joss and lowered his voice. "Something that no one here has been told to teach you is this: our greatest skill is keeping our secrets. The only training for doing so is in the field, I'm afraid. Get to know my daughter, but practice keeping your secrets over the next few days. It'll help you in the long run. More, I'd wager, than learning how to wield a stake or block a bite. Though those do come in handy from time to time."

Joss shifted awkwardly in his seat for a moment, trying to find the right words to describe his hesitancy. He'd never really had friends—unless you counted the books on his shelves. And he wasn't exactly comfortable around girls. Especially girls with wild purple and blue hair, who seemed extremely comfortable around him. The idea of being alone in a house with Kat for two days set his stomach in knots. Knots that he couldn't explain, exactly.

"Something wrong?"

He met Sirus's eyes then and sighed, rubbing the back of his neck absently. "It's just . . . I'm not sure how to act. Around Kat, I mean."

A protective glint flashed across Sirus's eyes then. "She's my daughter. You act with respect and kindness."

Joss's eyes widened at the insinuation that he'd do anything but. "No, it's not that. I just mean that I'm not sure what to talk about. I mean. She's a girl."

Sirus laughed softly and shook his head. "Some-

day, my young friend, you'll find out that girls are actually people, too. Just like you and me."

A crease found its way onto Joss's forehead then.
Because he was quite certain that Sirus was wrong.
Girls were more complicated than boys. Girls commu-
nicated in a language that only they understood. And
Joss wasn't sure at all that he would ever understand
them.

Apparently, Sirus found his expression amusing,
because he laughed again and said, "Let's get you over
to the other cabin before Abraham comes back."

Joss slowly stood, mindful of the burning on his
back. He started a gentle shuffle toward the door, and
cast a sidelong glance at Sirus. "Do you really have the
authority to tell Abraham what he can and can't do?"

Sirus shrugged. "You'll find there are decided ranks
within the Society, Joss. My station as the caretaker of
this clan is an important and powerful one. But don't
be mistaken. Your uncle has seniority as a Slayer here.
He's in charge. Not me. I can fix you up, but it's up to
Abraham to ensure you learn the required skills necessary to your training, and to dole out punishments
when needed."

Joss took another step toward the door, his back
stinging terribly, and winced at the pain his purification had caused. In all honesty, Joss didn't feel any
more pure than he'd been before Abraham had starved

and whipped him. But he knew better than to say so. He couldn't help but marvel at the pain as he moved, and wondered something that he would never dare speak aloud.

If this was what it felt like to be purified, to be accepted as one of the group . . . what was Abraham's idea of punishment?

· 11 ·

HEARTS OR SPADES

The smaller cabin was nothing at all like the larger one, expect for the fact that it, too, wasn't actually a cabin, but an historic house. It was smaller than the Victorian, and Joss got the feeling it was newer, too. This one didn't feel so formal in style, somehow. It felt cozy. It felt right.

True to her word, Kat had set up a nice area for Joss in the den, and he was now settled into a cozy couch, marveling at the differences between this cabin and the other, and blaming it entirely on the fact that no one but Sirus and Kat ever stayed here. Paintings adorned the wall—fantastic artwork depicting faraway places that Joss had never even dreamed of. Dramatic brushstrokes gave the images life, and Joss wasn't entirely surprised to see Sirus's name painted in the bottom corner of each piece. It seemed fitting that someone as kind and courageous as Sirus would be an artist as well. Joss had never painted anything . . . unless you counted the sad finger paintings of his kindergarten year, or his bedroom walls when he was in the fourth grade and Dad said he could help. In fact, Joss had never really done anything creative at all. He had written in his journal, but that was more like purging his thoughts rather than creating something . . . wasn't it? And he had started a pretty incredible collection of various insects—collecting, categorizing, mounting them on displays—but that was more science than creativity . . . wasn't it?

Kat set a tray in front of him on the coffee table. It was overflowing with various cheeses, crackers, apple slices, and grapes. After she set it down, she disappeared into the kitchen and returned a moment later with two bottles of water. Plopping down on the floor near the table, she smiled brightly. "Sirus said to take care of you. So eat."

Joss looked over all of the food and nodded with appreciation. "I'm not hungry now, but maybe in a little—"

"Eat." Kat's eyebrows came together in a way that reminded him of his mother when she meant business. "Please."

Joss stretched out his hand and grabbed something from the tray. After he took a bite, he realized it was cheese.

"Do you wanna play cards or something?"

Before Joss could decide if he did or didn't or even form a response in his head, Kat had a deck out and was shuffling them loudly on the table. He was beginning to wonder if she ever let anybody else make their own decisions.

Or maybe she just didn't think of stuff like that. He looked at her and cleared his throat softly. "Actually, Kat? My back really hurts. Could you maybe find me some Tylenol or something?"

Without a word, she bounded from the room and returned a moment later with a prescription bottle that was half full of pills. As she twisted the cap off, she said, "Sirus said you should take one of these every four hours until tomorrow. Then you can switch to ibuprofen."

The frightening thought that he was about to take strange pills from someone he hardly knew flitted through his mind and then disappeared again. He opened his hand and took the pills, then popped one into his mouth and swallowed it dry. If he could trust Sirus, he could trust Kat. After he'd swallowed it, he turned back to her and said, "Thanks."

"Well, if these are the same pills Sirus gave me when I broke my arm, you won't feel a thing in about twenty minutes." She smiled and cocked her head to the side, her eyes gleaming.

"How'd you break your arm?" he asked. The combination of the cheese and medication left a horrible taste in his mouth, so he sipped from the bottle on the tray, hoping to rinse the foul taste away.

Kat shrugged. "I was in a car accident when I was five. My mom was driving, hit some ice—the country roads in Michigan are pretty slick in the winter—and we skidded off the road into a big ditch. Mom didn't make it. I got out of it with a broken arm."

Joss swallowed hard, the bitter taste remaining on his tongue. He wasn't exactly certain what he should say or do. Kat had just shared something deeply personal with him, and all he could think to say was that he was sorry. Was that what she wanted? For him to empathize with her? Or had she just said it because he'd asked about her arm?

Before he knew it, too much time had passed with his silence, and saying anything at all would have proven even more awkward. So Joss took another drink of water and waited for Kat to speak again.

"It's no big deal. I was in a cast for a few weeks, and at the end of it all, it brought me and Sirus closer. We hadn't been before that. I mean, he may have been my father, but he was never really my dad until after I came to live with him. So everything happens for a reason."

"So Sirus wasn't married to your mom or any-thing?"

"Well, yeah. Actually, he was. For two years. But it didn't work out. They stayed close friends though. And after she died, her will said that I should go live with him, if he wanted me to. He did, so I did." She shrugged once again, her eyes speaking of a sadness that her words wouldn't hint at. Then she looked at Joss questioningly. "So are you going to tell me what really happened to you, or should I go on pretending that you lost to a mountain lion in a slap fight?"

Joss's throat seized and, for a moment, it felt as if all of the air had been sucked out of the room. By the time he'd recovered and placed a lie on the tip of his tongue, Kat had folded her arms in front of her as if she'd danced this dance before. "I got in a fight with one of the other . . . guys . . . and lost."

Only his words hadn't come out in the form of a statement. More like a question. Even he didn't be-lieve what he'd just said.

"Mm-hmm. Right. You either wrestle mountain li-ons or get in random fights with guys in the woods, and Sirus is just here to cook for his so-called friends and pass out Band-Aids on occasion." Her cheeks flushed pink in irritation. "I don't even know why I'm here. I should be at home, categorizing some beetles or something. But no, instead I'm stuck here with people who won't even talk to me about whatever it is that's going on. Do you know I left a perfectly preserved hairy fungus beetle just lying on my desk unmounted to come here?"

"Beetles?" He squeaked, with probably a bit too much excitement. "You're into entomology, too?"

"Are you kidding? I love it! Ever since I caught that Schaus swallowtail butterfly when I was six."

After a pause, one that was filled with elated heartbeats and so many questions that he thought he might burst, Joss leaned forward slowly, his back burning, and picked up the deck of cards. He shuffled them thoroughly before meeting her eyes. "Hearts or Spades?"

She sat down on the floor by the coffee table with a sigh. "Hearts."

He dealt their hands and unfolded his behind cupped palms. "At home, I have quite an impressive collection of insects. In fact, it's probably my favorite thing in the world to do."

Kat nodded and reached for a slice of apple. "I hear ya. Collecting, categorizing, mounting. I love it. It was a hobby at first, but it's kinda an obsession now. I got into it pretty hard core about two years ago with butterflies. It's interesting stuff, y'know? I kinda wanna be an entomologist when I'm older."

A strange, fluttery feeling settled into Joss's stomach then. It felt light and airy and so unusual that Joss wasn't certain if he were nauseous or just a little dizzy from happiness. Maybe it was the medication. "Me too."

Suddenly, his chest felt a bit tight, like he couldn't breathe. He'd never be an entomologist. Not now. Not with his future as a Slayer laid out before him. There was no time for a normal life. He had a duty to mankind . . . and to Cecile. "I mean . . . I did."

Kat grinned. "Seriously?" When Joss nodded, she said, "You are officially too cool for words, Joss McMillan."

Too cool for words. No one had ever described him that way before. He was alone, without friends, and looked down upon for being interested in things like books and insects and how they get along in this big, bad world. It was nice to know that someone on the planet—if only for a moment—admired him for just that. He smiled warmly at her. "I don't know why you're here, Kat, but I'm really glad you are."

"You won't be after this hand," she chuckled.

She was right.

For the next four hours, they played hand after hand of Hearts, and Kat won almost every time. And the only time she didn't win, Joss had a sneaking suspicion she'd let him win, and pity hands don't really count, as Cecile let him know long ago.

Kat shuffled the cards expertly. "Come on. One more. Maybe you'll get lucky."

But Joss's back yanked the strings of his resolve.

He winced. "I think it's time for some more meds. My back is killing me."

Kat handed him the bottle then and watched as Joss tossed another pill back. "Can you at least tell me why you can't say what really happened to you?"

Joss looked at her and shook his head. It wasn't that he wanted to keep this a secret from her. He had to. "Kat . . ."

She held up a hand. "Just tell me if it was a thing or a person."

He mulled it over for several minutes. She clearly already suspected that he was lying outright about what exactly had injured him so badly. What would be the harm in answering this one question? It wasn't like he was revealing the Slayer Society's existence or anything. He was just answering whether or not it was a thing or a person who'd hurt him. He could see no harm in answering the question at all. Crossing his fingers with hope that he was right, he said, "A person. But you can't ask me any more questions."

Her voice dropped to a whisper then. "It was Abraham. Wasn't it?"

Joss shot her a stern warning glance.

"You don't have to say anything. I just know it. I could sense it about him. He just comes off as a mondo-abusive jerk." Kat set her jaw, her eyes shining. "I'm sorry he hurt you, Joss. And I wish you'd tell me why or how, but I know you won't. I won't bring it up again. I just . . . you don't deserve whatever he did to you. And I'm sorry."

But he did. Joss did deserve every lick of the whip that Abraham had doled out. For not being there the moment that monster had entered Cecile's room. For freezing in fear when he saw it's horrible fangs. For not being able to recall its face clearly. And for falling asleep and letting Malek get killed. Let's not forget that one.

He deserved each painful lash and more. Cecile had given his life meaning. No one had ever looked upon him with such unrelenting love and devotion as his little sister had, and when she was ripped from his life, so was the joy of living. He should have been there. He should have stopped the vampire from hurting her. He deserved to hurt so much more than she had even in her last moments.

He lay on his stomach, clutching one of the pillows to his chest that Kat had thoughtfully placed behind him on the couch, and closed his eyes. "I need to sleep now, Kat. I need my rest."

His voice cracked on the last word, but he fought like hell to keep his tears contained.

After all, Slayers didn't cry.

Kat was quiet for a long time. Then she stood and removed the tray, wordlessly slipping back into the kitchen. He could hear her turning off lights as she moved upstairs, and then, just before closing her bedroom door, she said in a soft, concerned voice, "Good night, Joss."

No. It wasn't. And no night would ever be good again, until he righted the wrong that he'd committed the night he let a monster murder Cecile.

Joss laid in the darkness and waited for sleep to come. When it eventually did, it brought with it the same nightmarish images that it had every night for three years.

Cecile. Dying.

Again.

· 12 ·

TRAINING BEGINS

In the morning, Joss's alarm clock was the sound of the front door slamming, followed by raised voices. "I don't give a damn about your title or your reluctance to the cause, Sirus! He's my nephew and I know best what he needs. Sitting on a cushy couch while your daughter waits on him hand and foot is no path to becoming a Slayer."

"Be reasonable, Abraham. The boy just experienced a beating at the hand of a relative. You don't think he needs a little time to recover?" Sirus's voice sounded much calmer than his uncle's, but it was still raised. Mostly, Joss suspected, so that Abraham would hear him over his own shouts.

Then Abraham's voice quieted. But the tone brought not even an ounce of comfort to Joss, who lay very still on the sofa, eavesdropping. "He's done. Now get him up and outside so his training can begin. I'm done with your games."

Their voices fell silent. The silence was broken only by the slamming of a door and Sirus's sigh. Then footsteps as he moved into the den. He didn't seem surprised to find Joss wide awake. With another sigh, he leaned against the doorjamb and shook his head. "I'm sorry you had to hear that. Your uncle is a stubborn man, and reasoning with him can be challenging."

Joss sat up. His back ached, but it felt much better than it had the night before. "What exactly will training entail?"

"You'll learn defensive maneuvers, attack positions, tricks to dealing with vampires, and how to wield a stake. We don't generally teach these things in a step-by-step fashion, but rather it's dependent on what you're ready for, and what we have time for. You'll also learn how to forage for food and how to survive in the wild, care for any injuries you may receive—"

He glanced up at Sirus and could feel an eager buzzing in his chest. "And how to kill vampires?"

Sirus paused before answering. "Yes."

"Good." Joss nodded. "How long will my training be?"

"That depends on you, and how well you absorb the lessons given." He frowned slightly; it looked strange on him. Someone like Sirus always looked pleasant, if not genuinely upbeat. Behind his frown was an enormous wall of concern. "Joss . . ."

Joss swallowed hard. He wasn't sure he wanted to hear what Sirus had to say. "What is it?"

Sirus moved closer, and then crouched next to the couch, holding Joss's gaze. He spoke quietly, as if not wanting anyone to overhear. "I meant what I said the other day. You can still walk away from this. You don't have to become wrapped up in the web of the Society just to avenge your sister's death. Cecile might not want her brother killing creatures and endangering himself. Did you ever think of that?"

Joss practically jumped to standing and threw on his shoes. As he did, he barked at Sirus, "Don't talk about her. You don't know anything about her. You don't know anything!"

He went to the front door and yanked it open, but before he could step outside, Sirus reached around him and closed it again. "I know that becoming a Slayer won't bring your sister back. And I know a few other things as well. You may not like what I have to say, but I have to say it. Because nobody told me these things when I opted to follow this path, and someone damn well should have."

Joss's heart was racing with anger. Sirus had no right to talk about his sister, and certainly no right to keep him here.

"You're in over your head already and don't see it. You can't see it. You won't see it. Not until it's too late." He leaned in closer, his expression grave. "You'll take lives, Joss, and each time you do, it'll kill a small piece of your soul. No one—not your uncle or any of the other Slayers—will admit to the pain and heartache that slaying brings. They'll only speak of the glory and duty and honor of it all. But no one will tell you how difficult it is to look in the mirror each day after doing the Society's bidding. You'll grow to hate yourself, as we all do. That's what you're choosing, Joss. Can you live with that?"

Joss ran his hand over the back of his neck, visions of his sister racing through his mind. He realized Sirus was just trying to help, but Sirus had no way of knowing, no possible way of understanding what it was like to watch someone close to you have their life stolen away. He couldn't possibly understand Joss's motives. No one could. "I can't live with knowing the monster that killed Cecile is still out there. So . . . yeah. Yeah, I can give up my soul to put her at peace. It's worth it, Sirus. To me, it's absolutely worth it."

Sirus grew quiet for a moment, and then, as if making a difficult decision, he stepped back and opened the door once again. "Ash and Morgan will meet you in the same clearing where you had your purification."

"Sirus?"

Sirus met his eyes silently.

"Thank you. For warning me, I mean. I know you're just trying to help. But I have to do this. I just have to." He plucked the clean shirt from the back of his chair—likely placed there for him by Sirus—and slipped it slowly, carefully over his head. Then he stepped outside and crossed the yard to the trailhead, ignoring the sting in his back.

As Joss moved into the clearing, he was met by Morgan's beaming grin. "Welcome to what may potentially be your last day on earth, kid."

Ash stood to Morgan's left, shaking his head. His demeanor was much more subdued than Morgan's, and something about his posture told Joss that he was hoping this wouldn't take very long. "Instead of helping the others, we're here with you. So, let's make this quick. Today you're going to learn about weapons and explosives."

Joss dropped his eyes to the wooden case at Ash's feet. It could fit in his backpack. The lid had been opened and inside, on purple velvet lining, were a wooden stake, various bottles, a cross, a small gun, and a gleaming silver hatchet. He drew his attention from one weapon to the next before looking back at Ash. "I don't mean to be insulting, but other than a wooden stake, why would you bother with other weapons or explosives? I mean, a stake will take down a vampire, right? So . . . isn't anything else just a waste of time?"

Ash nodded, looking a little less impatient, as if it might just be worth his time to remain here a bit longer. "A stake is classic and, yes, extremely effective, but what if you drop it?"

"And what if you're dealing with a large group of vamps? How many do you think you could stake before they take you down?" Morgan was carefully coiling a long bronze cord along the length of his forearm. Joss recognized it from a television program he'd watched months ago as detonation cord—basically dynamite in rope form.

Ash folded his arms in front of his chest. "Our point is that you want to keep your options open. We're here to teach you a bit about those options."

"And, hopefully, to keep you in one piece while you're doing so." Morgan tossed the cord onto the ground and Joss winced. He was almost certain the cord required a charge to do any damage, but it was a bit unsettling to see Morgan throwing it around like it wasn't something that could kill them all in a microsecond.

"Now, your basic weapons fall into two categories." Ash crouched in front of the case on the ground, but not before flicking a glance at Morgan. "Barring explosives, of course."

Morgan's grin merely grew. It was easy to see how much he loved his job. "Of course."

Ash gestured for Joss to crouch down, too, and then gestured to the items inside the case. "There are direct weapons, and stealth weapons. If you look closely enough, you'll see that all effective weapons against vampirekind fall into one of those two categories. For instance, a stake punctures the vital heart organ, so it affects its target directly. But garlic juice invades the system and destroys from within, so it's more stealth. A silver bullet is direct, but holy water is stealth. Got it?"

"Totally." Joss nodded, his eyebrows coming together in a question as his gaze moved from weapon to weapon. "But what about the ax?"

"Hatchet. An ax is much bigger, far too heavy to wield easily." Ash met and held his gaze for a moment, as if making certain that Joss understood the difference. "The hatchet falls under the direct category; its purpose is to remove the head."

Joss swallowed hard. He hoped he'd never be faced with that situation, because he wasn't certain that he could ever behead anything living. The very thought sent his stomach rolling in nauseous waves.

"Now, something to remember is that you want to use the more effective of the two weapon categories first. So . . . first act directly. If that fails, then utilize stealth. Consider it your backup."

Pushing his nausea down, Joss looked more closely at the wooden case which contained the antivampire weaponry. "This case isn't exactly easy to carry around, is it? I mean, it seems kinda bulky and heavy. Are we supposed to have it with us all the time?"

Ash shook his head. "Not necessarily. The case is meant to store the weapons, yes, but there are other ways to carry them. Traditionally, Slayers carry the case their first year, but after that, they can request a holster pass, which is pretty much a concealed weapon permit from Headquarters."

"Look, kid, most of your weapons information is in the guide. You'll get one from Abraham. But explosives . . . those are a delicate issue." Morgan shifted his feet. He looked jumpy with excitement, as if he could contain his love of all things explosive no more. Throwing a glance at Ash, he said, "Do you mind?"

Ash closed his case and picked it up as he stood. As he turned and walked away, he released a sigh—one that seemed a bit like he was relieved that his part of this training was over for the moment. "By all means. I have better things to do anyway."

Morgan smirked and called out to him, "Sure you don't want to stick around, be the kid's target?"

Ash didn't answer. Joss got the feeling that

Ash didn't care much for either him or Morgan. Or both.

Standing, Joss looked at Morgan, an eager tension filling him at the idea of learning all about explosives from someone who seemed to enjoy them a little too much. "What are we going to blow up?"

Morgan sighed happily and slapped Joss on the back. "Kid . . . you just said my seven favorite words."

· 13 ·

DEFENSE

Setting explosives the day before had been im-measurably entertaining—and terrifying—but when Joss woke to a note from Uncle Abraham that said to meet him in the clearing, he was certain that this day was going to be drastically different than yesterday in tone. He wasn't sure what to expect, but he did know that his pace getting to the clearing was a bit slower than it had been the day before.

As promised, he found Abraham in the clearing. Joss gave a wide berth to the shed where the whip now hung, and approached his uncle with false confidence. Abraham looked him over, seeming to size him up, and nodded. "I told Sirus he was wrong about you.

Now . . . before we begin, I want you to start thinking about why you are doing this. And when you find yourself at the darkest point, I want you to hold on to that reason, and it will get you through to the light. Got it?"

Joss didn't have to think long. This was for Cecile. This was all for Cecile. He nodded at his uncle, who returned his nod and said, "Good. Now . . . let's start with basic defense."

Joss nodded, but didn't speak. He had a feeling his uncle liked it that way.

"Vampires are allergic to sunlight, so your best defense is to stay protected and hidden once the sun goes down. Of course, some missions call for nighttime confrontations, so in that case, you'll want to be armed with your basic weapons: garlic and a stake." He held up a small vial of cloudy yellow liquid. The aged label on the side read *Garlic Juice* in scripted text. Next he gestured to the stake in the holster at his hip. Joss found himself marveling that the things he'd seen in cheesy movies were right about vampires. The stake was handsome. Elegantly carved wood entwined with silver vines. The tip was sheer silver, too, and looked very, very sharp. He wondered briefly if Abraham had made it himself, or if it was some kind of gift or something, but didn't bother asking. Slayers don't question; they act. "They're allergic to garlic, too. Some are more sensitive to sunlight than others. But garlic . . . that'll kill any of them if they swallow it or it gets in an open wound."

Joss stood without speaking, wondering what else he'd seen on TV that was real. Were there really were-wolves? Monster clowns? Shape-shifters? The possibilities were both endless and frightening. After all, if one thing existed, why couldn't they all?

"But your best defense is this little number right here." From within his jacket, Abraham pulled a small book. Its cover was rich, brown, worn leather. Embossed on the front were the initials S.S. "This is your field guide. It contains every protocol, every rule, every regulation put forth by the Slayer Society. If you have a question, this book contains the answer. It's a Slayer's most valuable tool. It's also where you'll make notes about vampire encounters—there's a journal section at the back. Once a year, you'll get a fresh copy. Keep up on those notes. The Society deems every bit of information to be extremely valuable."

"Now," Abraham said, a shadow passing over his face—one that sent a cruel chill down Joss's spine, "shall we begin?"

Joss was about to ask what they would be beginning exactly, but there was no time. Abraham lunged at him, grabbing him by the throat. As Joss gasped for air, clutching his fingers, Abraham seethed. "When you're out there on your own, no one will come to your rescue. No help will come. You'll be on your own, fighting against an almost impossible foe. Defend yourself, Slayer."

Before Joss could ask how, Abraham shoved him back by the throat and Joss fell to the ground, almost howling from the pain in his back, coughing wildly, trying desperately to get air into his lungs. He stayed there, crouched in the undergrowth, until his coughing had subsided, then looked up at his uncle, whose eyes were filled with pure disgust.

"Defend yourself. Because this time, I will not stop, just as our enemies will not stop. These monsters won't cease in their attack just to spare the life of a young boy. They kill all humans—young and old. Grandmothers, infants . . . they are evil incarnate, and we are mankind's only hope of protection. If you won't defend yourself, how can you be counted on to defend the entire world? Now defend yourself!" Abraham shot his arm forward, aiming for Joss's throat. He connected, but this time, Joss managed to wriggle from his grasp before he could get a good grip.

Joss rolled away from him, his back screaming, and hurried to stand. His throat ached, but he wouldn't give Abraham the chance to grab it again if he could help it. He faced his uncle, eyeing him down, wondering what Abraham would do next, or how far he would take this lesson of defense. Would Abraham go so far as to put his life in danger?

He examined his uncle's face for a moment before

nodding. Yes, he thought. Abraham would kill him before he'd let Joss leave a coward.

Without warning or words, Abraham flew across the clearing and attacked Joss, punching him in the gut, the side, the jaw. He hit Joss solidly in the center of his wounded back, sending Joss all but crying as he fell to the ground. "They know your weaknesses. They can read your thoughts. And they will exploit both."

Abraham raised his fists again, and Joss's heart raced. He panicked, curling into a ball, as if by closing in on himself, he might escape his uncle's attack somehow. Then he held his arms up in front of him, trying his best to block the skilled blows.

Neither helped.

Abraham growled as he beat bruises into Joss's flesh. "Show me what you're made of, Slayer. Defend yourself!"

Pain shot through Joss's side as Abraham's fist connected again, and Joss cried out, forgetting about the wounds on his back entirely. He was almost certain he'd cracked a rib that time, and was definitely convinced that Abraham wasn't about to stop. Like he'd said, he'd continue . . . just like a vampire would continue. Joss swung his arm back, balled up his fist, and brought it forward as hard and fast as he could manage. His knuckles grazed Abraham's jaw, but just barely. He swung again, this time with the left, and connected. Abraham rubbed his jaw and stepped back. There was no emotion on his face.

"That's it for today." Abraham turned and moved down the trail, leaving a blinking, confused, wondering Joss behind.

Joss looked around at the clearing, blinked some more, and hurried to catch up with his uncle. "What do you mean? We're done?"

Abraham's steps didn't even slow as Joss reached his side. "For today, yes. I suggest you grab some lunch."

Joss rubbed the aching muscles of his lower back as he walked. The last thing he wanted to do was to question his uncle's methods, be he didn't really feel like he had much of a choice. "But . . . Uncle Abraham . . . what exactly was the point of that?"

Abraham sighed. "I set out to teach you a lesson today, and it's clear you've learned it. So we're finished. For now."

They'd reached the bottom of the hill and as Abraham stepped up on the porch, Joss said, "What was the lesson, exactly?"

"You had to come to understand that your opponent will never stop unless you fight back. And you did."

Joss bit the inside of his cheek absently. It seemed to him there were probably better ways of teaching someone that lesson, but he couldn't argue with age-old traditions that had apparently been proven time and time again. Still, the urge was in him to do just that.

Abraham met his eyes, a look of approval on his normally stern face. "Get some rest, and prepare for a long day tomorrow. I suspect that lesson won't come as easily."

▸ 14 ◂

THE LIES WE TELL

U se more black, Joss. Otherwise you look less like the forest and more like the Hulk." Paty's tone had a hint of laughter, but Joss could tell she was doing her best to keep it contained.

Joss dabbed his fingers into the black crème and rubbed crude lines onto his cheeks. Paty's camouflage was flawless, but when he looked in the mirror, all he saw were several colors smudged all over his face in no particular order, like a kid who'd gotten into his mother's makeup. He sighed heavily, hoping the lesson would soon be at an end. "Is this all there is to camouflage? Playing dress-up?"

As soon as the words had crossed his lips, he regretted them. Luckily, if Paty had felt the sting of insult, she didn't let it show. Instead, she smiled and handed him a moist towelette. As he rubbed the greens, browns, and black from his face, she said, "Actually, the most important aspect of camouflage is hiding our sounds, and at times, our scent."

He reached for another towelette, having destroyed the first, and said, "How do you do that?"

Paty began gently removing her makeup as she replied. "Well, to hide our sounds, we learn to be light on our feet, watch where we step. Scent is a bit more complicated, especially when keeping our scent hidden from vampires. They can smell our blood, determine that we are human, even detect our blood type. So we can only mask it so well."

"How?"

"You may regret asking." Paty sighed, capping the small dishes of makeup as she spoke. "Suffice it to say that death helps to mask it."

Joss furrowed his brow, confusion filling him. "I'm not sure I get your meaning."

"How can I put this delicately?" She sighed again, this time looking to the ceiling of the dining room, as if the answers were written there. "I can't. So . . . the truth, then. Gross as it may be. Basically, if you rub yourself with a dead animal, it throws vampires off your scent."

Joss's stomach turned slightly, nausea seizing him. "That's disgusting."

At this, Paty chuckled. "Well, there's always dung, but it doesn't work as well. Besides, you'd be amazed what you'll resort to when a monster is hunting you and closing in."

He mulled this over for a bit, wondering if she was right. What was it like to be hunted? Would he be desperate and afraid? Would he resort to methods of hiding that he currently deemed beyond his limit of tolerance?

He was still mulling this over when Abraham opened the back door. "Joss. Outside. We have hand-to-hand combat to practice."

Paty muttered something—something about beating a lesson into Joss—but when Abraham flashed her a certain look, she packed up her camouflage tools in silence. She moved out of the room quickly, without a further word. Joss was sorry to see her go. Despite his frustration with applying makeup, he'd been really enjoying their time together. But Abraham was waiting, an expectant look on his face.

Something told Joss that the longer he kept his uncle waiting, the worse his training would be.

That night, Joss stumbled down the hill in the darkness, his ribs screaming, his mouth filling with the sick, metallic taste of blood. He spat on the ground twice, but still couldn't get the taste out of his mouth. It was hard to navigate the dark woods, but somehow, he managed to find the cabin's back steps. With a groan, he stepped up onto the worn wood, pausing only when he unexpectedly heard a voice—Kat's voice—in the darkness. "Joss? Are you okay? Oh my god, what happened to you?"

He turned slowly toward her, images filling his head of just what had transpired to put him in this state. He'd been called to training early in the day, and Abraham had begun working him over, stopping only to catch his own breath. They'd fought for hours, until Joss had passed out from the pain, and then Abraham had started in again, and again, until Joss had become convinced that he would die if his uncle didn't stop. Abraham's final words to him before he'd released Joss from the torment he called training, had been, "Now you've learned how to take a beating, what it feels like to truly hurt. Because we've covered two lessons, you can have tomorrow off."

And Abraham was right—Joss had learned his lessons. He now knew exactly what pain was, and how unmerciful someone could be if they wanted to. And he knew how to take a beating, which really wasn't something he could take credit for. For one, Abraham had refused to let him leave. For two, every time he considered making a break for it, Cecile's face would grip his imagination, and he'd turn back to face his uncle head-on.

Lessons learned, if not entirely engraved upon his being.

"Joss? What happened?" Her eyes were so full of concern, so wide and fearful of whatever it was that had hurt Joss in this way. He could barely stand to look at her. He didn't deserve her pity, or her friendship.

"It was a mountain lion, Kat. Just another stupid mountain lion." He turned and opened the back door, then shuffled inside, all the while wondering where Sirus kept the bandages.

To her credit and Joss's relief, Kat didn't follow him inside. There was also no sign of the other Slayers as he rummaged through the medicine cabinet, looking for something to clean and cover his wounds. After knocking over several jars, bottles, and small boxes, he located a small tin of Band-Aids, a tube of Neosporin, and a little brown bottle labeled IODINE. Part of him was almost certain the Neosporin would be the right choice for all of his scrapes and cuts, but he could vaguely recall his mother using iodine on his knee when he'd scraped it learning to ride his bike a few years before. After putting everything neatly away, he left his choices on the counter, and took a long, hot shower. The water burned on his skin and felt like knives on his wounds, but it was healing somehow to feel that pain. Maybe there was something to that whole purification ritual after all. Maybe Joss was learning the right way to be, and in that, he might just find the strength to go on, and to find peace.

After he was clean, he turned off the water and stepped out of the shower, patted himself dry ever so carefully, ever so gently, and slipped his boxers back on. Then, loading his arms with his dirty clothes and medical equipment, he moved silently through the dark house and up the stairs to his room, where he changed into some fresh pajama bottoms and began cleaning his wounds. With a growling curse, he learned very quickly that iodine might clean your wounds, but it also feels like acid is eating its way through your flesh. Not to mention the delightful added bonus of dyeing your skin bright orange. With a grumble, he tossed the small brown bottle into the wastebasket and reached for the Neosporin. Gently applying it to the scrapes and cuts on his legs, arms, and chest, Joss counted to himself. Forty-three. There were forty-three visible wounds that he could find on his body, and who knows how many more on his back.

And every one was worth it. Each scar, each bruise was simply a check mark on the list of things it took to become a Slayer. Joss was determined to move down that list as quickly as possible and to grit his teeth through every pain.

There came a soft tap on his door and Joss lifted his head, speaking just as softly as the sound that had invaded his nurse work. "Come in."

Sirus pushed the door open and poked his head inside, his eyes moving quickly over Joss's injuries. "Kat mentioned you weren't feeling well. I thought maybe you could use some assistance."

Joss tightened his jaw. He didn't want anyone's help. In fact, all he wanted was to show his uncle that he was perfectly capable of taking care of himself, even after taking a beating like that. "No thanks. I've got it."

A look of immediate doubt crossed Sirus's eyes, but he didn't give voice to it. He merely asked, "You were out all day without any breaks. Are you hungry?"

Moments later, Joss was at the dining table, where Sirus had placed a large bowl of chili in front of him. He may be perfectly capable of tending his own wounds, but the fact was that Joss hadn't eaten anything since early that morning, and his stomach had been rumbling its protests all day.

Sirus handed Joss a utensil and he dug in, spooning bits of steak, beans, and various peppers into his mouth. The chili was spicy but delicious, and Joss quickly polished off one bowl and then another. He was working on his third when Sirus said, "I need to go into town tomorrow for supplies. You're welcome to join me, if you'd like. It's not far, but I'll need some extra arms to help load the truck."

Joss chewed another mouthful and swallowed before nodding. "Sure. I have tomorrow off. I guess that would be okay."

"Kat will be joining us. I hope that's all right." Sirus filled a glass with lemonade and slid it closer to Joss.

"I have a feeling you two could become good friends, given time."

Joss slowly set his spoon in the bowl and let Sirus's words sink in. He'd never really had a friend before. With all the moving his family had experienced, it had been difficult for Joss to make friends. It would be nice to have a friend besides Henry. Even though the idea of spending any extended amount of time with her sent his stomach into knots. Kat was bold, outgoing, and seemed to have no concern at all about asking him questions. And that was the last thing a guy on his way to becoming a Slayer needed.

Still . . . she was pretty nice and very friendly. He took a sip of lemonade and nodded to Sirus. "What time should I get up?"

"I'll wake you at seven. We'll leave around eight." Sirus stood and cleared Joss's dishes away. "By the way, I should warn you. Kat is a very curious soul. She may ask questions that you cannot answer."

Joss wiped his mouth on his napkin and looked at Sirus, mulling over exactly how to phrase his next sentence. "To be honest, she already has."

Sirus's eyebrows rose. "Oh?"

Joss nodded. "She knows that we're not on some hunting trip, and she suspects that you and I haven't been completely honest with her. But I don't think she'll push to find out what's really going on. I have to ask though. Why did you bring her here? I mean, it seems like a really strange way to keep the Society's secrets, bringing your daughter to a training camp."

Sirus said, "Every summer, I leave Kat behind. As you can probably imagine, she gets very lonely. After all, she has only me. No mother, no siblings. Just me. She stays with a friend of mine, but it's not the same as having family around. We exchange letters all summer long, but hers always grow more and more troubled as time wears on. Then a month ago, Kat tearfully made me promise not to leave her this summer. She didn't want to go to summer camp or on vacation with her extended family. She wanted to be with me. I couldn't promise that I wouldn't leave her, but I also couldn't abandon her again. Not knowing how much it was hurting her to be away from me for so long. When you have children and you love them, it's impossible to refuse them and even more impossible to knowingly cause them pain. So I brought her with me."

Joss furrowed his brow. He could only imagine how his uncle had reacted to the surprise news that a normal teenage girl would be joining them for the summer. He imagined Abraham's reaction had probably contained a string of obscenities.

Sirus smiled, as if guessing his thoughts. "Abraham was furious, of course. He threatened to report me to the Slayer Society. Then I reminded him of a few secrets of his own that I'm privy to, and he conveniently forgot my transgression. But if Kat finds out who we are and what we're really doing here, I will be reported and taken into custody."

Joss swallowed hard. Without him even realizing it, his voice dropped to a whisper, and he leaned forward in his seat. "What would they do to you?"

"If they're feeling kind, the Society will simply excommunicate me. But if they're not feeling particularly forgiving, I will be punished." The corner of his mouth tugged up slightly, as if Sirus were trying to make light of a very serious situation.

"How?"

"I'd rather not say." Sirus waved his hand and shook his head. "You're young. You should cling to your innocence while you can."

Joss sat back in his seat, crossing his arms in front of him. "I thought you wanted me to have an honest view of the Society before I joined."

"I do. But some things you shouldn't worry about until you're faced with them. And hopefully you never will be." Sirus met his eyes then, and Joss knew that the Society would kill him for betraying them. His life would be the price of not keeping their secrets. How he'd be killed, Joss had no idea, but he imagined it would be in the worst way possible. Sirus patted him on the arm and said, "It's time for bed. I suggest you take some Tylenol before lying down. Tomorrow, I'll take a good look at your injuries. Now get some sleep."

He nodded at Sirus, and yawned. He had no idea what time it was, but one thing was for certain.

This was going to be the longest summer that Joss had ever experienced.

· 15 ·

EARLY-MORNING ADVENTURES

C ome on, little brother." Cratian smiled at Joss across the breakfast table. It was still dark outside, but technically, it was morning. Five in the morning. Joss had slept for maybe an hour, and he'd been tormented by Cecile's restless spirit the entire time. When he awoke, he was famished, and Sirus had been happy to whip him up a nice breakfast. The house was quiet, but for Cratian's voice. "It's time to play. Chazz and I are going to search the hills for that hive. Thought we'd bring you along for the ride, if you're feeling up to it."

Sirus turned away from the stove then and gave

Cratian a look that said Joss wasn't going anywhere. The look made Joss's heart sink. Truth was, bruised or not, he really wanted to get out there and do some training, to further learn what it meant to be a Slayer.

Cratian put up his hands in surrender. "I swear, no training. But he might learn a few things by tromping through the woods with us. Just for fun, I promise, Sirus."

Sirus seemed to mull it over for a while before pointing a finger at the three of them. "No maneuvers. His muscles need the rest."

Cratian looked from Chazz back to Sirus. "Can we at least go for a hike? He can watch me kick Chazz's butt in the clearing."

Chazz looked up from his plate briefly. "Hey . . ."

Joss finished chewing a bite of breakfast and said, "I want to go, Sirus. I promise I'll be back before eight, so we can still go to town."

Sirus turned back to the stove without another word. Cratian grinned. Chazz shoveled in another mouthful of omelet before standing and giving Joss's shoulder a healthy smack. Surprised into swallowing a bite of hash browns, Joss coughed, took a sip of orange juice and hurried to clear his plate away.

Just a few minutes later, they were in a clearing in the woods, and Cratian was stretching his arms above his head. "The key to maintaining your strength is keeping the blood flowing, the muscles loose and limber, and the endorphins up. Before I head out on a hunt, I like to do at least twenty push-ups, and get some good stretches in. It's a good habit to get into."

After watching Cratian for a moment, Joss followed suit, stretching one arm over his head, and then bending it at the elbow to stretch out his triceps.

Cratian moved closer as Joss began to bring his arm down. "You're not holding it long enough. You should feel a good burn, count to ten, then release it."

A muscle in Joss's back started to cramp, but he brought his arm back up, refusing to show any sign of weakness to his fellow Slayers. Cratian caught his wince, though, and began to rub the muscle out for Joss. "Looks like somebody had a bit of hand to hand with Abraham last night."

Joss shrugged, his back muscles losing their tension some. "It wasn't so bad."

Cratian and Chazz exchanged looks that said that they knew just how full of crap Joss was at the moment. Then Chazz chuckled. "I remember the first time I faced off with your uncle. I couldn't see out of my left eye for a week. He has a hard right hook."

"Don't take it personally, little brother. It may seem like Abraham has it in for you, but he's just trying to teach you the only way he knows how." Cratian slapped him on the back before turning to Chazz. "Go on. Give him your tips before I kick your butt."

Chazz rolled his eyes as he turned back to Joss. "Despite what this meathead would have you believe, winning a fight is seventy percent mental, and only thirty percent physical. And preparation is key. For instance, look at Cratian and tell me what you see."

Joss moved his attention to Cratian and frowned. All he saw was a formidable opponent.

Cratian flexed his bicep and beamed. "He sees perfection, of course."

A chuckle escaped Joss. "I see . . . I don't know. He's fit. And bigger than I am."

Chazz nudged him with his elbow. "Look closer, Joss. What's he wearing?"

Cratian was dressed in jeans and a button-down shirt. On his feet he wore a pair of ratty-looking sneakers. Before Joss could reply, Chazz leaned in close and spoke quietly, so that their opponent wouldn't hear. "The materials are cotton, which can be forgiving, but jeans? A button-down shirt? Neither is a stretchy material, and both will inhibit his movement. Notice I'm wearing sweatpants and a loose tank top. I have a clear advantage over him in that regard. It may not be much, but it's something. And when you're fighting someone, you have to focus on the positive and keep your morale high."

"Are you girls done whispering? I'd like to get to this today, Chazz." A gleam was in Cratian's eyes—one that told Joss that he loved a fight. Even one between allies.

Chazz shook his head, the corner of his mouth lifted in a smile. "Keep your skirt on. We're talking."

Joss had to hide his grin. It was hard to believe that he could become so broken the night before, only to find himself truly enjoying himself the very next morning—after hardly any sleep, and tortured sleep at that.

Chazz said, "Now, look around the clearing. There isn't much to see. No stones, no sticks. Not really anything that can be used as a weapon. But there's something we can use to our advantage. Any guesses what that might be? What do we have in abundance?"

Joss swept the clearing with his eyes. One thing stood out above the rest. "Dirt. Lots of it."

With a nod, Chazz said, "And with a handful of that, an opponent can be momentarily blinded. Long enough to escape or to subdue them in another way."

Amazement filled Joss. These were things he never would have thought to look for before. Who paid attention to what type of clothing an opponent was wearing, or what clever use of dirt one could apply? Only a skilled fighter, it seemed.

Chazz straightened his shoulders and took a step

closer to Cratian. "Okay, we're ready now. Or do you need a few extra minutes to fix your hair, pretty boy?"

Cratian shook his head, a smile on his face, and rushed at Chazz. Before he could make contact, Chazz reached down and whipped a handful of dirt into Cratian's eyes. Cratian cupped his face and swore loudly, swinging blindly with his fists. Joss dodged out of the way, but kept a keen eye on the scene before him. As Cratian stumbled, his eyes watering, Chazz whipped around him in a circle and caught Cratian in the knee with his foot. An audible crack came just seconds before another foul word escaped Cratian's lips. Breathless, Chazz beamed at Joss. "And that . . . is how you handle a loud-mouthed buffoon with an attitude problem."

After allowing Cratian a few moments to calm down, Chazz and Joss helped him to his feet. Joss wondered aloud, "Think Sirus will have enough time to bandage that knee before we head into town?"

Chazz glanced down at the affected leg. "Sirus will make time, I'm sure of it."

Through gritted teeth, Cratian said, "Chazz, you are so dead the next time we face off. But thanks for teaching our little brother here all your dirty tricks. He'll need 'em."

Chazz and Joss exchanged smiles. Then they moved down the hill, toward the cabin. Despite the excitement, a yawn snuck up on Joss, and he stretched as well as he could with a grown man weighing down his right shoulder. Maybe, he hoped, there was time for a nap before their trek to town.

A nap, he hoped, without dreams.

▶ 16 ◀

CONFRONTING THE BEAST

oss studied the Slayer Society manual for a while, waiting for eight in the morning to come. He hadn't slept, but just lying down seemed to be enough to rest him. He'd just gotten to an interesting chapter on drudges—or vampires' human slaves—when his stomach rumbled loudly. He bounded out of bed and headed down the stairs after a quick shower, a full hour before Sirus said he'd wake him. He wasn't exactly sure what had filled him with the peculiar energy—maybe it was the adrenaline rush of early-morning training—but he was in a good mood, that much was for certain. He mused that maybe it was the fact that his uncle had been enormously challenging to him in the past few days, and Joss had been man enough to rise to the occasion—something that likely surprised Abraham as much as it did Joss. But part of it—a small part, he was certain—was probably because he'd get to hang out with Kat today. And even if the very idea of friendship scared him, he was kind of excited about the mere possibility of having someone to call his friend. Even if she did ask a lot of questions that he couldn't answer. Even if she was a girl.

Sirus turned his eyes toward Joss as he made his way into the kitchen. Joss shrugged. "Any way I can get another omelet before we go to town?"

"Not a problem. It's good to see you have an appetite." Sirus quickly, but happily, set an omelet pan on the stove and started organizing his ingredients.

Joss grabbed a small glass from the cupboard and poured himself some orange juice. As he put it to his lips and sipped, he looked across the room to Sirus, who was busying himself at the stove. "Easy to have an appetite when you cook such great food, Sirus."

A smile settled on Sirus's lips as he turned to face Joss. "Thank you, Joss."

Sirus made him the most delectable cheese and ham omelet known to mankind, along with a side of crispy hash browns. Joss had just swallowed a second mouthful of hash-brown goodness when he cast a glance around the room and noticed that no one had joined them or even shuffled through the house since he'd been downstairs. "Where is everyone?"

Sirus shrugged as he filled the omelet pan with soapy water to soak for a bit before washing. "Our fellow Slayers have already started their day."

Joss chewed thoughtfully for a moment. "But . . . where did they go? What do you all do when there's not a new Slayer around to train?"

The air around Sirus seemed to fill with tension, as if Joss were entering into semidangerous territory, but Joss couldn't understand why. He was just curious. When Sirus spoke, though, it was casual and calm, without the smallest hint of tension. Maybe Joss had been reading too much into it. After all, he had been going through a lot lately, and getting a read on others' emotions when you've been run ragged is too much to ask of anyone. Sirus was fine. It was just his wildly overactive imagination. Probably. "They're searching for a hive—that's what we call a base of operations for creatures of the night. There's been evidence over the years that the hive is somewhere in this area of the Catskills, but we haven't narrowed its precise location down yet, I'm afraid."

Joss scooped another forkful of the delicious, steaming omelet into his mouth and chewed. The cheese was so hot that it almost burned his tongue, but he couldn't help but eat more. His parents' idea of cooking was calling the local pizza joint. Apparently

McMillans can do anything, except cook. His mom used to make a mean French toast but hadn't done that since Cecile had died. "What happens when they find it?"

Sirus was quiet for a while. He'd rinsed all of the pans and loaded the dishwasher before answering. That strange air of tension was back, and Joss began to wonder if Abraham had been onto something when he hinted at Sirus's lack of loyalty to the cause. He wondered if it were possible, when one was older, if one decided that belonging to the Society was no longer in their best interest, to leave, to walk away from Slaying forever. He doubted it very much. Likely, the only way out was through death's dark door. The thought sent a shiver up his spine. Sirus met his eyes—he looked exhausted, as if the subject were one he was tired of dealing with on a regular basis. "The hive will be set aflame. Any vampires who manage to escape will be destroyed."

"Why?" Curiosity filled Joss. Not that he disagreed that the task was necessary. He just wanted to know why exactly they were killing the beasts and not caging them up like animals at the zoo.

"Why?" Sirus sighed deeply. "That, my friend, is a dangerous question. Questions, in fact, are all dangerous to ask of the Society, but 'why' is perhaps the most dangerous of all. You'd do well not to wonder why we do the things we do, Joss. Your job is not to question.

Yours is to follow orders. 'Why' can get you in a lot of trouble."

Joss felt the fork slip from his fingers but couldn't make himself grip it. He was leaning forward in his seat, eyes locked on Sirus, who seemed so close to telling him something important. He parted his lips and said, "Sirus . . . did *you* ask 'why'? Is that what made you change your mind about the Society?"

Sirus's eyes were very dark. He looked troubled. "It wasn't the 'why' that did it, I'm afraid, my young friend. It was the reply that I received."

"What was the reply?"

But it was too late. Sirus broke away from the darkness and smiled a pleasant smile over Joss's right shoulder. "Good morning, Kat. Care for an omelet?"

Kat flopped into the chair next to Joss and laid her head on the table. Joss got the feeling she wasn't much of a morning person. "If by 'omelet' you mean 'Mountain Dew and a Snickers bar,' I'm totally on board."

Sirus shook his head and reached for a clean pan, the hint of a smile on his lips. "An omelet it is."

"But, Sirus"—her voice was full of a whiny tone—"I don't want eggs and cheese. What I want is sugar and caffeine."

He cracked two eggs into a mixing bowl and picked up a beater. "That's not a healthy diet, Kat. You should eat a better breakfast, something high in protein. An omelet is just that."

She narrowed her eyes. "You're one to talk."

Joss found his fork again and continued eating.

There was a clank on the side of the bowl as Sirus dropped the beater and turned to flash his daughter that don't-mess-with-me parental look. The silence between them seemed to stretch on forever. Joss filled it with chewing his food and hoped that the awkward quiet between father and daughter would soon pass. It did, once Kat sighed dramatically and returned her head to the table.

Sirus went back to cooking, tossing shredded cheddar, chopped onions, and diced bell peppers into the bowl. As he mixed the ingredients together, adding in bits of smoked ham and pepper jack cheese, he said, "Maybe we can pick up some Mountain Dew while we're at the store today."

Kat turned her head toward Joss and smiled, then sat up again. "So what kind of supplies *are* we picking up today?"

Sirus sprayed the pan with Pam and poured the egg mixture into it. "All kinds. Dairy, dry goods, meat, fruits, and vegetables. I'd like to get enough to get us through another two weeks, if possible. The men eat quite a bit, as you can imagine, and if I don't stock up, I'll be running into town every two or three days."

Joss finished cleaning his plate, took it to the sink, and rinsed it. As he turned to Sirus, he said, "Do you want me to make a list so we don't forget anything?"

Sirus flipped the omelet over with a spatula and nodded. "A novel concept, Joss. I was going to rely on my memory. But memories cannot always be trusted."

Joss grabbed a pad of paper from the counter and listed as many basics as he could think of, like eggs, milk, and cheese. Sirus added to the list, indicating how much of each they'd need to get for two weeks. By the time he'd reached the end of the list, he and Kat were adding their own list of supplies.

"I think we could use six pounds of chocolate and a gallon of something heavily caffeinated to wash it all down, don't you?"

Joss laughed wildly, wiping a tear from his eye. It was almost as funny as the two-story tall bag of marshmallows he'd added just moments before. "A gallon? You're thinking too small. This has to last us for two entire weeks. We're gonna need an entire drum of something heavily caffeinated."

Kat tilted her head thoughtfully. "Does Mountain Dew come in drums?"

This gave Joss pause. "I'm not sure."

He also wasn't exactly sure where the Slayer Society got their funding for such things. Houses, food, medical supplies—who paid for it all and how? He'd approached the subject with Malek before but hadn't gotten a straight answer, so his impression was that it was, frankly, none of his business. Not yet, anyway.

Sirus had finished quietly cleaning up the kitchen,

and turned back to them at last with a bemused smile on his face. "If you two are quite ready, we need to get into town. And no, I'm fairly certain that Mountain Dew does not come in drums."

Once outside, they piled into Sirus's truck, and Kat put a scratched-up CD in the stereo. She turned the volume up really high and Sirus turned it back down a bit so their ears wouldn't bleed. Joss wished very much that he could say he'd heard of the band they were listening to, but honestly, he had no idea who they were and why they seemed so determined that some guy named Bela Lugosi was dead.

Twenty minutes later, they pulled into the sparsely populated area that Sirus kept referring to as "town" and came to a stop in front of a small market that looked as though it had seen better days. Joss looked out the passenger-side window at the sticker-covered glass door and shook his head. It was highly doubtful that this small shop would have everything they needed, let alone a drum of Mountain Dew. He opened the door and stepped out, ready for a disappointing shopping trip.

Sirus looked over the list. "Kat, you head over to the eatery and pick up muffins, bread, cookies, and crackers. Make certain you get two cheesecakes and maybe some sandwiches for tonight, if they have enough. I'm going to run a few errands and meet you both back here in an hour. Joss, you're in charge of the rest of the list. Feel free to pick up a few treats for you and Kat."

Over Sirus's shoulder, Kat mouthed "Mountain Dew," and brought a smile to Joss's face.

Sirus glanced back at her with a question in his eyes before withdrawing several hundred dollars from his wallet and splitting it between the two of them. "Try to keep it under an hour, okay? Let's make it snappy and get back to the cabin before lunch."

Joss gripped the list in his hand and pulled open the glass door to the store. As he stepped inside, a rather hairy man behind the counter grumped, "We got no meat today."

At first, Joss blinked. Then he wondered briefly whether or not he looked like the kind of person that desperately needed a steak or two. He looked at the man and said "Okay" before proceeding farther into the store.

He looked over the list again and was surprised to find things like oranges and bananas in such a small shop like this, in the middle of nowhere. He could see only five aisles, but each of them was packed to the brim with items on Sirus's list.

There were no shopping carts to speak of, so Joss took his time filling one small handheld basket after another until he'd piled ten of them on the counter for checkout. The grumpy-looking man scanned everything and bagged it into six brown paper sacks. As he took the money from Joss, he spoke again, his voice only slightly less grumpy than before. "We'll have meat tomorrow. If you're interested."

Though he was extremely tempted to ask the man what it was about him that made him look like a guy with outrageous carnivorous needs, Joss merely nodded and retrieved his bags. "Thank you."

Someone that he couldn't see opened the door for him and though he almost dropped all of the bags on his way to the truck, he somehow managed to set the bags in the back unscathed. After he did so, he breathed a loud sigh of relief and looked around the small parking lot. Kat and Sirus were nowhere to be found. He waited awhile before ducking his head back inside the store and checking the time. His shopping had taken just forty minutes, so he was a bit early yet.

At the corner just up the street was a small tented booth, containing a table piled high with baked goods. Joss wandered over and smiled at the two little old ladies sitting behind it in lawn chairs. The rounder, blue-haired woman nudged the thinner, gray-haired one and smiled. "Oh, isn't he precious? He reminds me of Bertha's boy. What's his name?"

"Terrence? Or do you mean Thornton?"

"No, the other boy! You know the one." She smiled broadly at Joss and nodded. "You look just like him. Any relation?"

Joss had to fight a chuckle. "I'm sorry, ma'am, but I don't even know anyone named Bertha."

"Oh." Her smile deflated some. "Well, that's a shame. Bertha's very nice. In fact, she usually donates to the bake sale every summer. Of course, this year she's sick with something awful over at the hospital. What's she got, Emmie? Bronchitis? Tuberculosis?"

The other woman shook her head. "I don't know. Something awful, that's for sure."

"I hope she feels better soon." Joss swept his eyes over the bags of cookies and various Saran Wrapped yumminess. "What's the bake sale for?"

The blue-haired woman puffed out her chest with pride. "We're raising money for our library. Would you care for a brownie? They're only a quarter."

Joss's ears perked up. He loved libraries. Nowhere else in the world felt so safe and homey. Nowhere else smelled like books and dust and happy solitude quite like a library did. "Do you have two brownies?"

"We have four. How many would you like?"

As he walked away with all four brownies in his hands, Joss felt a peculiar warmth spread through him. In a strange way, coming to the Catskills for the summer had freed him and given him something that he couldn't find within his own quiet home life. He'd found a challenge in Abraham, a mentor in Sirus, a friend in Kat, and strange sense of belonging in the sleepy little town of Phoenicia. And he was liking it more and more here. Yes, Abraham at times seemed to have it in for him, but he knew if he could just keep chipping away at that frosty exterior, he and his uncle could bond in a way that he had never been able to bond with any of the McMillan family—not even his cousin Henry. And yes, Kat was nosy and bossy, but she was also super funny and incredibly interesting. Joss was full of so much hope for the future, he felt his chest might burst.

Then he turned his head and saw a familiar face peering out from behind the funeral home across the street. Dark, brooding. The face of a killer. It was the vampire who'd attacked Kat just two weeks before.

Well, not attacked, exactly. But it had chased after her. It had scared the daylights out of her and had made him shake from the inside out. What was that thing doing still lurking around? It clearly knew that Sirus was a Slayer. Why stay in a town where people were out for your blood and hunting you? Why not move your so-called hive to a safer location? Joss didn't know, couldn't even fathom something resembling a sensible reason for putting your life in danger like that. But he was determined to find out.

Plus . . . he had been training lately, and his skills were developing nicely—even Sirus had said so. And what better way of impressing Uncle Abraham than taking down a vampire on his own, just days into his training?

Joss walked over to the truck and set the brownies inside on the dashboard before turning back to where he'd seen the monster lurking. As he approached, he kept a close eye on his surroundings, carefully making sure that he wasn't being followed. After all, he was fairly certain he could handle one vampire. But any more than that and he'd be toast.

He moved around the corner of the funeral home as silently as possible, but it turned out there was no need for sneakiness. The vampire was sitting on a stump, as if awaiting his arrival. It smiled at Joss as it rubbed sunscreen on its skin. "It's warm today, my Slayer friend. I've had to reapply sunscreen twice already and it's not yet noon. It would be no wonder to me if the sun chases me inside by early afternoon."

Joss stood very still, saying nothing. He hadn't expected the thing to attempt a conversation with him. Let alone a casual, friendly conversation about the weather. The creature finished rubbing sunscreen on its skin before capping the bottle and slipping it in its inside jacket pocket. Then it smiled at him again. He could see no sign of fangs, but knew that they were there somewhere, lurking within its monstrous mouth. It looked so human, so . . . normal. But Joss knew that it was anything but.

He could feel the corner of his mouth twitch as he parted his lips to speak. Even as he did so, he wasn't exactly certain what he was going to say. He only knew that he had to say something, so it would know why he was here. "So we meet again."

Great, Joss. If that wasn't the most stereotypical response to a mortal enemy, he didn't know what was. But it was out there now, hanging in the air between them. To his greatest disgust, the monster visibly suppressed a smile.

Of course it was amused by his antics. It had probably faced Slayers like Abraham and Sirus. What threat could a boy spewing cheesy movie lines possibly provide?

The vampire met his eyes and again Joss was stunned by how distinctly human it appeared. If he hadn't already witnessed this monster's fangs once before, he might be doubting his actions now. The very thought was unnerving. It removed its jacket and placed it casually on an old stump to its right. Before Joss's training, he might have dismissed such an act as nothing notable at all, but now he knew better. It was preparation for a fight. The fabric might inhibit its movement slightly, and it didn't want to get its jacket dirty with Joss's blood. Joss casually glanced around the yard, noting areas of escape: back around the side of the building, into the woods, or through the open window. Few options and none of them smart choices. But there were weapons available: a small hatchet was stuck in a nearby log, sharp branches lay strewn about the edge of the yard, and a hose was attached to the back of the building. Maybe he could wash away the sunblock and let the sun take care of his work for him. The point was, there were options. And Joss was seeing those options—something he took great pride in.

When his eyes found the vampire again, it was perching on the stump, its hands folded in its lap. Perhaps it was excited about the idea of feeding from him and trying to keep its hands from trembling. Joss didn't know. All he did know was that judging by the sounds and sights and smells around them, they were alone.

It smiled warmly, like they were old friends. "I wouldn't be a gentleman if I didn't ask your name, boy. So? What do they call you up there in that house in the hills?"

It knew where he was staying, where they were staying. Joss swallowed hard at the realization. After the briefest of pauses—one to consider whether or not answering the creature could possibly compromise himself as a Slayer or the Society as a whole—he said, "Joss. And you are?"

He didn't think admitting his name would compromise them. After all, it was just a name . . . right? It wasn't like he was revealing deep Society secrets.

The monster clucked its tongue, shaking its head. "Curious about a vampire, are you? Abraham would be disappointed, to say the least. He doesn't believe we even have names. At least he's never cared to learn mine. May I ask why you're so intrigued?"

Joss shrugged. "I wouldn't be following protocol if I didn't find out everything I can about your kind. Plus I'd like to have a name to give when I report to my uncle this afternoon."

It leaned forward, a bemused sparkle in its eyes. "And just what will you be reporting, Joss?"

Joss leaned forward, too, his jaw set. "That I found a vampire lurking around Phoenicia and killed it."

Its eyes widened in surprise and bemused laughter boiled over from within it. Joss could feel insult and anger threatening to take him over, but instead he managed to stay calm and breathe deeply. "Are you going to give me your name, or should I just refer to you as 'number one'?"

Its smile quickly faded, replaced by fury at Joss's insinuation. "Look, *boy*, I am over six hundred years old. Six hundred and twenty-three to be precise. You should be mindful of who you threaten."

"What." When the monster blinked at Joss, he said, "I should be mindful of *what* I threaten. After all, you're not a person. You're just a thing. An animal. A monster."

The creature paused for a moment before nodding

slowly, as if agreeing that they were at an impasse. "Zy. My name is Zy."

Joss nodded, bracing himself for what he knew was coming. "It's time to perish, Zy."

The creature nodded once more, a dark shadow passing over its eyes—one that Joss regarded instantly as a fusion of hunger and pure, unadulterated hatred. "If you insist, Joss."

It moved so fast that Joss had no time to react. All of his plans, his forethought came crashing down around him as the monster gripped him by the throat and slammed him down on the ground. The back of Joss's head met with the earth harder than he could have imagined, and for a moment his vision was blotted out in varying sizes of black polka dots. Then the thing leaned in close, close enough for Joss to smell the metallic hint of blood on its tongue—it had fed recently. "If you're wondering why I've allowed you to live this long, it is because I have a message for your uncle. A message that I cannot deliver to him personally without risking my life or his. And so I am tasked with giving this message to the weakest in that Slayer crew. You, my dear boy. Joss, as it were—I'm not so prejudiced that I refuse to acknowledge your name. You, Joss, will deliver this message to Abraham. And I will let you live . . . for now. Are we clear?"

Joss tried to wriggle free, but he couldn't move as much as an inch. The beast had him pinned. It gave his throat a threatening squeeze and his vision wavered. It was a warning. Don't move. Don't even blink.

Out of sheer terror that this might be his last moment on Earth, Joss obliged.

His heart beat in his ears so loudly that he feared the monster's words would be drowned out by the sound of it, and he wouldn't know what message he was supposed to deliver to his uncle. But the vampire waited—it looked as if it was listening—until Joss's heartbeat settled some before it began to speak again. "Tell your uncle that we are well aware of their activities here, and they have reached the edge of our patience. We are giving them—you—exactly one month to pack up camp and leave. If you do not comply, we will skin you all alive, starting with you, my dear boy. Tell him this and mean it. If they do not adhere to our wishes, I shall find you and rip the skin from your bones myself. Do you understand?"

A fleeting, empowering thought entered Joss's mind then: the Slayers must have been getting close to the hive. Too close for comfort, and that's why the threat was coming now.

It released its grip on Joss's throat, and he sucked in a lungful of air before nodding. He wasn't sure that he could have spoken at that moment. His throat burned painfully, so it might not have been possible. Not to mention the fact that he was also terrified that if he did speak, it would come out in a high-pitched shriek rather than the calm, strong tone that a Slayer should use. Saying anything would completely crush any amount of false confidence that he had left, so he stayed silent.

"If you're smart, you'll stay here until I've gone. Count to ten. Then return to the truck. Tell no one but Abraham the message that I have bestowed upon you. If you're not smart . . ." It peered down on him, tilting its head to the right, as if it were examining his features and committing them to memory. Then it clucked its tongue. "Well . . . let's hope you're smart, Joss."

As quickly as it had taken Joss down, the thing disappeared again. The thought briefly crossed Joss's mind that he should follow it, track it, but he pushed that thought way down deep inside of him, in a box marked "stupid, dangerous ideas" and closed his eyes, counting to ten and thanking the stars that he was still alive.

· 17 ·

SECRETS TO SHARE

The trip back to the cabin was long, and silent on Joss's part. He could sense that Kat knew something was off about him, and every time she'd look out the window, Sirus would cast him a glance that was full of questions. *Is everything all right? Are you okay? Did something happen while we were apart that I should know about?*

He didn't have to ask the questions aloud. Joss could read each and every one on Sirus's face, and in his eyes. And to each one, Joss gave him a look that he hoped would answer him in the most broad and general manner possible. *Everything is fine. I'm fine. There's nothing to talk about.*

Each silent reply was a blatant lie, but a necessary one. He felt terrible for lying—albeit silently—to Sirus. Especially since Sirus had been nothing but a good friend to him since the moment he'd arrived. He told himself that he'd explain everything to Sirus later, after he'd passed on the vampire's message to Abraham. But even that only managed to comfort him a little bit. So he looked out the window and watched the trees as they wound their way up the mountains to the grand house that they all referred to as a cabin. As his eyes fell on the house, he marveled at the lies they told each other every day. It was a cabin—not a grand spectacle of a house. They were just friends and family, gathered for a summer of hunting and cookouts. They were just regular people, like those in town. The only danger lurking in the woods was a mountain lion. Lies. All lies. And each one had been so easy to tell.

The thought made him feel somewhat queasy.

The truck came to a stop and Kat slid out the passenger-side door. She loaded three bags of groceries into her arms and headed for the house without another word, but Joss could tell she felt cut off from something, from him. He instantly hated that he had to make her feel that way, but there was little he could do about it. Not without exposing the entire Slayer Society, that is. And even though he hadn't been a part of their group for long, Joss felt a growing sense of loyalty to them. He belonged to them, believed in their cause. They were good and just and right. And more than that, they were his path to laying Cecile's tortured soul to rest, which was worth the cost of any friendship.

He got out of the cab of the truck, noting the distinct absence of his uncle's car, and closed the passenger-side door. Sirus was waiting for him near the open tailgate. "What's happened, Joss? You seem troubled. Shaken, even. So badly that even Kat has noticed. What is it?"

Joss reached for a bag, but Sirus placed a firm hand on his forearm. "Joss . . . tell me. Please. I'm concerned."

He shook his head. "Not yet, Sirus. I need to speak to my uncle first. Then I'll tell you everything you want to know."

After a moment, Sirus nodded and released his grip, though something in his eyes told Joss that he was reluctant to do so. They each grabbed several bags and carried them to the kitchen. As they entered the house, Sirus called out to a few of the Slayers and soon, the truck bed was completely empty, the groceries tucked neatly away. Once they were finished, Kat disappeared out the door and Joss took a seat on the front porch, hoping that his uncle would return from wherever it was that he'd gone off to. The burden of the vampire's message weighed heavily on him, so heavily that it consumed his thoughts, filling his head with dark, murky clouds. He ached to be free of it.

Joss lost himself for a while in the pages of the Slayer Society manual. He absorbed rule after rule, and absorbed the message of loyalty and justice. There was an insistence on protocol—of following the correct channels to report any interaction between himself and vampirekind. There was also a list of punishments for those who dared to defy that protocol. Ugly, awful things. Joss didn't envy the man who went against the Society, but he knew the rules were important to the cause. After all, rules were in place for a reason. Without them, the world would fall into chaos.

In the journal section of the manual, Joss noted his encounter with Zy, every detail. And he waited for his uncle for what seemed like an eternity.

Two hours later, headlights lit up the house as Abraham's car pulled into the parking space beside Sirus's truck. Joss waited quietly until his uncle left his car and made his way to the house. Abraham's steps slowed when he noticed Joss on the porch, but it was Joss who spoke first. "I have a message for you, Uncle."

Abraham eyed him keenly for a moment before responding. "What an ominous-sounding welcome."

When Joss didn't say anything, he sighed, as if bothered by Joss's very presence. Then he withdrew his pipe from his inside jacket pocket, filled it from a small leather pouch, and lit it, taking a puff and blowing out the smoke in small circles. The circles dissipated into the air as he sat beside Joss on the porch steps and sighed again. "What's the message, boy?"

Joss's throat felt dry as he opened his mouth to speak again, but he knew that what he had to say was important, so he forced the words out, despite the difficulty they were giving him. "They know we're here, and they know what you're doing."

A dark cloud passed over Abraham's face then and as it did, Joss felt a cold tickle race up his spine, like the fingers of the dead. Abraham spoke again, but this time, his tone indicated that he was taking his nephew seriously. "How were you contacted?"

Joss could feel the weight—the burden of the message he'd held in secret for much of the day—lifting from him. He already felt lighter and safer, knowing that his uncle would soon be aware of all that had happened. Abraham wasn't exactly the friendly type, but he was definitely a take-charge kind of guy, and someone who Joss knew he could count on in the heat of battle. "After getting supplies in town, I saw one lurking behind the funeral home. His name—"

"*Its* name." Abraham's glare was sharp. Sharp enough to cut right through him. "They are things, Joss. They are monsters. You know this perhaps better than any in our group. They are animals. Beasts. Not people. Don't start referring to them as he or she, or else it'll make them that much harder to kill. They look as we do. The things even sound like we do. But they are not human, and it would be a grave weakness to start thinking of them as such. Do yourself a favor. Keep that distinction in the forefront of your mind. Always."

Joss nodded his understanding, his face warming as it flushed pink with embarrassment. He should have known better. The things his uncle was teaching him could save his life someday. If only he would listen. "Its name is Zy."

"Is?" Abraham raised a sharp, questioning eyebrow. "You mean it's still alive?"

Joss flicked his gaze around the porch, feeling very much like a complete idiot. How could he tell his uncle about his cowardice without disgracing himself completely? There was no way.

Abraham calmly took a puff of his pipe and rested his elbows on his knees, a newfound patience lurking in his eyes as he looked at Joss, who was fidgeting with a hole in the knee of his jeans. "What happened exactly, Joss? Point by point. I need to know every detail."

Joss blew out a sigh and with it came words that he had not expected. He explained in full detail about exactly what had transpired earlier that day with the vampire that called itself Zy, and as he came to the end of his tale, the last remaining bit of weight on his shoulders lifted with each word.

When he was finished, Abraham silently smoked

his pipe for several minutes. The sight of it was oddly comforting to Joss. It meant that his uncle was mulling over their situation, and planning, strategizing what to do next. The more time he spent with Abraham, the more Joss came to respect him as a leader.

Abraham withdrew his pipe from his lips and bit the end thoughtfully before speaking once again. "Let's gather the troops. And when we do, I want you to repeat every word you just said to me verbatim. Then we'll form a plan of action."

Action. Yes. Abraham was nothing if not a man of action—something that Joss greatly admired, something he very much wanted to be.

An hour later, every Slayer in their group was gathered in the living room, poised and listening to Joss recount his tale. Only Sirus refused to meet his eyes, and Joss had a feeling it was because Joss had insisted on telling his uncle first, despite the fact that he and Sirus were absolutely closer than he and Abraham. He hoped Sirus would understand—it was important to follow protocol. And the only way that he could advance through the ranks of the Society was by doing just that.

But still it weighed on him how disappointed Sirus seemed. Or maybe he was wrong about it being disappointment in Sirus's eyes. Maybe it was just concern for Joss's well-being and shame that he hadn't been there to take the vampire down.

Joss finished regaling them with his tale, and as he spoke the final, crucial words, Sirus met his gaze at last. "If we're not gone within a month, they say they'll skin us all alive. Starting with me."

Ash shook his head. "Why are they warning us? Why not just attack? It's not like bloodsuckers to give their prey time to escape. I don't trust it."

Paty stood up from her perch on the arm of the couch, eyes alight with flames. "Neither do I. I say we set fire to the woods, flush them out."

Sirus shook his head in disgust. "Are you actually suggesting we stage a wildfire?"

Her voice was a growl. "What if I am?"

"As our Californian brothers in arms have proven time and time again, wildfires do nothing to flush out vampires. They only damage the forests and homes that surround our fellow humans."

"Then what would you suggest, nursemaid?" As they argued, the two of them grew closer and closer. It was clear that neither thought much at all of the other. Like Sirus as he did, Joss was on Paty's side. The only way to deal with the vampires was drastic action.

At last, Abraham held up a hand, silencing them both. All eyes fell on him with respect and awe—except for Paty and Sirus, of course, who were still glaring at one another with seething disgust. "Perhaps we should count our blessings, Slayers, and regroup elsewhere. There's nothing saying that we can't use this to our advantage. After all, they'll likely send a scout to check the house in a month to ensure we've gone. So let's give them what they want. Leave. But watch the house from a distance and trail their scout back to the hive, where we'll dispatch them all."

At this, Paty nodded and Sirus relaxed his shoulders some. From the back of the room, Cratian spoke up. "Abraham, do you think this hive has anything at all to do with the Pravus myth we've been hearing so much about lately?"

Abraham's calm face turned instantly red with anger. He whipped his head around, but before his eyes could even fall on the Slayer who'd spoken, two others had already dragged him out of the room. Abraham looked at Joss and said, "Forget you heard that."

Joss nodded, but despite his silent promise, a word, strange and somehow meaningful, rang in his ears, and he couldn't help but wonder what it meant. It was a word his mind would replay again and again as he laid down to rest that night, watching the moonbeams dance on his pillow.

Pravus.

What on earth could it mean? And why did it make his uncle so furious?

▸ 18 ◂

FACING THE ENEMY

The next morning, Joss opened his eyes to Paty, who was standing at the foot of his bed. She tossed a pair of jeans at him and barked, "Get dressed. Your uncle wants you in the clearing in fifteen minutes."

She stormed out, as if Joss had said something to really irritate her, and Joss sat up in bed, rubbing his eyes. The clock on his nightstand said that it was just quarter after six, but instantly, he understood what had Paty all annoyed. Most of the Slayers were out the door by four in the morning. He wasn't sure why Abraham indulged him in extra sleep. He only knew that if Abraham wanted him in the clearing in fifteen minutes, he'd better be there in ten.

He slipped out of bed, throwing on clean clothes as he made his way to the kitchen. Sirus was standing at the stove. "I'd offer you some toast, but it looks like you've been summoned."

Joss nodded, casting a longing glance at the warm pan of apple cinnamon muffins that were cooling on the counter.

Sirus smiled and ruffled Joss's hair. "Don't look so forlorn. I'll make you a good lunch—whatever you want. Now get out there before Abraham starts screaming."

Joss darted out the back door without a word and into the woods toward the clearing, cursing himself aloud for having forgotten his shoes. By the time he reached it, his uncle was already looking irritated and well on the verge of anger. "Joss. It's about time."

"Sorry," he said breathlessly. "I was . . ."

Joss searched his still-waking mind, but couldn't seem to grasp anything of importance that he'd been doing before he ran out the door on his uncle's whim. So he grabbed what he could and ran with it ". . . putting pants on."

Cratian and Chazz, who were standing on either side of Abraham, exchanged looks, and then smirked at Joss's admission, but Abraham spoke as if he hadn't heard Joss's excuse. "There will be times when you will face multiple foes at once. Today's lesson, my nephew, is intended to prepare you for those times."

Joss blinked, uncertain of Abraham's meaning. Then Chazz and Cratian split apart, moving equal distance around the clearing, and he knew full well what today's lesson would entail. Joss was going to have to fight his way out of this clearing. He was still half asleep, hungry, and wearing no shoes. But he was going to have to fight for his life against well-trained, well-rested, well-fed, and odds were, well-armed opponents. His uncle had wisely dropped him into a likely situation for any Slayer to face. It was the perfect test. Even though Joss was terrified to take it.

He glanced around the clearing for possible resources, but found nothing at all that would prove useful to him. Every rock and stray stick had been cleared away. The only potential weapons available were in the hands of his opponents. For the first time, it really hit Joss hard that he could die here. He could lose his life in a moment, all for a need for vengeance. His heart pounded inside his chest and, though he'd never dare admit it out loud, for a moment, Joss wondered if this was the right path for him, or if he was foolhardily chasing after vengeance that he might never obtain. Or worse, if he might die here in the clearing, leaving his parents completely childless. But any choice that he might have had before he got to the clearing was gone now. He was faced with two options, and only two. Live or die.

This wasn't about Cecile. Not now. It was about survival. And perhaps that was a lesson worth learning as well. After all, when he was out in the field, there would be no one there to help him, no one to save him. He'd be on his own, and if he died, no one would know why. Just like when he'd confronted Zy behind the funeral home—an act of pure stupidity. And what had he learned?

He eyed his opponents—that's all they were at the moment; not his uncle; not his comrades; just the Enemy and nothing more—and readied himself, knowing that his bare feet would be a weakness on the weed-infested, uneven terrain. Chazz moved forward with more speed and agility than Joss was ready for, and whipped the stake from the holster on his hip, swiping it at Joss. Joss heard a sound like air being sucked through a tube, and realized that he'd gasped aloud. Instinctively, he jerked back, away from the weapon, away from the Slayer. The eeriest feeling came over him then. Almost like he knew what vampires must feel like when they are hunted by the Society. It was a feeling of pity—one that sank into Joss's stomach and nauseated him to no end. How could he feel pity for monsters that killed little girls in the dead of the night? How could he feel pity for creatures whose sole purpose was to destroy human life. Instantly, he hated himself, and swore that he would never again show an ounce of pity to a vampire. Disgusted with his momentary weakness, Joss was too distracted to see the second swipe of Chazz's stake. It caught him in the bicep and he screamed. Blood poured from his arm and he whipped around in a moment of pure fury, grabbing the stake and throwing Chazz down hard on the ground. It took him a moment to realize that he was holding Chazz's stake in his hand. When he did, he thought about what Uncle Abraham had said about Slayer's having a natural agility, and knew that he was right, even though it had never occurred to Joss that he might be special in any way.

Not that he was special. Only Cecile had made him that. He had been her protector, her brother, her mentor. And her failure. Just a coward who couldn't even stop someone from hurting her. From killing her. If he hadn't hesitated when he heard her cries, he could have stopped the beast from taking her life. But he had.

Joss turned back to Chazz, but was blindsided by Cratian, who tackled him. Joss flew backward, time slowing to a crawl as his body became airborne. When his back hit the ground, the air in his lungs came out in a gush, a groan its only company. Cratian sat atop Joss, his eyes alight with certainty, his stake in his confident hands. There was no emotion on his face. He was as removed from this situation as he could be. Joss imagined that that was another lesson of sorts—that a Slayer couldn't let emotions dictate his actions. He had to commit to the task of killing vampires and not allow himself to feel.

He imagined it would be the most difficult of all lessons for him to learn.

Quickly, he ran down his list of resources, but it didn't take long—mostly because he had so few. Namely, one. Chazz's stake was still in Joss's grip, but he wasn't exactly certain what to do with it. Ash hadn't yet taught him anything practical about weaponry, like how to wield a stake. Was this another thing that would come naturally to him? What he'd read in the Slayer Society manual was that a Slayer's stake was a weapon that had to be earned, that one didn't just grab a stake and go off chasing vampires. It was a gentleman's weapon, and something to be held in the highest regard. In short, you had to build to that.

As Joss struggled against Cratian, he waited for the miraculous knowledge of how to beat his fellow Slayers without a weapon to come.

It didn't.

The most he could hope for was that Cratian would grow tired and give up, but something about the way his face didn't show any sign of strained effort told Joss that was unlikely. So Joss weighed his choices and did all that he could do.

As he bit down hard on Cratian's hand, Joss wasn't proud. Nor did he think it was a particularly brilliant fighting move. Really, it was kind of chicken, and more akin to a catfight than Slayer-to-Slayer combat, but it was the only thing that Joss could think of to do with his limited resources. Fortunately, judging by the surprised cry and hesitation, Cratian hadn't seen it coming either.

Cratian yelped and sat back, relaxing his grip on Joss's wrists just enough for Joss to shove him back. He fell over, a look of surprise locked on his formerly emotionless face. As he fell back on the ground, Joss whipped the stake in his hand forward, stabbing the ground next to Cratian. Then he beamed. "You're dead, Cratian."

"As are you, nephew." Something cold and sharp pressed against Joss's throat. Abraham was standing behind him, holding a blade against his tender skin. And he wasn't exactly being gentle about it. Joss swallowed hard, his heart racing, and felt blood trickle down his neck.

He took a slow, shallow breath, followed immediately by another. Then, without thinking, he reached back and grabbed Abraham by his left shoulder, flipping him over so that Abraham flew through the air, landing on his back in front of Joss.

The moment Abraham's back hit the ground, shock filled Joss. He was stronger than he'd thought.

Joss straightened his shoulders, pride filling him. He'd been challenged by three well-trained, highly skilled Slayers and had won.

It took several seconds for Abraham to stand, and when he did, he didn't look at Joss at all. He merely walked out of the clearing without a word. As Joss watched him leave, his heart sank with every step. Breathlessly, he called out, "Uncle Abraham? What is this? What is this supposed to teach me about hand-to-hand combat?"

But Abraham was gone.

Chazz had stood and was still brushing the dirt from his pants when he said, "Run ten laps on the long trail. And don't come back to the cabin until you do, little man."

Joss rubbed the back of his neck absently. He was still wondering what exactly he'd done to upset Abraham, and he had no idea where to find the so-called long trail. "Where is it?"

Cratian was breathing heavily as he walked by, knocking his shoulder into Joss's with a playful flare. "When you find it, start running."

▸ 19 ◂

RUNNING ON EMPTY

Joss stumbled toward the back door to the cabin in the morning light on wobbly knees. His lungs were burning so badly that it was difficult to breathe, so much, in fact, that his chest ached. His legs were throbbing with intense pain. The hurt of his day and night spent running couldn't even be masked by the rush of adrenaline coursing through his veins. It had taken him a long time to locate the long trail that Chazz had instructed him to find, and a couple of hours to run it once, let alone ten times. He was reasonably sure he'd been alone on his run, but knowing the Slayers, they were watching him, so stopping and lying about his run wasn't exactly an option. Besides, it was the principle of the thing. He'd know that he'd lied, that he hadn't lived up to their expectations, and that he just couldn't live with.

He'd thrown up on his third pass around the trail, and almost gave up on his sixth, but he realized something while he was standing in the woods, breathless and hurting and so homesick that he almost cried—he, Joss, who never cried, not even on the day of Cecile's funeral, though he'd desperately wanted to, desperately needed to. He wouldn't let himself cry, wouldn't allow himself that release of pain. He deserved to hurt, deserved to suffer.

He realized on the trail, when his lungs were aching so bad that he thought he might actually keel over and die, that this too was a test, but more than that, it didn't matter how many tests he passed or how much he impressed his uncle. He would never have Abraham's approval, and Abraham was simply waiting for him to fail. Maybe hoping that he would. Maybe knowing that he would. And Joss wasn't about to give him the satisfaction.

This was about more than a desire for vengeance for Cecile now. It was about him and Abraham and this strange tension between them. It was about Joss proving himself to no one but himself, and showing Abraham who was the better man in the end.

His thigh muscles screamed as he stepped up onto

the back porch, and his shoulder screamed again when he reached out to grasp the doorknob. He stepped inside, his eyes first falling on the clock in the kitchen. It was just after six in the morning. Which meant that he'd been running, hurting, and puking his guts out for almost twenty-four hours straight.

Sirus was standing at the sink, rinsing out some pans—probably some that he'd used just a few hours ago to make the other Slayers breakfast. When he turned to Joss, his face went white. "Joss, you look awful. Are you okay?"

Joss's legs wobbled a bit more, and he found his way to a chair in the dining room. If he didn't sit down soon, he was going to fall down. And if he did that, he might never get back up again. And then Abraham would win, wouldn't he?

When he replied to Sirus, his voice sounded gravelly, as if he'd been eating sand. It also sounded strangely distant, as if they weren't really his words at all. "As okay as I can be after ten laps on the long trail, I suppose."

Sirus shook his head, a look of disgust settling into his eyes—disgust, Joss would have bet, for Abraham and his idea of training. "I had no idea you didn't come in last night. I thought you came back after I'd gone to bed. I thought you were still upstairs asleep. If I had known—"

"You'd what?" Joss snapped, then sighed, feeling

immediately awful about taking out his frustrations on his best ally here at Casa de Slayer. "There's nothing you can do, Sirus. No one can do this for me, and no one can swoop in and rescue me every time I'm challenged. I have to do this on my own."

Sirus watched him in silence for a few moments, then moved back into the kitchen. Joss heard cupboards opening and closing along with the refrigerator door, and assumed that Sirus was making him a sandwich. A few minutes later, Sirus returned, and Joss realized that he was only half right. On a small plate in Sirus's left hand was the most delectable looking turkey sandwich that Joss had ever seen. In his right hand was Joss's Slayer manual.

On the plate beside the sandwich were three pills—Joss raised an exhausted eyebrow and Sirus slid a glass of water closer to him. "They're vitamins. After a night like that, you need to replenish your nutrients. Take your vitamins and sip your water. Small sips, but drink a lot—I'm sure you must be dehydrated. Then eat your sandwich, slowly. I want you to spend the day resting."

"I don't need to rest," he snapped, despite his gratitude toward Sirus.

"Then you'll study." Sirus dropped the journal in front of him loudly, his patience clearly at an end.

Joss reached for the pills, and as he closed his hand over them, he met Sirus's eyes. It touched him that

Sirus seemed to care about him—so much more than his own parents ever had in the last three years. It meant more to Joss than Sirus would ever know. He wanted to speak again, to thank Sirus for every shred of kindness he had afforded him, but the words refused to come. So instead, he nodded to Sirus and popped the vitamins into his mouth, swallowing them dry.

He was just taking his second bite of the sandwich and marveling that something as simple as turkey, bread, and assorted veggies could taste so delectable, when Sirus spoke again. "Survival isn't an easy thing, especially not in the wilderness. You have to know what to eat, what to drink, and how to shelter yourself. Meat is always your best bet—high in protein and, as long as it's a fresh kill, you don't have to worry about contaminants. Stay away from mushrooms. Many are poison, and though they'll fill you up, they won't do you as many favors as some other plants will in the wild. If you have to drink water, boil it first, unless it's fresh rainwater or from a running stream. You'll find many tips in the survival section of your manual, but don't be afraid to add things as you learn them."

Joss chewed the mouthful of sandwich and swallowed slowly. "What about berries?"

Sirus shook his head and tapped a finger on the cover of Joss's journal. "Only if you know what you're looking for. I've scribbled a few descriptions and images in the back of your journal to help you along, but you really ought to study up on the different species of edible plants."

Joss nodded, but paused to raise a questioning eyebrow. "How am I supposed to boil water in the middle of the woods?"

"Didn't your father ever take you camping?"

He shook his head, biting into his sandwich again. Embarrassment engulfed him. Was that what dads did with sons, when sons weren't invisible? Took them camping? Showed them how to start a campfire?

Sirus furrowed his brow in concern. "No Boys Scouts? Nothing like that?"

Joss swallowed again and shook his head, wishing it were possible for him to disappear completely.

From within his pocket, Sirus withdrew a small metal instrument. It looked a bit like a nail file. He held it up for Joss to see before laying it on the table. "This is a Swedish FireSteel. It contains a magnesium alloy that sparks to make a fire. Takes some practice, but once you've got the technique down, it's foolproof. Keep it. It's yours."

"Thanks, Sirus." Joss closed his hand over the FireSteel, his heart welling with gratefulness. It wasn't just the gift that had him feeling emotional. It was Sirus's unfailing kindness. "For everything."

Abraham walked into the dining room then, looking well rested, clean, and well fed. He looked very much like he hadn't been out running all night long just to prove himself. Unlike Joss.

Joss lifted the sandwich to his mouth once more. It was almost impossible to keep his composure, to not scream and rant and yell at his uncle for everything he'd been put through. But somehow, he managed. He kept his cool. And just as he was taking that third bite of turkey yumminess, Abraham said, "Cut and stack the firewood."

Joss immediately set his sandwich on the plate and stood, his muscles and joints screaming for him to let them rest, please God, just let them have a moment of stillness. Sirus shot Joss a look—a look that told him that it was okay, to sit down and finish his sandwich, that he needed his rest and Sirus had the power to force that on Abraham—but when he did, Joss shot a look back. He hoped that his look was full of meaning, that Sirus could understand without a single word that this was more than training now.

Without a word to Abraham, he pushed open the back door, letting it slap closed behind him. And though it wasn't the most mature thought that he had ever had, Joss wished very much that the sound had hurt Abraham's ears. It would be something, at least.

Outside, Joss found the ax stuck in the top of a stump. Beside it lay the trunk of a tree. It had been cut into three long logs and the branches had been trimmed away. Against the back of the house was a quickly dwindling stack of firewood logs. Joss looked over the new logs and wondered how long they'd been lying there. Probably close to six months. Maybe a year, even. But he was betting they were seasoned and ready for the fire. If you didn't wait long enough, the wood would be too wet and wouldn't burn right, wouldn't burn long enough or hot enough. But this looked ready. And more than that, it looked like hickory, which was a nice wood for burning. Joss may not have known much about surviving in the wilderness, but he knew all about cutting wood. His grandfather had shown him how to do it two years before. It had been one of the last things that Grandpa had taught Joss. Before his life was taken by a vampire—like Cecile. Since then, it had been one of Joss's chores at home. He had two woodcutting seasons under his belt now. So if Abraham thought he was challenging Joss in new and unexpected ways, he had another think coming.

Of course, all of Joss's woodcutting had been turning logs into firewood, not turning entire tree trunks into logs. But he was reasonably sure that he could do it. After all, how much of a difference could there really be? Rubbing his hands together, Joss yanked the ax free and approached the first log with a confident step.

An hour later, sweaty and broken and so frustrated that he really wanted to kick something, Joss knew exactly how much of a difference there was between cutting logs down to size and cutting trunks into logs. Huge. There was a huge difference. Enormous. Because while it was difficult hoisting larger logs onto the tree stump and chopping them straight through the middle, it was almost impossible to hack away at a giant piece of hickory in hopes of cutting it into large disks that he'd struggle to lug onto the stump in hopes of maybe, just maybe, chopping that stupid thing into quarters, just so he could chop those quarters into usable logs. Never mind the fact that Joss hadn't slept. Never mind the fact that he'd only had three bites of a turkey sandwich and not a single drop of water in twenty-four hours. Never mind the fact that he'd just run he didn't even know how many miles and was now expected to do chores for his uncle—an uncle he was coming to loathe with every fiber of his being. And now he had to chop another hunk from another log, lug it over to the stump, struggle to lift the stupid thing and drop it on the stump without dropping it on his foot, and then cut that stupid thing into stupid pieces that would fit nicely inside Abraham's stupid fireplace. Joss held the ax over his head and swung it down hard with a frustrated growl. It hit the stump and stuck in deep.

"Remind me not to be reincarnated as a tree around you."

Joss jerked his head up to see Kat, who was standing several feet away, smiling at him with that crooked, sarcastic grin. Any other time, he might have been happy to see her. But right now he was tired and hungry and sore and just about as miserable as anybody on planet Earth could possibly get. Which meant that despite the fact that he was feeling extremely lonely, all he really wanted was just to be left alone. "What do *you* want?"

Kat's smile wilted, but only slightly. She wouldn't be easily sucked into his misery. "I want world peace, Joss, but that isn't likely to happen."

In her hand, she was holding a butterfly net. Hanging from her belt was a jar. Several fluttery creatures moved within the glass confines. Joss hesitated—not wanting to be drawn into conversation, just wanting to be left alone, really—and pointed to the jar, unable to resist his obsession. "I see you've been out collecting."

She smiled brightly again. "Yeah. Some interesting species up here. You should come over tonight and help me categorize them. Unless you have plans to wrestle another mountain lion, of course. What's with the ax murderer routine anyway? Reminds me of a preview I saw for this movie called *Psycho Slasher Chain Saw Guy from Hell*."

Joss raised an eyebrow and looked at her, his confusion overshadowing his frustration for the moment. "Wouldn't he have a chain saw?"

Kat nodded enthusiastically. "And an ax. And a pair of hedge clippers. It's supposed to be brutal, but doesn't come out for a while. Maybe when it does, we can go see it. I mean, you know, if we like visit one another this fall or something. You know, if you want to."

He shook his head. They couldn't visit one another. They couldn't be friends. Joss was about to become a Slayer. He couldn't have close ties, blossoming friendships. It would make it that much harder for him to move around, to leave people behind. There was no way he could risk becoming close to someone. He never should have even started.

With a glare at Kat, he yanked the ax out of the stump again. "Get out of here, Kat. We're not friends. We never were friends. We'll never be friends."

Kat stepped back, her eyes wide, as if he'd just punched her in the gut. Wordlessly, she shook her head, but she didn't leave.

Joss screamed, "Get away from me!"

Her eyes welled up with tears—tears that were soon burned away by her hateful glare. "Fine! I will!"

Joss swung the ax as hard as he could into the log and it split. Then he turned and watched Kat race into the other cabin, slamming the door behind her.

He knew that everything he'd said had hurt her, but what she didn't realize was that he'd probably just made her life a whole lot easier—and a whole lot better—by removing himself from it. She didn't want to be friends with a Slayer, let alone with a boy who wasn't capable of protecting anyone. Even himself.

·20·

J'ACCUSE

Joss tossed the last two logs onto the cord of wood lined up against the back of the house. The palms of his hands were now home to several splinters, and Joss had discovered a type of exhaustion that he hadn't known existed. His shoulders were burning, even though he wasn't really using them anymore. For a long moment, once the wood was all in place, he simply stood there in a daze. The sun had set two hours before, and Joss had taken few breaks—none of them to eat. At one point, Sirus had brought him a few jugs of water and insisted that he drink, but that was all that Joss was willing to do. There would be a time for food and rest, and that time would come once he was finished with the task at hand. Not one second before. Now that he was done, all he really wanted to do was sleep, or at the very least, lie still on his soft bed and think about the choices he'd made that had brought him to this place, to this moment. He turned toward the house, knowing that his efforts wouldn't coax so much as a single word of gratitude from his uncle, and lifted his left foot, ready to begin the small journey that would take him inside the house and up the stairs to his bed.

But then he heard a noise. A noise that sounded like movement in the trees. A noise that sent a shiver up his spine and goose bumps crawling all over his skin. It could be a vampire—or worse, several vampires—and no one was here but Joss.

Sure, he could have flung open the back door and called to the others, but part of him knew that Abraham would frown with disapproval at a sign of weakness like that. So instead, Joss picked up a large, thick splinter of the wood he'd been chopping and headed soundlessly into the woods, toward the noise. It was probably really stupid of him to try and face a vampire on his own, but maybe if he could take the thing out of commission, Abraham might start showing him just an ounce of respect. He had to try, anyway.

When he reached the edge of the woods, his movements became even more careful. One snap of a twig and the beast would be on him in seconds. He had the advantage right now. He just had to ensure that he kept the advantage.

His fingers were wrapped so tightly around the large splinter that the wood bit into his palm. He wasn't shaking at all, but on the inside, he felt as though he were quivering like a coward. He might be walking into a trap. He might be willingly provoking his own death. And he had absolutely zero control over any of it, except for the sounds he made as he worked his way through the thick brush. He held his breath for as long as he could, then very slowly let it out, breathing in another lungful of air just as slowly, and holding it until he couldn't hold it any longer.

The woods were pitch-black and full of sounds that hadn't been there in the daytime. Frightening sounds. Sounds that could be anything or anyone. Hungry sounds.

Joss swallowed hard, gripping the splinter even tighter, and edged up to a large oak tree. When he peered around the side, he saw a light in the distance. It looked like a campfire, but he couldn't be sure from this distance. As he moved closer, he heard voices. Familiar voices. He relaxed his shoulders and slipped the splinter into his back pocket. Until he earned a stake, it was a good idea to keep some kind of weapon around. Who knew when a vampire might be lurking just around the next corner? He had to be prepared.

He turned from the fire, but stopped when he

heard Abraham speak. "I remember my training days, and no one ever went so easy on me. You're all soft on the boy. Joss will never become a great Slayer if you Slayers keep coddling him."

Coddling him? Abraham was acting like the other Slayers had been spoon-feeding Joss berries every breakfast and treating him to movies and popcorn every night. He ran his hand over the back of his neck, looking down the hill to where he'd entered the woods. He was certain his uncle wouldn't want him eavesdropping, but since Joss seemed to be the subject matter, didn't he have every right to listen in? After a moment spent debating with himself over the morals of purposefully overhearing a conversation that one isn't supposed to be privy to, curiosity got the best of him and Joss crept silently forward, determined to take in every word. He got close enough that he could see the Slayers' faces clear as day, but not so close that the light or heat from the fire would touch him. After he was in position and fairly certain he wouldn't be caught, Joss's eyes fell on the small pile of logs beside the fire pit. As if in acknowledgment of all his back-breaking labor, his palms throbbed. He made a mental note to ask Sirus for some bandages to cover all the blisters.

Morgan tossed another log onto the fire. "It's not like we're tucking him in with a teddy every night,

Abraham. But he is just a boy. You're too hard on him."

"Besides," Paty interjected, "he's talented. Given enough time, he could be one of the best. If he gets a chance, that is. If you don't kill him first."

Abraham shot her a look, and everyone grew quiet for a long while. Then Chazz shook his head, a bemused smirk on his face. "I think he'll survive. But his parents might suspect something about his summer activities if the boy ends up in traction, like you did, Cratian."

The Slayers roared with laughter. All but Cratian, who looked more embarrassed than anything.

Ash took a swig from a label-less bottle and wiped his mouth clean on the back of his hand. "We have to be rough on Joss. Otherwise he could stray. Look at Sirus, for example."

Several Slayers grunted and nodded their agreement. Abraham tensed, the semipleasant expression on his face vanishing in an instant. "Exactly why I'm being rough on my nephew. I've officially reported Sirus twice this year already. He's been beyond his training days for years, and still needs to be reminded of the cause."

Morgan shook his head, as if something critically obvious were escaping Abraham's attention. "You let Sirus get away with too much. What about the girl?

You let him bring his daughter to our training facility. His non-Slayer daughter. Being in charge, that's enough to get you reprimanded by the Society."

"Don't tell me what will get me reprimanded and what won't, Morgan. I report to the Society, not you," Abraham snapped. "You're not all privy to certain information, so just keep your speculation in check. There's a reason the Society's allowing it. Or am I to understand that you're questioning their good wisdom?"

Morgan's eyes went wide, and Joss guessed that questioning the Society was a major no-no. "Of course not. I would never question. I was merely curious."

Abraham tossed another log onto the fire, flashing Morgan a heated glare as he did so. His tone was full of warning. "Don't forget what curiosity did to the cat, Morgan. I'd hate to lose another member of my team."

Joss took a slow step back, and was about to begin his descent down the hill and his journey to his soft bed, when Cratian spoke again, stopping Joss in his tracks. "We need to talk about Malek."

Paty shook her head. "I think it's fairly obvious that Malek's death was a message from the hive, from that vampire called Zy."

Cratian threw another log on the fire. Sparks burst up and out, dancing on the tips of the flames. "Maybe. But let me remind you of a certain new recruit six years ago. She turned on us in a matter of weeks to help the vampires. We have no reason to believe Malek's death wasn't an inside job."

A mutter raced through the group, and by the looks on their faces, Joss could see that they all agreed—all, that is, but Abraham, who looked disgusted at the very idea that a Slayer would dare take another Slayer's life.

Could it be true? Could Malek's horrific murder be the act of one of the Slayers, someone who slept every night in the same house as the rest of them? Joss didn't know if he would ever sleep again, knowing that the person who could do that—rip a fellow Slayer limb from limb—might be sleeping just down the hall. Or maybe not sleeping at all. Maybe plotting quietly which Slayer they'd take out next, and how.

The thought sent a wave of cold nausea through Joss.

Abraham spoke, his tone as curt as it could get. Joss could tell he was irritated. "I doubt that a man could or would take such a violent approach to murder. His body was in pieces."

Cratian shrugged. "What better way to drive their message home than by making one of our own the messenger? A man might not be capable of tearing someone limb from limb . . . but a Slayer might."

Abraham stared at the fire for a long time before speaking. "And just whom do you think it could possibly be, Cratian? The nine of us have known and trained together for years. Which of us would turn on the others?"

Chazz shook his head. "Not Sirus. He may be a wild card, but he's loyal. He may not be here tonight, but only because of his parental duties. He and I have discussed our concerns at great length, and I can tell you, the man is one of us. Besides, I've seen him fight. There's no way he could have taken Malek down, let alone tore him to pieces. There's a reason Sirus is a nursemaid."

A few of them chuckled, but all sound stopped once Ash said a name. Every animal in the woods was silenced. Every crackle of the campfire ceased. Even Joss's heart stopped beating when the name was uttered in an accusing tone. "What about Joss?"

A long silence went by. It took a lot of guts for one of them to accuse Abraham's nephew, Joss could tell. But accuse him Ash had.

"He's new to the group," Cratian piped in. "Strong, talented. He's a nice kid, but he did meet with that vampire, and walked away with a message and not a single drop of blood on his hands. It could be him, Abraham."

To Joss's utter shock and amazement, Abraham nodded. "Watch him. Closely. If he was the one to take Malek down, if you even think you see any evidence of a lack of loyalty on his part, come to me. I'll take care of him."

Joss slowly, silently moved down the hill and across the yard, his mouth hanging open in utter shock. He knew that his uncle hadn't meant that he'd punish Joss and send him on his merry way, back to his parents, back to his life.

Abraham was going to kill him.

▶ 21 ◀

DETERMINATION

Despite his bruises, despite his exhaustion, Joss tossed and turned for most of the night. The little bit of sleep that he did get was tormented by terrible nightmares. In one, a shadowy figure crept down the hall to his room, where it proceeded to rip Joss to shreds. In another, his uncle staked him through the chest as the other Slayers gathered around, laughing wholeheartedly. And then there was Cecile, always haunting him, always blaming him for her horrible fate.

By the time the sun had come up, Joss was ready to get out of bed and away from his pillow. He was also very much in need of Sirus's company and counsel.

After all, what good were friends if you couldn't go to them for advice?

As he moved down the stairs, he glanced at his still-aching palms, and remembered the blisters. Maybe Sirus would have some antibiotic ointment as well. The other Slayers could call Sirus a nursemaid if they wanted, but the fact was that training and fighting and all of their hard work would be nothing without someone to patch them up at the end of the day. Joss wondered if they viewed Sirus as less than manly for his caretaking responsibilities. If so, he thought, then they had no idea what it really took to be a man.

The stairs creaked below his feet, and by the time he reached the bottom, he noticed that something was different this morning. No breakfast-y smells greeted him. No sounds of pots and pans and cupboards and movement filled his ears. The kitchen, he realized when he entered it, was completely empty. No sign of Sirus remained, but for a note taped to the cabinet which read, "Joss, I had to run to town for last-minute supplies. Sorry about breakfast—I left some cold cereal and milk for you. Abraham left instructions for you to run ten laps today, but I believe you need a day off. I leave that decision up to you. Why don't you go say hi to Kat? I'm sure she misses your company—Sirus."

Joss read the note over again before filling a bowl with chocolate and peanut butter cereal. He read it a third time while pouring cold, crisp milk over the contents of his bowl, and a fourth as he devoured his breakfast. Then he moved upstairs, took care of his many blisters, showered, dressed, and headed outside. But not before putting on a pair of running shoes.

A wise man might say that he was not just running into trouble, but away from his problems, away from Kat. And that man might be right. But wisdom wasn't always the driving force in Joss's actions. In fact, most often his actions were driven by pure gut instinct. And instinct told him that it would be better if he stayed as far away as possible from Sirus's daughter until they parted ways at the end of the summer. Better for her. Better for him. Better for everyone.

Besides, he had a feeling that Abraham would be watching him carefully today, wondering if he would choose to run or take the easy way out. So running was the only option.

Joss had carried with him six large bottles of water and stashed them by a tree where the overgrown trail met the long trail. He stretched his muscles then, carefully, taking his time, and within fifteen minutes, he was ready for his run, ready to give it his all, ready to prove to himself that the first run hadn't just been a fluke. That he was tough enough to do it again, and this time, to not feel like dying after he was finished.

Not that he was a total wimp. After fighting against three skilled Slayers and hours spent locating the right trail, followed by running his first ten laps barefoot, hadn't he slipped some shoes on his aching feet and gone on to cut and stack an entire cord of wood? And with barely any sleep at all, wasn't he readying himself for another run of his own free will? Nothing about that said Joss was a wimp, despite what some of his fellow Slayers might say. It didn't make him weak, didn't show the slightest hint of lack of loyalty to their cause. Still . . . he wondered why they'd accuse him of taking Malek's life, and why Abraham would so readily agree with the possibility that he might be working with the enemy.

Shaking his head to clear the troubling thoughts away, Joss began to run at a steady, sure pace. He kept his mind free and open, focusing only on the sound of his feet as they hit the earth.

At the end of his second lap, Joss grabbed one of the bottles and drank until he'd emptied it. Staying hydrated was making it easier this time, and Joss was surprised to be enjoying the run somewhat. Even though he strongly believed that one should only run when one is being chased. And only then if it's by something bigger and faster and meaner than you are. He started up again and by the end of the fifth lap, his side was hurting like crazy, like his left lung had broken free and slipped down, squashing all the organs below it. Pressing his hand into his side, he finished the lap, but just barely. By the seventh lap, he thought he might die, but something in him, something dark and primal, moved his feet along the trail, pushing him with all its might. He had to finish, had to prove to himself that he could do it.

He stopped to drain the remaining two bottles of water—having guzzled the other three at various points along his gut-wrenching trek—and a feeling settled into the pit of his stomach, causing the tiny hairs on the back of his neck to stand on end. Joss was being watched.

As he finished the last bottle and dropped it to the ground, Joss's eyes swept the surrounding woods, but he could see nothing. No Slayers, no vampires, no Kat. Nothing. So he began his final lap, tired, aching, sore, but proud of himself for having almost completed the task at hand. And while that strange feeling that he was being watched refused to leave him, Joss shook it off with every running step he took along the trail. His tenth lap. He was almost done.

A sound to his left caused Joss to turn his head, but he had no time to recognize what had made the noise. An arm clotheslined him, sending him back, then down onto the unforgiving ground. He hit so hard that, for a moment, the air rushed from his lungs and his throat tightened, refusing him as much as a single, relieving breath. He tried to inhale, but the small amount of air that managed to fight its way into his lungs burned painfully. The second breath came easier, but only just. The arm that had stolen his ability to breathe came down again, grabbing him by the collar of his T-shirt and dragging him to his feet. Just as his eyes fell on the familiar face, Ash swung his fist forward, clocking Joss in the left eye. Joss's head snapped back, the muscles of his neck tensing. The pain was immediate and intense, but faded quickly, first causing Joss's eye socket to feel like it was engulfed in flames. The heat was immediately followed by an unsettling tingle that made it feel as if his skull was vibrating.

Joss didn't analyze the situation. He didn't look at advantages and disadvantages, didn't think about why Ash had attacked him or the possible repercussions of fighting back. He simply acted.

Balling up his fist, Joss swung forward as hard as he could in a right cross that caught Ash in the jaw. Ash stumbled backward, but just long enough for Joss to start thinking he was pretty tough. Then Ash leaped toward him, knocking him to the ground, pinning him there, battering his face with repeated blows. At first the pain was almost too much to bear. Each hit crushed his will to fight back, and he shrank inside himself, wishing it away, wishing it all away. But then something—something deep inside of him—caught fire, and as that fire moved up and out, it grew by enormous measures until it was a raging inferno of leave-me-the-hell-alone. Joss brought his knee up as hard as he could. When he connected, Ash's face went white. A look of surprise crossed his eyes before they rolled back into his head. A strange squeak escaped his throat and he fell to the side with an *oof*.

Joss slid out from under him and stood, brushing the dirt from his clothes. He kept a wary eye on Ash, who was moaning and holding the place where Joss had kicked him, wondering all the while exactly what had provoked the attack. Ash had accused him at the fire—was that because of some deep-seated hatred of him or something? He couldn't remember having done anything that might tick Ash off in recent days, or ever, if he was truthful. That might be the fault of his memory, or maybe he just hadn't been paying close enough attention to the things he'd said and done since he'd been here and how it might affect the other Slayers. Whatever it was, he now really wished he had been paying attention and that he hadn't made Ash so angry.

Joss rubbed the back of his neck absently and looked at the trail ahead of him. He wasn't altogether certain he should get going. In fact, he was reasonably sure that the smartest thing to do would be to help Ash up off the ground, find out what had provoked him, apologize, and then head back to the house. He turned back to Ash, whose color had pretty much returned to normal, and parted his lips with an apology on the tip of his tongue. Before he could say anything, Ash said, "You'll never finish. Just because you took me out doesn't mean you'll finish this lap. You'll fail, and then you'll be sent home. You're not a Slayer. You're just a boy."

Joss felt his temper warm his ears. He bent down and said, "A boy that put you on the ground. And a boy that kicked you in a not-so-happy place. Twice."

Ash's eyebrows came together in confusion. Joss pulled his foot back, aiming a second assault, and kicked him hard.

As he started running again, abandoning the idea of apologizing completely, he thought about what Ash had said. Would Abraham really send him home if he didn't finish this run? If that were true, why not send him home before this? What was so important about this run in particular? And that still didn't explain why Ash had attacked him so viciously.

After a few minutes, his eye was throbbing in time with his heartbeat. Joss started counting them in an effort to block out his thoughts. He'd only just reached fifty-eight when someone grabbed him by the wrist and spun him around, flinging him hard into the trunk of a paper birch tree. Joss's right shoulder took the brunt of the hit. It felt like something was burning its way out from the inside, so he imagined that he'd probably ripped a muscle or tore a ligament. But at least he still had his breath this time. He turned around to face Cratian, and then Joss blinked in surprise. He'd thought that Ash had likely caught up with him with a want for vengeance. He never dreamed that a second Slayer would attack him on the trail.

Cratian grinned like he was really enjoying this already, before whatever he'd planned had even begun. "You owe me five bucks, kid. I didn't think you'd make it past Ash. So now I'm out five bucks in the pool because of you."

Joss shook his head slowly, completely lost. "I . . . I'm sorry . . . ?"

Cratian's grin spread wider across his face until it seemed he was all teeth. "Maybe not yet. But you will be."

Before Joss could blink, Cratian came at him with a high roundhouse kick, catching Joss in the left ear. A high-pitched ringing sang through Joss's skull as he fell to the ground. It was almost beautiful. It might have been truly lovely, if it hadn't been for the lightning bolt of pain that shot through Joss's head. He hit the ground, but the lightning kept coming, crackling through the bones of his skull, singeing every nerve within his head. He heard a moan, and it took him a second to realize that he had made the sound. Just as he acknowledged his moan of pain, Cratian's foot came down hard on his forearm and he cried out. He scrambled away from Cratian, stopping only when his back met with another birch tree. To his horror, Cratian was advancing on him again, that same stupid grin on his face. Joss dug his heels into the ground, scrambling to stand. When he was finally upright and on his feet again, he kicked desperately at Cratian, to no avail, missing him by three feet. He wanted Cratian to just stop, to go away, but he had no idea how to make him change his mind about beating Joss to a bloody pulp.

Then, like a cartoon lightbulb had flickered on over his head, Joss understood exactly what was going on here. It was a test. Another stupid test. And he had no choice but to finish it. He had to complete the last lap of this trail, no matter whom or what was standing in his way. Because if he didn't, he'd never be a Slayer. He'd never have what it takes to get revenge for his sister. He'd never be a man.

He understood why his uncle had set up this lesson—and the others preceding it—without explaining what the lessons were. Because part of being a Slayer, part of being a man, was figuring things out on your own and dealing with them without counting on help from anyone else. Sirus had said that being a Slayer was a lonely job. And Joss imagined that he was right. But you were lonely for a reason. Because in the end, you had to take care of yourself—and the cause—and no one and nothing came before those things. You were alone because you had to be. Because being alone means being strong, and Joss was most definitely that.

Or he wanted to be, anyway.

Again, he kicked at Cratian, but this time, he connected with Cratian's right knee—the same knee he'd seen Chazz take out not long ago. Cratian swore loudly, bending down, cupping his knee, and Joss saw his window of opportunity.

He grabbed Cratian by the ears and brought his knee up as he was bringing Cratian's head down. There was a distinct crack as the bones connected and the hit made Joss's leg light up with pain, but it did the trick. Cratian howled, one hand on his knee, the other clutching his head. He cursed Joss's name repeatedly, but Joss didn't stick around to find out what Cratian planned to do about it. He took off like a rocket, racing ever closer to the end of the trail. How many Slayers would he be forced to fight with? All of them? Would Sirus be among them?

No. Sirus would never do anything to hurt him.

Joss rounded the corner, honestly amazed that no one jumped out and grabbed him. He was merely yards from the end of his run. From where he was, he could see the empty water bottles sitting at the base of the tree. He picked up the pace, sprinting toward the tree.

Abraham stepped out from behind it, a bemused smirk on his face. Joss's steps slowed. His heart all but stopped. He was going to have to fight his uncle. And he couldn't. Abraham was too skilled, too eager to win, too serious about everything. He'd hurt Joss badly. He might even kill him.

Joss swallowed hard, but didn't speak.

Abraham looked past him, furrowing his brow. "Chazz, you missed your mark! Don't tell me you fell asleep waiting for the boy. Or didn't you think he'd make it this far?"

Joss waited, not speaking, not wanting to provoke any kind of reaction at all from Abraham, keeping his eyes on his uncle the entire time. Mostly on the silver-tipped stake in the leather holster on his hip.

Abraham shot him a look—one that confounded Joss completely—and darted off down the trail. After about twenty yards, he dove into the trees on the left side. Joss blinked, and followed, his steps hesitant. When he reached his uncle, his stomach felt like it was made of lead. Abraham was standing over Chazz's body. Chazz was dead, his eyes staring lifelessly into the surrounding forest. Abraham pinched the bridge of his nose and squeezed his eyes shut, as if trying to snuff out even the smallest show of emotion.

Joss had a feeling it was all an act. Abraham had killed Chazz, because Abraham was really the rogue Slayer. After all, it was the perfect ruse, wasn't it? Point all blame to his nephew with the knowledge of a past new recruit's betrayal—something that would only fuel the fire. Joss was an easy target. And Abraham had had easy access to both Malek and Chazz. He glared at his uncle, sizing him up, wondering if he had the power to take him down for the good of the Society.

Behind him, Joss heard the rustle of branches and undergrowth. He turned to find Cratian and Ash entering the woods. Both looked shocked when their eyes fell on Chazz's corpse. Joss opened his mouth to outwardly accuse his uncle, but before he could, Abraham looked at the Slayers and nodded toward his nephew. They slanted their eyes and Joss knew that he was in trouble.

Abraham had just pinned a second murder on him.

·22·

A DYING FLAME

Cratian and Ash grabbed Joss by each arm, yanking him wordlessly from where he stood. He could feel their anger, and sense their questions, but neither uttered a word. As they dragged him through the woods and along the trail, Joss didn't speak either. He merely clenched his jaw tight, not certain what to say or what to do. It wasn't like he could outwardly accuse his uncle now of these horrible acts, of betraying the Slayer Society in the worst way possible. For one, he didn't have any evidence to support his theory, just an intensely strong gut feeling—and everybody knew that intuition wasn't exactly counted as a valid argument in a court of law. For two, this was Abraham

McMillan—one of the most highly regarded Slayers of his time. The Society counted on him, and barely recognized that Joss even existed. Why would they take his word over his uncle's when he had no proof, just a sickening feeling? They wouldn't, and that was the truth of it. Joss was trapped, and there wasn't a damn thing he could do about it but see it through until he'd gathered some hard evidence.

They were taking him to the house. Joss felt a small flicker of hope ignite inside his chest. Sirus was at the house. Sirus would make them listen to reason. After all, Sirus was sure and strong and honest. He liked Joss, and he'd listen like no one else would and convince the other Slayers of the hypocrisy that was taking place right inside their own group. As Cratian kicked open the door, Joss clung to that flicker, and allowed it, just for a moment, to grow into a small, hesitant flame.

Cratian tugged Joss through the door and Ash moved behind him, pinning his arms, as if he were a prisoner who had been daring an escape. In truth, Joss hadn't fought against them at all. He knew better. These men were skilled trackers, skilled hunters, skilled killers. And what's more, Joss was innocent. The innocent never run, so he made a point to cooperate fully. But still they yanked on him, practically carrying him through the kitchen as if he'd fought against their efforts with mad force.

Sirus was standing at the stove. He'd looked up when the door had been kicked in, and when his eyes fell on Joss, they filled with a questioning look. Joss tried to communicate silently with him, hoping the expression on his face would explain enough to his friend that he'd realize that Joss needed him, needed his help, like never before. Sirus didn't nod, didn't make any facial expressions that showed that he understood or that he'd do whatever he could to help Joss out of the mess that he'd gotten himself into. His face was blank as he looked at Ash. "What's happened?"

"We found Malek's killer." Ash needlessly tightened his grip on Joss's forearm. Ever since the day that Malek had been found murdered, Ash had never liked Joss. He shouldn't have been surprised that it had been Ash at the campfire that night to accuse him of murdering Malek. But he was. Maybe because they had become more than co-Slayers in the past weeks. They had become family. And now his family believed him to be a murderer. A betrayer in the worst of all possible ways.

Sirus's eyes went wide. He flicked his gaze from Ash to Cratian, but kept his eyes off of Joss. The small flame of hope within Joss's chest began to waver, suffocated by fear. "Really? Joss?"

Cratian nodded, an air of sadness hanging over him. "He may have killed Chazz, too. We just found him on the trail."

Joss swallowed hard, resisting the urge to dispute what Cratian had just said. Technically, the body had been in the woods, not on the trail. And technically, it had been Abraham who had found it. And wasn't that convenient? Abraham had been the closest to Chazz while Joss was running and defending himself from Cratian and Ash. It would have been easy for Abraham to take Chazz out. So why wasn't anyone else seeing it?

Because, Joss thought, the Slayers loved Abraham. They knew him. He was one of them, and Joss wasn't. Joss was just a boy who had been thrust into their routine, invaded their peace. They didn't like him. They didn't even want him here, despite the camaraderie he felt with them during his training sessions. He was alone in this. Not even Sirus seemed to care. He'd been a fool to count them among his family. He didn't have a family. He was just the invisible boy. Nothing else. The flame died out completely and Joss lowered his head.

As Ash and Cratian dragged him through the kitchen into the dining room, Joss lifted his head for a moment. He just couldn't believe that Sirus wasn't going to help him. He'd thought Sirus was his friend. Had the entire thing been nothing but a ruse? Some twisted kind of test set up by Abraham from the beginning?

No. He refused to believe it.

He looked at Sirus, wishing like anything that they could have ten minutes alone, so that Joss could explain everything. Sirus met his eyes. Joss had expected to see that the eternal kindness had faded away, like a mask ripped off after a masquerade. But there it was in Sirus's eyes, compassion, understanding, and concern. Inside Joss's chest, that flame flickered again. It was small and uncertain, but it was there.

Ash released Joss's arm and Cratian practically threw him into a chair. Then Ash pointed at him, his finger so close to Joss's face that it tickled his eyelashes, and said, "Make one move and I'll tie you to that chair, boy."

Joss said nothing, but relaxed his body, trying to retain some sense of calm, and hoping it would show the Slayers that he wasn't about to attempt an escape. Ash stood back, folding his arms in front of him, keeping a close, watchful eye on their prisoner.

Moments later, the silent room was filled with sound as Abraham entered the house, bringing the remaining Slayers with him. No one spoke—clearly Abraham had briefed them all before bringing them back to the house—but the sound of their boots on the aged hardwood floors reminded Joss of thunder. It was fitting, he thought, because a storm was coming. One that Joss might not survive.

Once all the Slayers were in the room, some seated on chairs around the table, some standing—all of them wearing expressions of anger, hurt, and disbelief—Abraham's voice boomed through the room. "Joss Mc-Millan, I accuse you of the foulest deed. Turning on your fellow Slayers, betraying our trust, and taking the lives of both Malek and Chazz. How do you plead?"

"Let's not forget protocol, Abraham." Sirus's voice was hushed, but nevertheless, it commanded the attention of every Slayer there. He was seated across the table from Joss, his hands folded neatly in front of him, his head bowed slightly, as if in prayer. He raised his head and looked pointedly at Abraham. "According to Slayer Society rules, one cannot be tried by his individual group, merely accused. It's up to the Society to try and convict a Slayer. What's more, Joss isn't an indoctrinated Slayer, so he isn't held by our rules."

Abraham's face went white. Daggers shot from his eyes into Sirus, which told Joss that his uncle wasn't used to being wrong. "True. Joss hasn't been indoctrinated. But if he is guilty of taking the lives of two Slayers, then something must be done. A person cannot simply commit crimes and evade justice."

Sirus shrugged, his voice eerily calm. "So involve the police."

Abraham's response wasn't nearly as loud, brash or boastful as before. It was as if Sirus had somehow managed to take a bit of the wind out of his sails. "You know we can't do that, Sirus. Local authorities would complicate the Society's plans."

"Besides, this is your nephew we're talking about, and you wouldn't want him to go to prison, would you, Abraham?" Sirus met and held Abraham's gaze. It was a dare. Almost as if he and Sirus had previously discussed just this, and Sirus was bringing it up again just to prove a point. The very thought made Joss's heart flutter. Had his uncle actually expressed an ounce of care about him? No. He doubted it strongly. Abraham didn't care for him. He didn't even like him.

Abraham dropped his eyes to the table for a moment. "My relationship with Joss has nothing to do with this hearing."

"Doesn't it, Uncle Abraham?" Joss stood slowly, pushing his chair back and placing his palms on the table's surface to keep them from shaking. He had put up with so much up until now. Abraham's seeming disappointment in him from the very start. The accusations of murder. The personal training sessions that seemed more like Abraham's method of punishing him for something he couldn't identify. And now he was being put on trial without even being asked whether or not he had any idea what was really going on. It was too much to bear, and Joss could no longer stay silent. "If you ask me, I think it has everything to do with it. You've never liked me, and certainly never hoped that I would be the next Slayer in our bloodline. You've been after me the entire time I've been here. It's like you want me to fail. Like you don't want me to ever be indoctrinated into the Society and are determined to punish me for trying. And isn't it convenient that Slayers start dying off the moment I show up? What an easy way to be rid of the embarrassment of me for good."

A low mutter raced through the crowd, one that Sirus gave voice to. "What are you saying, Joss? That Abraham knows who took the lives of Malek and Chazz?"

Joss met his friend's eyes. As he readied the words on his tongue, a shock of fear shot through him. Fear of their reaction, mostly, but also fear of what Abraham might do or say. Not to mention fear that he'd put Sirus into a very uncomfortable position with the Society. "More than that, Sirus. I think Abraham killed them and is using me as a scapegoat."

The room fell so silent that Joss could hear his own heart thumping inside of his chest. No one moved, no one breathed for a very long time. Then Abraham shook his head slowly. "It's senseless. It's asinine. Why would I wait twenty years to start taking the lives of Slayers?"

"Maybe you were waiting for the right moment. Or maybe your loyalties have only recently shifted." Joss tilted his head some as he met his uncle's eyes.

Abraham moved so fast that Joss barely had time to register it before his uncle was just inches from his face, gripping the front of Joss's shirt. "Are you actually questioning my loyalty to the cause? You haven't been training for half a summer yet. What do you know of loyalty, *boy*?"

Joss's heart was racing. He knew his uncle was capable of killing him, and at the moment, he got the impression that Abraham was anxious to take his life. But he had to remain strong, had to stay vigilant. It was the only way to prove his innocence to the others. To Sirus, who didn't need for him to prove it at all. "I know that the vampire who spoke to me in town knew you by name and acted as though you'd interacted several times."

A look crossed Abraham's face then—one filled with shock, confusion, and amazingly, fear. He released Joss's shirt and stepped back, shaking his head. "This is ridiculous."

Joss's eyes were locked on his uncle's. Because there was something else, something that surprised even him. He was looking into the eyes of an innocent man. Shaking his head, too, admonishing himself for having jumped to such a drastic conclusion when the answer to the recent Slayer murders was so obvious, Joss said, "It may be ridiculous, but it doesn't feel good to be accused, does it?"

Abraham paced the room for a moment before turning back to Joss, his voice calm. Almost as calm as Sirus's had been a moment before. "Did you kill Malek, Joss?"

"No."

"And Chazz? Did you take his life?"

"No, Uncle. I didn't." Joss held Abraham's gaze, hoping that he would see the innocence in Joss's eyes the way that Joss had seen it in his.

Then Abraham sighed, shaking his head. He tilted his face up toward the ceiling and sighed again. "So who did?"

While Joss was certain that the question was completely rhetorical, he took his seat once again and said, "If it's not you, Abraham, and it's not me, then maybe it's the obvious."

The surrounding Slayers blinked at him, overwhelmed by recent events and the loss of their friends. They needed guidance, and Joss was happy to give it to them. "Vampires. There's a hive nearby. Maybe they killed the Slayers. And what's more, wouldn't doing so in a way that made us accuse one another be a brilliant way of spreading doubt among our ranks? It would weaken us as a whole, *has* weakened us as a whole, and isn't that the way to really take down a well-oiled machine?"

Joss looked from one face to the next—his fellow Slayers, his family. They were broken, but could be mended. And Joss wanted more than anything to lead that charge. He loved them. Here, among his fellow Slayers, he was anything but invisible.

One by one they nodded, accepting his theory. It

was so obvious, and such an embarrassment that they would turn inwardly rather than toward the enemy in a time of crisis. Sirus relaxed in his seat, looking more than a little bit relieved that the accusations hadn't gone any further. Something told Joss that being put on trial by the Slayer Society was the last thing that he wanted to experience. Abraham stepped closer and extended his arm, shaking Joss's hand. His eyes were warm and apologetic. "I relinquish my accusation, nephew."

Joss smiled, but it was fleeting. Smiling hurt too much with all the bruises he'd received on his run. "Ditto, Abraham. We're cool."

"Joss? What have they done to you?" Kat dropped the box of medical supplies she been carrying over from the other house and rushed into the room, her horrified eyes locked on Joss's face, which was still crusted with dried blood and the filth of the trail. She looked worried, and that suspicion was still there in her eyes.

As she hurried across the room to Joss, Abraham caught her by the arm and tossed her backward. "I don't recall inviting you to this gathering, miss."

Kat tightened her jaw stubbornly, defiantly. Her eyes were bright and clear, her hair shining in the afternoon light that was pouring in through the window. For the first time, Joss thought that she was beautiful, absolutely stunning. She practically hissed at Abraham, "I don't remember asking your permission for me to be here. Now what have you done to Joss? He's covered in bruises and blood. His eye is all puffed up. That gash on his forehead is oozing. He looks awful! If you hurt him, I swear, I'll—"

"You'll what?" Abraham's tone was cool and crisp. Joss knew he didn't care much for Kat, but he wasn't even trying to hide his displeasure at her company now. "This, my dear, is none of your concern."

Without warning, Kat slapped Abraham hard across the face, the noise sounding out into the room, shocking them all. Joss sucked in his breath in a surprised gasp.

Abraham reached up, touching his fingers lightly to his cheek. Then he drew his arm back, as if to backhand Kat a good one, but Sirus and Joss were on him in an instant. They pulled him away from Kat, who stood there glaring at him defiantly. The other Slayers didn't interfere, just watched quietly, as if waiting to see how this whole thing might play itself out. Finally, Abraham wrenched himself free of their grasp and turned to Sirus. "Either she leaves tomorrow . . . or you do."

A sick feeling filled Joss's insides. He knew that Abraham wasn't just saying that Sirus would be packing his bags and leaving. He was saying something horrible, that Sirus would be kicked out of the Society. Or worse.

He wasn't sure if his uncle had been implying death, but he wasn't about to rule it out as a possibility. After all, he had yet to put all the Society's rules to memory. Maybe Sirus's insubordination over the years had been more serious than Joss had realized. Maybe Sirus's life was in danger, all because of his inability to leave his daughter again for an entire summer. Joss hoped not, but he really had no idea what Abraham had meant, other than the obvious: get Kat out of here. Now.

Sirus moved to Kat and gently guided her out the back door by the elbow. As Joss followed, he glanced at Abraham, not wanting to anger him, but knowing that he couldn't leave his friend alone. Not now. But Abraham wouldn't meet his eyes.

As Joss moved out the door, he could feel the heat and fuming anger pouring off of Kat. That, coupled with Sirus's tense silence, made for an awkward walk to the cabin next door. By the time they reached it, Joss was certain that Kat's head was going to explode.

Sirus opened the front door and Kat stepped inside. Once Joss had come in and closed the door behind him, she turned to him. "What did they do to you? It looks like you've been wrestling or fighting or something. What happened? And don't give me another one of your stupid vicious wildlife stories, because I'm not buying it. What really happened to you, Joss?"

He looked at Sirus, who folded his arms in front of him. Sirus's voice was hushed, as if he were trying to contain his emotions. "Kat, I want you to go upstairs and pack your things. I'm putting you on a train home tonight. It's for the best."

Kat's jaw dropped. "The best? Who says? Abraham? Come on, Sirus, you can't send me home. You promised we'd spend the summer together!"

Joss watched Sirus carefully. He looked as though he'd crumble at any moment. He needed help. He needed strength. He needed a friend. Joss looked at Kat. "I think you should do what he says, Kat. Your father has very good reasons for everything he's done. You should trust him, and just go pack your things."

Furious tears filled Kat's eyes and for a moment, Joss was certain that she'd slap him even harder than she'd slapped Abraham. Then Kat turned and ran up the stairs, slamming her bedroom door behind her. He turned back to Sirus, to try and offer some kind of comfort to his friend, but Sirus just shook his head and walked away. Joss took that as his cue that Sirus very much needed to be alone.

As he exited the cabin, Joss inhaled a deep breath and released it into the outside air. His insides felt heavy, but he wasn't exactly certain why. Kat would be safer away from this place, and Sirus would be safer without her here. Joss and Abraham had been cleared of any murderous accusations. And, smallest of all, Joss had managed to complete his run and was reasonably certain he'd passed his test. All, for the moment, seemed right with the world.

So if that was the case, why did he feel so upset, so lost, so angry? There had to be a reason he was feeling this way, and it couldn't just be the fact that vampires were lurking nearby, picking off Slayers one by one. He wasn't homesick—the comforting feeling of home had left him long ago, with the loss of Cecile. And though he was physically injured, it hadn't bruised his ego. Quite the contrary, in fact—Joss felt really good about his ability to stand up to two extremely talented fighters. So if none of those things could be the cause of his upset, then what could?

As Joss crossed the yard, he turned back to Sirus's and Kat's cabin. Slowly, he realized exactly what was wrong. He was going to miss Kat. Despite the fact that he'd pushed her away, and told her to listen to Sirus and pack, he was going to miss her more than he'd ever admit to. Because she was his friend, his first real friend. He knew with absolutely certainty why his chest felt so heavy and his stomach ached.

Because pieces of your heart clearly weigh more when they're sitting shattered at the bottom of your stomach.

·23·

FOR YOU, CECILE

Joss woke after a blissfully dreamless sleep and rolled over in his bed, reluctant to open his eyes. He'd tossed and turned for much of the night, repeating to himself every moment that he and Kat had shared, despite his reluctance to even think about her. Thinking about Kat hurt, and thinking about the fact that he was a large part of what was making her leave made him hurt even more. But despite his efforts not to have her in his thoughts, there she was, with every breath, every heartbeat.

He'd never really had a friend before, and certainly had never felt about anyone the way that he felt about Kat. He wanted to protect her, the way he'd wanted to protect Cecile. And the only way to do that was to push her away. The only way to save her was to hurt her, and that hurt him as well.

More than he would ever dare admit to.

Finally, reluctantly, Joss cracked open his eyes. Abraham was sitting quietly in a chair beside his bed, but spoke as if they were continuing a conversation. "You're quite right about that, nephew. I never hoped that you were the next Slayer in our bloodline. I'd hoped for your cousin Greg, or even his brother, Henry. But not you. You were the runt of the litter, so to speak. Greg was virile and quick, with a steady hand and a confidence that normally pervades our family. Henry was less confident, less physically apt than his brother, but with some training and direction, he would have made a fine Slayer. Then there was you."

He didn't say it with any intended hurt or malice. His words simply *were*. They rang of truth, a truth that could not have been easy to share. Nor were they easy to hear. "You were born a month early, too eager to come into the world, too impatient. And there were signs of weakness even then. You were born jaundiced because of a slight liver problem. It cleared up within months, but other weaknesses followed. You learned to walk much later than your cousins and had a reluctance to run from a very young age. But then . . . you found your legs, and I saw that you could outrun anyone around you. I wanted it not to be true—your incredible agility—waited for it to prove itself false, but there it was. You had a Slayer's agility, and later, a Slayer's skill with a weapon. You blew everyone away at archery, whether it was at camp or in school. And I knew that you were one of us, and that I'd have to train you, despite your remaining weakness."

Joss sat up in bed slowly, wrapping his arms around his legs, clutching his knees to his chest. He wasn't angry. He wasn't sad—not about the things that his uncle was saying. He was just disappointed in himself for having been such a . . . well . . . disappointment. "What weakness? What weakness do I still possess?"

Abraham sat forward in his chair, his eyes expressing a sorrow that Joss didn't quite understand. "You care about people, Joss. And though that is an admirable quality for a normal person to possess, you are a Slayer. Closeness, caring, these things can only harm a Slayer in the end, and will prove a terrible weakness in the armor of the Society. In truth, I'd hoped you'd fail at enough tests that I would be forced to send you home, to convince the Society that I had made a mistake about you, that you weren't a Slayer after all."

Joss rested his chin on his knees, watching his covers with false interest. He took in his uncle's words and realized that by hoping he would fail, that by doing everything within his power to make Joss fail, Abraham had actually been trying to protect him. From what? Vampires, certainly, but more than that. From everything that Sirus had been telling him. From a lonely, dangerous life without anyone to share it with. But then, didn't Sirus have Kat? Surely he'd been close enough to someone in order to have a child. Surely there was a chance—even a small one—that Joss could live a basically normal life outside his Slayer duties. It was possible. Wasn't it?

"Initially, I tried to talk Headquarters out of their decision that you were the next Slayer in my blood-line, but they were adamant. And then, when I asked what would become of you should you desert the Society after your induction, they instructed me to take your life."

Joss met his eyes, surprise and fear filling him.

Abraham nodded. "It's protocol for such situations, but I had to ask. Once I received my instructions, I turned to leave, but by the time my hand touched the door, my mind was set. I knew I could not allow my nephew to perish, and that with your sensitivities, your weaknesses, you would be better off living a life without the binds of the Society. I turned back to the man in charge and pleaded with him to grant me a single favor. And he did. He said that if you should fail at your training before induction, you could go free."

Joss's heart raced with the knowledge his uncle had shared. Was it true? Abraham had only been so hard on him so that he could save Joss from a life in the Slayer Society? Why hadn't he just told him in the beginning? But Joss didn't have to ask that. The Society wouldn't want Joss to have an easy out, so Abraham had likely been sworn to silence.

"I thought it would be easy to make you fail." Abraham spoke softly, with more kindness than Joss had ever heard his uncle use before. "But then you passed my tests, at times with flying colors. You've bested men with skill beyond their years of experience and succeeded in ways I had not deemed even remotely possible, especially not for a boy with such incredible weakness. But despite that weakness, you have an inner strength unlike any I have ever seen, Joss, and I will be proud one day to call you a Slayer. That is . . . if you still want to after hearing all that I've told you—which I shouldn't be doing."

Joss lifted his head and met his uncle's eyes, which were shining with pride. Suddenly, his insides felt lighter. He had something he'd convinced himself that he'd never have—his uncle's approval and the love of a family member. For a moment, he forgot about Kat and everything that had happened. He forgot about his healing wounds and the way his muscles ached. All he focused on was the admiration in Abraham's eyes.

It was wonderful. So wonderful, in fact, that a large lump formed in Joss's throat, rendering him unable to speak.

Abraham reached out and patted him on the shoulder roughly, an almost-smile on his lips.

When Joss found his voice, it came out with a croak. "I do. Very much, Uncle. I want to be a Slayer."

"That day is fast approaching, Joss, but there are still a few tasks at hand that need tending to."

Joss could feel moistness in his eyes, but blinked it away before his uncle could notice. "What tasks? I'm game."

Abraham patted him again and stood. "Meet me in the clearing in twenty minutes. In just three more minor tasks, you can be indoctrinated into the Slayer Society. And these last three are where it gets fun. The worst of your training is over."

Joss clung to those last seven words like they were a lifeline. The worst was over. His uncle had said it. And Abraham wasn't a man to lie about something like that. Joss pulled the covers off and hurried out of bed, a permasmile on his face. "I'll shower and be right out."

Abraham chuckled. "Grab some breakfast first. After yesterday, you certainly earned a good meal."

Joss nodded, still smiling, and Abraham walked out of his room, closing the door behind him. After grabbing some clothes, Joss hurried through a shower and bounded down the stairs. Sirus was nowhere to be found, but after last night's ordeal with Kat, he wasn't exactly surprised. He made a mental note to stop over and check on Sirus once he'd completed the task that Abraham had set up for him, and then filled a bowl with cereal and milk. After wolfing it down, he headed outside and up the hill along the trail until he could see the clearing up ahead of him. A strange scent was in the air—like smoldering ashes and decay.

As he drew closer to the clearing, he saw why.

Abraham and the other Slayers were there—all but Sirus, of course—and at the center of the clearing were two bodies. Their skin was charred and their eyes stared unblinking up at the sky, but their chests still rose and fell. Joss's breakfast edged its way up his throat, threatening to leave him. He paused in his steps, looking away from the gruesome scene, trying desperately to ease his sudden, growing nausea. If he threw up, he'd never hear the end of it. Once his stomach had settled to a more manageable point, Joss continued into the clearing, standing to Abraham's right, waiting for his uncle to give him his task. A task that would, hopefully, take him far away from the charred near-corpses in front of him.

"Early this morning we located the vampire outpost. These two beasts were inside, unaware that they'd been detected. We waited until first light, then dragged them outside into the sun. Luckily, they were pretty allergic, but not enough to kill them. Only enough to subdue them. Which is actually really fortunate for you, nephew, as ridding the world of these monsters in very specific ways is part of your training." Abraham held up a small, silver hatchet. It gleamed in the morning light. The sight of that glint seemed abnormally sharp, like the metal itself. He held it out to Joss. "So . . . are you ready to take the next step to becoming a Slayer, nephew?"

Joss looked from the hatchet to the vampires. They looked so human. Two eyes, a mouth, two ears, hands, arms, legs. And hearts. Did they feel? Did they know how? Did they know how to love as much as they seemed to know how to hate and destroy? Joss didn't know. And all of a sudden he didn't know if he had what it took to be a Slayer. It was one thing to fight with his fellow Slayers. It was quite another to take a life.

He shook his head slowly and took two steps back. He needed to think. He needed to think about what he was doing and why he was here before he did something so drastic, so unbelievably horrific and violent. Before there was no turning back.

As he turned away from the clearing, Abraham's voice found his ears, stopping him in his tracks. "What ever happened to the vampire, the creature, the monster that killed your younger sister, Joss? Did it leave her room that night with a full belly, content with the murder it had committed? Do you suppose it felt any compassion at all for that sweet, innocent child before it ruthlessly took her young life? Do you suppose it was so overcome with regret that it gave up its vampiric ways and took its own life?"

Joss gripped his hands into fists, his body tensing at the memory of that night—the night he lost Cecile. "No."

Abraham stepped closer, dropping his voice so that only he and Joss were privy to his words. "No, it didn't. That bastard moved on to other children, other sisters and brothers, perhaps, and murdered each of them with a defiant, bloody grin. You know it did. Just as you know that one of those things lying in that clearing could be the one who did it. You can right the wrong it committed that night, Joss. But only you can do it. Only you can lay Cecile's soul to rest. So are you going to man up and do it, or has this all just been for show?"

Joss closed his eyes and images of his sister raced through his mind, flipping like photographs in an album. Cecile in her crib. Cecile taking her first steps—to Joss, of all people. Cecile leaving for her first day of kindergarten. Cecile . . . dead in her bed. A vampire whose face he couldn't recall, poised over her with bloodstained lips. Cecile's blood.

He opened his eyes and grabbed the hatchet from his uncle's hands, wordlessly turning back to the clearing. He approached the two charred creatures with a confident step, though his actual confidence was absolutely lacking. With a shuddering breath, he raised the hatchet high and whispered aloud three words that he clung to, three words that would get him through every act he could not face alone, to remind himself exactly why he was doing this, exactly why he'd come here in the first place. "For you, Cecile."

Then he brought the hatchet down as hard as he could, his aim sure, his arm strong. As he did, a piece of his soul fluttered off into the air, like ash in the wind.

Hours later, once the monsters had been beheaded and their remains disposed of, the Slayers sat around a campfire in that same clearing. Mugs were filled with foamy drinks. Songs were sung. And Joss sat on a large stone near the fire, his blood-soaked hands still trembling wildly. In his mind, he kept repeating his sister's name, but it brought him no solace. There was nothing comforting about what he had just done to those vampires, and nothing just about the way that he felt now. Afterward his uncle had assured him that the act would get easier, that everyone experiences doubt after their first few kills, but that he'd done exactly what he'd needed to do in order to ensure the safety of all of mankind . . . and to avenge Cecile. But Joss didn't want to hear his words of comfort and assurance. He wanted to forget that it had happened. He wanted to wash away the blood and go home to his mom and dad. But he couldn't. He was in too deep.

Abraham gave his shoulder a squeeze and held up his glass. The other Slayers followed suit. "Today, my nephew, you became a man. And due to your bravery and unfailing loyalty in the face of danger, soon we'll call you brother and count you among our ranks. Slayers! We drink to Joss!"

Morgan, Ash, Cratian, Abraham, Paty—every Slayer in their gathered group raised their mug then in excited pride, toasting to Joss and celebrating his success. But Joss couldn't raise his eyes to see them do so. All he could do was stare at the blood on his hands and wonder how much more there would be.

·24·

ABSENT FRIENDS

That night, after a long, hot shower, Joss retired to his room. He had been planning to speak to Sirus, but honestly just couldn't face anyone until he'd had some time alone. In the shower, he let the scalding hot water wash away the blood, sending it swirling down the drain and away from Joss's shaking hands. But the blood wasn't alone. It mixed with Joss's tears—tears that fell in steady streams down Joss's cheeks. He cried without mercy—for Cecile, for the vampires he'd murdered, yes . . . but mostly for himself. It was shameful to feel so much pity for one's self, especially in this case, but Joss couldn't stop the tears from coming. He hoped the water was loud enough to mask his weeping, but couldn't be sure. Once the worst of his self-pity was over, he turned off the water and toweled himself dry before heading to his room for some much-needed solace.

He didn't sleep. He didn't think. He didn't relive any of the moments of his day. He merely lay in bed and stared at the ceiling for eight hours, pushing away all emotion until the sun had risen again. Then he dressed and went downstairs to find Sirus, to see how he was doing and if Kat had left without a fight.

Sirus wasn't in the kitchen. Nor could he recall having seen Sirus at all the day before. Eerily, he saw no one on his way outside and next door, something he was consciously grateful for. He stepped up on Sirus's porch and knocked before opening the door and sticking his head inside. "Sirus? You home?"

But what he saw made his heart sink.

Sirus's paintings were gone, as were Kat's video games, butterfly net, and books. He stepped inside, moving from this room to that. The house wasn't empty, but Sirus and Kat were nowhere to be found.

"We suspect he left sometime yesterday." Abraham was standing near the front door, looking troubled. "I didn't want to say anything to you until you'd had time to recover a bit. A first kill can be—"

"Traumatic. I know. You said so." Joss pushed away his uncle's acknowledgment of his horrific act and shook his head, his heart sinking some at the idea that Sirus would have just abandoned him without as much as a word. "He didn't even say good-bye. Not a note or anything. I can't believe he'd just leave like that. We were . . . friends."

Abraham cast his eyes slowly around the room. It was the first time Joss had remembered seeing his uncle at Sirus's house. "Sirus's loyalty has been in question for some time. By both the Society and yours truly. But even I was surprised to find that he'd defected. Foolish. Stupid. He knows what awaits him."

Joss glanced at his uncle with a question. "What awaits him exactly? What happens to a Slayer who defects?"

Abraham didn't speak for a moment, but when he did, his tone was serious and deadly. "He'll be banished. But it's a bit more complicated than that."

Joss nodded, even though he didn't really understand what his uncle had meant, and moved toward the door. As he passed Abraham, his uncle stopped him with a hand to his chest. Abraham's tone was grave. "It would be best, nephew, if you learned now not to ask questions. Questions require answers. And answers can cause trouble. You wouldn't want the Society to view you as a troublemaker, now would you?"

Joss shook his head, feeling his heart flutter a bit in uncertainty and fear. His words came out in a whisper. "No . . . no, of course not."

Abraham removed his hand and Joss stepped outside. The air felt oddly heavy and stale, the sun too hot on his face. On the surface, it was a beautiful day, but what someone sees on the surface isn't necessarily what's real.

Sirus was gone. Kat, too. Joss was left with nothing but his duty to avenge Cecile. Maybe it was better that way. Maybe being alone with his utter hatred of vampires was what he really needed. Maybe Abraham had been right, and his caring compassion for other people really was a weakness. Joss wondered why he hadn't seen it before now, that his friendship with Sirus and Kat had been such a terrible distraction from his reason for coming here, his reason for moving on after Cecile's death. He vowed to himself, and to Cecile's restless spirit, that he would experience no further distractions. Not until he'd located the vampire that had stolen her away, and made it suffer like no other had suffered before.

Once they were both outside, Abraham leaned closer, his hand on Joss's shoulder, and said, "I have another task for you, if you're up for it. This one will bring you ever closer to your goal, ever closer to becoming indoctrinated into the Society. But it will take an amazing amount of strength, Joss. I won't lie to you about that, or cater to your fear. Yesterday you faced the worst of it, but today will be a challenge. I'll leave it to you to decide whether or not you want to face this task. There's no shame in it if you can't. If you can, meet us in the clearing after lunch. If you can't, there's a train ticket lying on your nightstand. You decide."

Abraham walked away then, leaving Joss staring up into the too-bright sky. When he finally looked away, his vision was marred by dots of light, spots of shadow every time he blinked. A passing thought entered his mind, remarking on the strange similarities between darkness and light, and he wondered what he was representing now—was he light? Dark? Was he doing the right thing, at all costs? For a while, he'd viewed Abraham's tests as a cruel fate, a form of sadistic torture, but everything that he had seen reflected otherwise. Abraham was doing good. He was doing everything within his power to train Joss to do what it was that he'd come here to do—to take down vampires.

Joss was weak. He knew that now. And he was wrong to question the Society's wisdom, wrong to question his uncle's motives. Joss wished deeply that he could be more like his cousins, Greg and Henry, who would never question the things that they were told, who would never hesitate in doing what had to be done. Their loyalty, like that of most McMillans, was unfailing and admirable. Joss was a rebel in that regard, and that fact deeply embarrassed him. His need to question, and his disgusting need to act on those questions. Dark questions invaded his thoughts, like a disturbing voice in the back of his mind that insisted on spreading rumors that only he could hear—rumors about his uncle's motives, rumors about whether or not he was acting wisely. Only through focus and determination could he squash that self-doubt, that questioning, and only through the wisdom of the Society could he avenge his sister's death. He was deeply ashamed of his tears last night and vowed not to cry again, not to give in to the shadow of doubt that loomed over his experience in the clearing. Beheading the monsters had been an ugly thing. But it had also been just. It had also been right.

Hadn't it?

Joss shook his head, willing that doubt away. No more. From now on, he would never doubt his actions. He would trust in the Society and follow their whims. And through that loyalty, he would be rewarded.

He crossed the yard and entered the cabin, moving quickly, silently through the house until he reached his bedroom door. On his nightstand lay the train ticket, as promised by his uncle. On his nightstand also sat the pocket watch, and beside that, a small frame. The watch was a reminder of his grandfather and everything that he had given for the cause of the Slayer Society—everything, maybe, that Joss would give someday himself. Captured within the frame was a photo of Cecile, a smile forever frozen on her young face. Joss picked up the train ticket and tore it in half, then in fourths, then in eighths before tossing it in the trash can. He was staying, for all the right reasons.

Then he sat on his bed and stared at the clock, waiting for noon to come. When it finally did, hours later, he moved through the house again, not stopping for food, and headed outside to the clearing. When he reached his uncle and the others, he was greeted with looks of admiration. Abraham stepped closer to him, a smile on his face. "I'm so proud of you, Joss. It takes a real man to face the evil of these monsters once, let alone repeatedly. And though you haven't yet been indoctrinated, we wanted you to know—and I speak for everyone here—that we count you among our ranks already. In your heart, you are a Slayer, and part of our group forever."

Morgan moved closer then, holding something silver in his hand. "We usually wait until after the indoctrination for this, but . . . we figure that won't be too far off anyway. Besides, as Abraham said, you're one of us now, forever a part of our family. So take this."

Then he handed Joss a silver hatchet that gleamed in the light. "It's your first weapon. Care for it. Don't lose it. And swing it with absolute purpose."

Joss tightened his grip on the handle, marveling at the heft of the tool. His first weapon. He could hardly believe it.

Ash moved forward and spoke then, his voice kinder than Joss had ever heard it before. "We want you to remember that no matter where you go, no matter what you face, you are not alone. We're with you, Joss. Always."

Cratian thrust a small item he'd been cupping in his hand into Joss's other palm. "Keep this safe. Keep it forever. It means you're one of us."

Joss slowly held his hand out in front of him and peeled his fingers back, revealing a thick metal coin. On one side were graven images: a crescent moon, a stake, and an infinity symbol. On the other were letters in an Old English script—S.S., for Slayer Society—along with a quote that Joss desperately wanted to cling to. It made him feel safe. It made his actions—even those of yesterday—seem just and right and good and necessary. It read, FOR THE GOOD OF MANKIND.

As Joss closed his hand over the coin, squeezing it tight in his fist, Abraham spoke again. "It's a Slayer coin. We use them to identify one another in the field. If you produce a coin and the person you're with doesn't, they're not one of us and therefore, not privy to discussing all the details of the Slayer Society. It's a time-honored tradition, going back hundreds of years. And now you're a part of it, nephew. Forever."

Cratian slapped Joss on the back and grinned. "Now let's go kill us some vampires."

Joss blinked up at his uncle. "There are more?"

Ash chuckled. "There are always more. Damn things are everywhere. And it's our job to snuff them out before they infect the entire planet."

"I just thought that the two from yesterday—" Joss swallowed, trying hard not to conjure up the images in his mind of charred bodies and blood. "I thought they were the only two from the outpost you found."

Morgan interjected. "They were. But we found another outpost this morning—a cave about halfway up the mountain. We would have gone in after them, but we were waiting for solid daylight. And you, of course. Wouldn't want you to miss out on all the fun."

As Joss swept his gaze over the group, he noticed that each was armed with a wooden stake. Cratian had his in a leather baldric that crossed his chest. Paty had hers in a leather strap around her thigh. Abraham's was in his leather hip holster. Each of them was well armed, and all that Joss was carrying was a coin and a hatchet. He suddenly felt inept and unprepared. "When will I get a stake of my own?"

Ash chuckled. "You have to earn your stake, and though you've performed admirably, you're not quite there yet, Joss. Get indoctrinated. Then the Society will decide when you're worthy of a stake."

Joss frowned, concern crossing his thoughts briefly. Concern that he didn't share with the others, but which was apparently written all over his face. Abraham patted him roughly on the back. "Don't worry—you'll earn it. We all did. For now, you'll be charged with beheading the beasts after we drag them outside. You've got a knack for wielding an ax, after all."

Joss's heart skipped a beat.

When Joss looked down at the hatchet in his hands, his heart skipped another beat, but he willed it to steady its rhythm and nodded to his uncle with a confidence that he didn't really feel. He slid the coin into his front jeans pocket with one hand and gripped the hatchet with the other. His hands were steady, but it took an immense amount of control to make them so. He would not show weakness in front of his fellow Slayers.

And he was one of them now. They'd said. And he would never again give them reason to doubt his loyalty. They were his family now. And he would face down any danger that threatened them, that threatened any human. He would do so without question, without doubt, and with more courage than he had ever dared to use before. Because their cause was a just one, and through them, Cecile would one day find salvation.

As they made their way up the mountainside, Joss kept his head clear. He didn't think about the task at hand, didn't relive his first beheading experience, didn't think about Sirus or Kat or the comforts of home. He merely hiked upward with his fellow Slayers, ready for whatever the day would bring.

The day was still bright, but as the sun drifted through the trees, it didn't seem as bright as it had earlier in the day. Joss could gaze up at the sky without it hurting his eyes, could walk in the beams of light without thinking they felt too hot, or that the air felt suffocating. Everything seemed clearer now. Joss had obtained a focus and clarity unlike anything he had ever experienced before. He was, as the Slayers had attempted to assist him with weeks ago, pure.

As they reached the crest of a hill, Abraham silently gestured to the other Slayers, all but Joss, and they split into groups, moving off into the woods. They must be close to the outpost. Joss looked to his uncle for direction. Abraham pointed to a large nearby oak and then to Joss, indicating that Joss should wait there until they withdrew the first vampire. Joss moved into position, clutching the hatchet tightly to his chest, and waited.

The sounds of the forest filled Joss's ears. Peaceful sounds, of birds and breezes and furry things moving about through the undergrowth. For a moment, the serenity calmed his nerves, but it was a false calm. One that offered a promise of a quiet, easy day. One that lied through the sweet sounds and smells of nature. But Joss wouldn't hear its lies. He was ready. Poised to act. Awaiting Abraham's signal.

A howl, accompanied by a sizzling sound, echoed through the trees, followed shortly by Abraham's stern voice. "Joss! Now!"

Joss whipped around the tree, his fingers tingling with numbness from clutching the hatchet so tightly, his heart racing with adrenaline and a fear that he refused to acknowledge. Abraham was standing over a vampire which looked as though it had been set aflame by means other than the sun. Two other Slayers had staked down its wrists in a clear effort to hold it until Joss had removed its head. Why they hadn't staked its heart, Joss had no idea. But he suspected that today wasn't just an ordinary job for the group— he suspected that this was another test, another means for Joss to prove his loyalty to the Society. He raised the hatchet high above his head and brought it down, blocking out the screams that echoed through the forest, not knowing if they had belonged to the vampire or himself.

When he was finished, Ash and Paty cleared away the remains, and Joss took his position behind the tree again. He didn't look at his hands and without realizing it, he was grateful that the forest contained no reflective surfaces, as he couldn't have stood to look at himself at that moment.

But he was doing his duty as a Slayer. All that he had done, and would continue to do, was for the good of mankind. And for the release of Cecile's tormented soul.

After three more vampires, Joss was feeling numb. He told himself that the beheadings were no different than cutting wood for the fire, and he got through each mindlessly, doing his job, pretending he was somewhere else, keeping himself removed from each terrible, horrific situation.

"One more, Joss. Get ready!" his uncle shouted.

A hand closed over Joss's mouth and yanked him away from the tree, spinning him about so fast that for a second, he could not breathe. When the phantom hand released him, Joss looked around, but didn't recognize the part of the forest he was in. There was no trail nearby, and no sign of his fellow Slayers. His breath came in frightened gasps.

"You *should* be afraid, little one. I warned you this would happen."

Joss turned around quickly, his eyes falling on a familiar face. The face of the vampire who'd spoken to him in town. Zy. Joss tightened his fist, but only then did he realize that the hatchet was gone.

The vampire shook his head, clucking his tongue like a teacher chastising a student. "You won't be needing that. Not that it would do you much good to have it."

Joss's eyebrows came together in confusion. The

beast really did have the ability to read his thoughts.

"Hear them, actually. Reading thoughts would be quite a bore, considering how dull most human thoughts are." It cocked its head to the side. "For instance, you'd be amazed how much humans think about food. But then, I suppose vampires aren't all that different from you in that regard. Just a different type of food."

Shock and fear filled him. Abraham had said nothing about vampires being telepathic. Had he? How could you hide anything from these things if they had the ability to hear every thought in your head? His heart raced.

It closed its eyes momentarily. "Now there's a happy sound. The truth is, Joss, you can't keep your thoughts from me, and I'm not entirely certain your uncle knows about our telepathic gifts either. Not that he'd care to know anything about us but where to put that damn stake of his. But you . . . you're different. You're not like your uncle."

Joss set his jaw stubbornly. "I am just like my uncle."

It shook its head, its eyes reflecting a sadness that Joss did not understand. "No, Joss. you're nothing like Abraham. He's . . . he's a monster. There's good in you. You possess a quality that so few humans retain into their later years. Kindness. Openness. Acceptance."

"My uncle is not a monster!" Joss's heart was ramming against his ribs. His breathing came in deep, angry breaths. "You're a monster! You're all monsters!"

It kept its voice calm, hushed, as if it were trying to reason with Joss. "Not all of us. But some, yes. Just as humans, we are not a perfect race. Some of us do cruel, horrible, and unspeakable things."

Joss glanced around, looking for anything that might act as a weapon, but tried to keep his thoughts clear, so that the creature might not read his mind. His eyes fell on a sharp, pointed portion of a branch that had apparently been the victim of a recent storm.

The creature took a step closer to him. Joss remained still, not wanting to provoke an attack. "Say, for instance, some of us creep into young ones' bedrooms at night and rob them of their life before their time has come."

Joss's heart skipped a beat. He forgot about the branch entirely and looked at the vampire with wide, knowing eyes. It knew about Cecile. And though Joss had no idea if the beast had merely plucked the memory from his thoughts or had been the evil beast in question, he only knew that this was the closest he'd been so far to having answers about his sister's passing. He didn't dare to speak, merely stared at the thing in front of him, wanting answers.

It spread its arms wide, its expression blank. "I wish I had them to give, but that's not up to me."

Joss moved before the thought could enter his mind. He grabbed the broken section of branch and twisted around, then thrust his arm forward. The makeshift stake entered the vampire's chest with a popping sound. Blood gushed out over Joss's hands and he jerked his arms backward, as if he could escape the spraying crimson. His efforts were futile.

Blood sprayed across his face and Joss jumped back, landing hard on the ground, scrambling for anything so he could to hit the monster again. But as his eyes fell back on the creature, his heart settled into a somewhat normal rhythm again. It was lying face up on the ground, the sharp makeshift stake sticking out of its chest. He'd killed it, and for all he knew, it might have been the monster that had killed Cecile.

In the distance, he heard the Slayers calling out to him. He stood, brushing leaves and dirt and grime from his legs and looked around, trying to locate the origin of their voices. A different, unfamiliar sound filled his ears, distracting from their faraway cries. A low, intermittent whistle. It wasn't a bird, or a train—the train tracks were miles from here. Just the strangest high-pitched whistle that would sound off for several seconds before breaking and starting over again. Joss turned, cocking his ear to the side, trying to locate it. Then he paused. The whistle was coming from behind him, where the vampire's body was.

Stiffly, slowly, and full of wondering disbelief, Joss turned back toward the creature. It sat up just as slowly as he had turned, its body drenched with blood, its fangs elongated, its eyes fierce. "That wasn't very nice, Joss. I'm afraid you force my hand."

Joss looked at its chest, confused. He must have hit a lung. It was the only thing that could explain the whistling, and the fact that the monster had survived. It leaped toward him, pinning him to the ground, its still-flowing blood soaking into his clothes, his hair. "Monster?" It growled. "Who's the monster now?"

It reared back, opening its mouth wide, exposing its fangs. Joss struggled uselessly beneath it, but there was nothing he could do. The thing meant to have him for dinner.

He wondered briefly if he would see Cecile again.

Then, through the monster's chest came a sharp gleam of silver as a stake burst out. Abraham stood over the monster and Joss, his stake triumphantly through the vampire's heart. Abraham pulled the dead beast away and tossed it to the side, helping a shaken Joss to his feet. Then he handed the silver hatchet to his nephew and said, "I believe you dropped this."

Joss moved over to the creature and raised the hatchet high, bringing it down again and again with terrified, furious shouts until there was barely enough left to burn. The forest began to swirl around faster and faster, as if it had been placed in a blender.

Joss's world closed over him in black.

▸25◂

THE DARKNESS

J oss opened his eyes briefly—just long enough to see Abraham's face and to realize that he was in an ambulance. His uncle pressed his lips together, a glimpse of concern crossing his eyes. "It's okay, Joss. It's going to be okay."

As the darkness dragged him under once again, he heard someone—the EMT, perhaps—ask about his wounds.

"A mountain lion," his uncle replied, and Joss laughed hysterically inside his mind. All of the Catskills was going to be on the run from make-believe mountain lions.

But the hysterical humor disappeared along with the ambulance, his uncle, everything. Joss was alone in the darkness, with nothing for company but the emptiness.

▸26◂

SECRETS REVEALED

The next day Ash opened the door of Abraham's car and helped Joss out. "What did the doctors say?"

Ash already knew what the doctors had said—as did all of the Slayers. Abraham had called them from the hospital last night. Three doctors examined Joss, and each expressed deep concern over his wounds, which seemed suspiciously like abusive wounds. But Joss had convinced them, for the time being, that he had an abnormal interest in hand-to-hand combat, and that none of his wounds had been at the hands of his uncle. After many shaking heads and lots of whispering, they deemed Joss to be severely dehydrated—thus the fainting. They also deemed that he was sleep deprived and under an unusually high amount of stress for a boy his age.

They didn't know the half of it.

He'd spent the night at the hospital for observation; now that Sirus was gone, the Slayers had to risk the authorities to get Joss the care he needed. Every time Abraham would leave the room, a nurse would enter and tell Joss that it was okay to talk to them, okay to tell them if his uncle had been hurting him. No, Joss insisted. None of these wounds had been Abraham's fault. They'd been his. And that was the truth.

Abraham answered Ash very matter-of-factly. "They want him to rest, which shouldn't be a problem. Joss's training is at its end. With one more task—a sole hunt and kill—it'll be complete, but that can wait until next summer."

Joss nodded, and moved toward the house. Several other Slayers said their hellos on their way into the woods. On the drive back from the hospital, Uncle Abraham had told him to head straight to his room and pack so he could make the noon train. It was time to go home.

The other Slayers would be staying here for the duration of the summer, in an effort to locate the vampires' hive. If they didn't find it, they'd move on to other jobs and Joss would join them again the following summer to continue their search, until every inch of the Catskill Mountains had been thoroughly explored. The idea that their efforts might not be fruitful even after years of searching was exhausting, but it was a matter of duty and honor, and the Catskills had proven to be a desired location for vampire-kind.

Joss lifted his suitcase and set it on his bed, tossing his clothes inside. He retrieved his toiletries from the bathroom and tucked them near the bottom, then plucked up Cecile's photograph from his nightstand. He ran the tips of his fingers across her face, drawing soft lines across it in the light layer of dust on the glass. Then he placed her picture inside his suitcase, and the pocket watch inside his jeans pocket, and zipped the suitcase closed.

He carried his bag down the stairs and set it near the front door. As he entered the kitchen to grab a snack, his eyes fell on the stove, which brought his thoughts back to Sirus, back to Kat. With but a moment's hesitation, Joss headed out the back door and across the yard. He wanted to say good-bye to Sirus and Kat before he left. Even if they weren't really there to hear it. For all he knew, he might never see either of them again, and he just couldn't bear the thought of leaving things unsaid. It was a weakness he still possessed, but he promised himself he'd work on it. He'd work on all of his weaknesses, until he became a Slayer that even Abraham would envy.

He pulled open the door and stepped inside, a

strange sadness settling over him. He felt like he was mourning his friends, not just saying good-bye, and couldn't put his finger on exactly why he was feeling that way. As he moved through the house, he thought about every happy memory they'd shared. By the time he'd reached the kitchen, he was smiling. The kitchen, more than any other room, reminded him of Sirus. The smell of cooking food and the sight of clean dishes being put away. The sounds and smells and sights of comfort and home. All of that meant Sirus to him. Sirus was a caretaker, after all, and he was very good at his job.

Joss leaned up against the counter, cursing under his breath when he realized he'd somehow gotten spaghetti sauce on his shirt. Sirus must have been cooking before he disappeared with Kat and gotten some on the counter without realizing. Joss moved into the bathroom and rinsed his shirt off in the sink, ringing water from the cotton, hoping it wouldn't stain. Musing that there might be something in the medicine cabinet to help remove the stain, he opened the cabinet door. To his surprise, he found it filled with six different kinds of sunscreen.

Joss furrowed his brow. That was an awful lot of sunscreen for just two people. Or maybe he'd been storing it for all the Slayers' use, for the duration of the summer.

A strange stillness filled him as his eyes fell on the

cabinet below the sink. Surely it would contain nothing more than bathroom cleansers. Nothing unusual at all.

He stretched out his hand—it seemed like it took hours to do so—and opened the cupboard door slowly. Inside there were neat stacks of tubes of sunscreen. Rows and rows of them. Joss slammed the door and heard the neat piles collapse within. He stood there for a long, lingering moment, trying desperately not to put the puzzle pieces together, wishing he'd never entered Sirus's house to say good-bye. What a stupid idea, anyway! Saying good-bye to people who were already gone. What was he thinking?

It meant nothing, had to mean nothing. Because if Sirus's large collection of sunscreen meant what Joss feared it meant, then that would mean that Sirus was a liar. And a rather stupid one at that. If Sirus was a—he couldn't bring himself to use the "v" word; not even in thought—then why wouldn't he take more care to hide his sunscreen? Or had he hoped that someone would see it, and maybe put him out of his misery?

He looked down at the stubborn stain on his shirt and pressed his lips together tightly before moving back into the kitchen. His eyes moved from the small smear on the counter to the refrigerator and never before in his life had he wanted to see spaghetti leftovers sitting on a shelf in a refrigerator so badly. He placed his hand on the refrigerator handle and took a deep breath, holding it in his lungs as he pulled the door open.

The refrigerator was almost completely empty.

Except for a single item.

Joss's hands shook as he retrieved the bag from the top shelf. It was plastic, full of a crimson fluid, and marked with various stickers—one of them a biohazard sticker. Another sticker read Type A Positive.

Blood. He was holding a bag of blood. And what's more, it was a bag of blood from Sirus's refrigerator.

At first, he tried to rationalize it. Sirus was the caretaker. Maybe he kept the blood around in case he needed to perform a transfusion of some sort. Maybe he was worried about not reaching a hospital in time. After all, they were in the mountains, and the hospital really was pretty far away.

But the voice of reason kept invading his panicked thoughts, reminding Joss that while he'd seen Sirus cook many elaborate meals, he couldn't once recall having witnessed Sirus eating any of those meals. And the sunscreen . . . so much sunscreen.

Joss dropped the bag to the floor. It landed with a splat, but the plastic held, still containing the blood.

Horror crept over every inch of his insides, piercing his soul. Sirus was a vampire. Joss had been duped this entire time. What's more, he now knew why Sirus had run. The Slayers had been getting too close to discovering exactly who had turned on them, who was responsible for the deaths of Malek and Chazz. Sirus had killed them. Sirus was now working for the enemy.

Sirus *was* the enemy.

Joss's heart pounded so loudly in his ears that he almost didn't hear the scream coming from somewhere in the direction of the clearing. Instinctively he bolted out the door and toward the clearing, stopping only when he saw his uncle on the ground, his right leg bending at an odd angle, Sirus crouching over him with his hands covering Abraham's mouth. Abraham's stake had been flung across the clearing, no more than three feet from where Joss was standing. Sirus was pressing Abraham's mouth hard, the look on his face one of panic. "Shut up, Abraham! Just shut up. Let me think."

Joss bent down and stretched out his hand, grasping the stake in his hand. It was heavier than he'd expected, and he blamed its heft on the silver that snaked its way around the wood, coming together at its silver tip. Then he looked at Sirus and said—in a tone that seemed so calm and determined, in a voice that he barely recognized as his own, "What's there to think about, Sirus?"

Sirus stiffened at first, then sighed heavily, his shoulders sinking some. "Joss. Of all of them, it would have to be Joss, wouldn't it?"

Joss waited, getting a feel for the weapon in his

hand. He knew what he would have to do, and reminded himself that it was Sirus who had brought him
to this. It was Sirus who was forcing his hand.

Then Sirus lifted a finger to his lips and gave Abraham a pointed look, telling him to hush. He stood
slowly and turned on one heel to face Joss. His friend.
"This isn't what it looks like. It's not what it seems. So
think about that before you stab me with that thing
and force yourself to live with a regret you may not
recover from."

Joss gripped the stake, comfortable with its weight
now. He turned it over in his hand and held Sirus's
gaze. "Are you a vampire, Sirus?"

Sirus's eyes filled with sorrow. "I'm not your enemy, Joss. Please. Put the stake down."

Joss felt a lump form in his throat. He needed answers, but wasn't getting them. "Did you kill Malek
and Chazz?"

"No. I swear to you that I didn't." Sirus held his
hands out in a pleading gesture. "Joss, you know me.
Do I look like a killer?"

In all honesty, he didn't. But Joss couldn't shake
the image of all that sunscreen—enough for hundreds
of normal people, not to mention that blood bag in
the refrigerator. But this was Sirus. His confidant. His
friend. Relaxing his grip on the stake some, Joss shook
his head. "I'm a little confused."

Abraham lay there quietly, his eyes squeezed tight,

as if he were in immense pain and doing all that he could just to remain conscious.

Sirus shook his head slowly, looking pained. "I was bitten three years ago. And though I resisted, I was sent here time and time again to gather information about the Slayer Society. This was supposed to be my last Catskills mission."

Suddenly, Joss knew exactly what had happened to Sirus. He'd been bitten, once, and turned into a vampire's human slave. The Slayer manual had spoken about such an occurrence. He remembered that it was referred to as being made into a drudge. And what a horrible fate it was, unable to resist your vampire master's every command, no matter if it went against your beliefs or morals. That had to be it. Sirus was a drudge, and his vampire master had sent him back here to spy on his fellow Slayers, against his will. He looked at Sirus, at his friend, and wondered if it were possible to free someone once they were trapped by the binds of vampire control.

And the sunscreen. It was so obvious. Clearly, Sirus had to keep sunscreen around for his master. Joss suspected that master was Zy.

"It was never my intention to hurt you or the others, Joss. I swear it. I had no choice." The truth rang through in each of Sirus's words.

Joss lowered the stake, not knowing what to do, only knowing that he could never harm a friend. Not exactly to his surprise, Sirus turned and took off into the woods, probably headed to warn his vampire master, as he'd likely been ordered to do. He moved over to his uncle and knelt beside him. "Abraham? Are you okay? I'm going to go call an ambulance."

Abraham opened his eyes wide, the intensity of his pain all over his face. He reached up and grabbed Joss by the shirt. "Go after him, Joss. Don't stop until he's dead."

Joss furrowed his brow in confusion. He wondered if it were true what they said about people who suffered delusions after breaking a bone. "Uncle Abraham, it's not Sirus's fault. He's just a drudge. We have to figure out a way to help him."

"Help him?!" Abraham trembled violently as his body slipped into a state of shock. "Don't help him, Joss. He's a vampire! I saw his . . . his . . ."

Joss's eyes grew wide in disbelief as his uncle collapsed into an unconscious state. But not before he whispered one final word.

". . . fangs."

·27·

THE HUNT

J oss ran through the woods in the direction that Sirus had fled, his self-created wind brushing back his hair and tickling his eyelashes. He gripped the stake tightly in his hand, running, going, moving forward, not knowing if he was making any headway at all, and cursing himself for ever having jumped to the easy, forgiving conclusion that Sirus was merely a harmless drudge. But still he ran, his thigh muscles on fire, his focus clear and sure. He had to find Sirus, had to forget about the friendship he'd been duped into believing they had shared, and had to stake him through the heart.

He couldn't think about Kat and wonder if she had

any idea that her father was a bloodsucking monster now. He couldn't think about the way that Sirus had made him feel cared for in a way that not even his parents had made him feel. He couldn't think about anything but the wooden instrument in his hand and his duty to the Society, his duty to mankind, and his duty to Cecile.

Because every time Joss killed a vampire, he was setting her soul just a little more free. And if it damned him, so what. Let him be damned. But let Cecile's soul rest.

Slowing his steps for a moment, Joss whipped around. He didn't recognize this section of the woods and after spinning completely around, he really had no concrete idea of what direction he'd been heading in. In short, he was lost, with no idea how to find Sirus, let alone the clearing he'd left Abraham in. Joss turned slowly, making a guess at which way he'd been running, and moved forward through the woods until he spied something he had never seen before during his forest treks here. A small log cabin sat at the bottom of a shallow valley. Joss watched it warily, wondering if there were any occupants, and if there were, whether or not they were human. To be safe, he crept silently down the decline and around the building, ducking below the windows, until he came to a small door on the side of the house. The area around the cabin was unkempt and grown over, so it was likely empty, but

Joss had to play it safe. Vampires, it turns out, were immensely crafty creatures. He'd rather tiptoe around and find out the building had been abandoned rather than throw caution to the wind and end up dead. Or worse.

And there was something worse than death. He could be made into a drudge. Or, even more terrible than that, he could be turned into one of the walking undead. A vampire. Joss couldn't even imagine the horrors of that existence, and didn't want to. He'd rather be dead than be a monster that fed on the innocent.

He turned the knob slowly and the small door swung open without a sound, as if its hinges had been recently greased. The room he entered was pitch-black, and it was only then that Joss realized that every window had been painted over, allowing no sunlight to pierce the glass. His heart picked up its pace, but Joss calmed it at once, not wanting to draw any attention from the vampires that surely must reside here, in this small, nowhere cabin, lost in the woods.

As he made his way across the room, he used his fingers for sight. The counter led him to the refrigerator, and when he hit empty space, he moved forward slowly, reaching out into empty darkness until the tips of his fingers found the table in the center of the room. Beyond that he found a blank wall, and then a door that was standing open a single inch. From within that next room, Joss heard voices. One of them very familiar to him.

"More bloodwine, Sirus?"

"Please." Sirus's voice sounded agitated and upset, as if he'd been terribly wronged and was consulting with his friends in order to find a solution to his dilemma. "Abraham still lives, but he shouldn't be a problem. I broke his leg. Not a clean break, either. He won't heal quickly from that."

"Better than he deserves," a third voice declared. "You should have killed him, drained him dry."

Sirus sounded bemused. "Is that what you'd have done, Boris?"

The third vampire snarled. "I'd have taken my time, slurped every drop from every one of his lovely little veins. But not before tormenting him with a bit of fire. It's the least he deserves."

Joss leaned forward and quickly counted twenty-four vampires gathered in the dimly candlelit room. Plus Sirus. So twenty-five. He was no match for twenty-five monsters. Hell, he was barely a match for one, and that one he'd needed Abraham's help with.

As he ducked away from the door, back into the darkness, he thought about Sirus and wondered how it was that none of the Slayers had recognized him as a creature of the night. His movements, his mannerisms, seemed so distinctly human, not at all otherworldly the way that the other vampires seemed to be. Then it hit him. Sirus must have been around humans for so long that he was able to adopt their mannerisms. Even if what Sirus had said was true, that he had been a vampire for just three years, then that meant he was just three years out of being human and into being a monster. Joss paused, his thoughts darkening briefly. What did that mean for Kat? Was she a vampire, too? Did her mother know about Sirus? Did he kill her and leave Kat motherless? He vowed then to find Kat and protect her at all costs. She was very lucky that Sirus hadn't yet given in to his evil hunger and devoured her in her sleep as he likely had so many others. Joss would find her, no matter what, and protect her. As he should have protected Cecile.

A new voice spoke from within the next room. "There's been news in your absence, Sirus. News having to do with the Pravus prophecy."

Joss raised a curious eyebrow. Pravus. The word that had made his uncle so angry. What did it mean?

Sirus chuckled. "I don't need to ask who shared this bit of information with you. Need I remind you gentlemen that the president of the Stokerton council is about as nutty as a hatter?"

"He may be crazy, but he says he has proof, and I'm inclined to believe him. Rumor says the Pravus may be located in a small town called Bathory." This voice was deep, and the sound of it reminded Joss of pictures he'd seen of Scotland. It was old and lyrical.

Joss sucked in his breath. Bathory. That was where Henry lived.

The deep voice spoke again. "Keep this between us. We can't have any nonbelievers getting involved. Or should I count you among their numbers, Sirus?"

Sirus sighed. "I never said I didn't believe. Just that I don't believe that he is a man we should follow blindly."

Joss stepped silently away from the door. He turned toward where he remembered the door being, but slammed into what felt like a stove. As it yanked away from the wall, he heard a hissing sound. The air smelled like gas. And from the next room, a ruckus broke out. "What was that?"

"It's that damned boy, I know it!"

The deep, Scottish voice shouted, "Sirus!"

Then Joss heard Sirus's voice, just as he'd reached the small door that led to the outside. "Go after him, Kinley. And when you find him . . . kill him."

Joss burst outside and took off at a sprint, running as fast and as hard and as far as his legs would carry him, not slowing down to catch his breath or to stop his heart from bursting inside his chest. He just ran and ran and ran and ran, with no regard for his health or what was surely coming up behind him, hungry for his blood. He ran like never before and prayed to any deity he could possibly think of to let him reach the Slayers' cabin, let him get to a place of safety. Even if it wasn't actual safety. Just someplace he could pretend.

But an uphill run was taking more energy and more effort than he ever deemed possible. He was still too close to the cabin, too close to the vampires, and too close to death.

Above him there was a rustling sound, and just as Joss was about to brave a glance upward, the vampire that Sirus had called Kinley dropped from the trees and landed easily in front of Joss. With speed so fast Joss barely had time to blink, the beast moved close to him, shoving him backward, until Joss tumbled down the hill, toward the cabin he'd been trying so desperately to escape. It advanced on him, growling under its breath, so animalistic that Joss feared it might claw him into pieces before it even took a bite. Then it opened its mouth wide, revealing saliva-coated fangs, and Joss froze in fear, knowing that it wouldn't just bite him. It wanted very much to kill him.

Joss recalled the heft in his hand and thanked the stars that in his terror, he'd gripped his uncle's stake even tighter, so tight that the veins of silver were surely now temporary imprints in his skin. He slashed forward as hard as he could, but just nicked the beast's shoulder. It screamed in a roar of rage and Joss stepped back, tripping over a rock that he hadn't noticed behind his foot. Joss fell onto his back and, as the creature leaped forward at him, its teeth bared, its hungry tongue lolling inside its ancient mouth, Joss brought his knees up to his chest, a scream tearing from his throat until his vocal cords burned. He kicked his legs out just as the beast came down and to the shock and terror that now belonged to both Slayer and vampire, Joss kicked the monster backward. It flew through the air for a moment, but before it could regain control of its form, it slammed mercilessly into a large fallen branch, the sharp wood plunging through its back, piercing its heart.

The beast went still.

Joss scrambled to his feet, still gripping the stake in his hand—even harder now—and started to climb the hill once again. Then, from behind him, came a terrible explosion. The heat from the blast picked Joss up as if he were but a leaf on the wind and tossed him casually into a tree.

Joss's world—once again—went dark.

▸28◂

NO APOLOGIES

The pain came before consciousness. It was immediate, intense, and filled his entire head up until it felt like a balloon. A big, painful balloon. The thought occurred to him that he might have a concussion, and moments later, Joss opened his eyes.

He was lying on his bed in the Slayer cabin, under crisp white linens. His wounds—the few fresh ones he had—had been carefully bandaged. And the Slayers were standing around his bed in a semicircle, his uncle Abraham at the foot end, near the door. His leg was in a cast, and he was leaning on a sleek black wooden cane.

Joss couldn't remember how he'd gotten here, or even if he was really here at all. Maybe it was all a figment of his imagination. Maybe he was hallucinating from his injuries. Maybe he'd died in the explosion. He only knew that he was glad to be here, glad to see these faces, glad to feel like he hadn't completely ruined everything. Even if it wasn't real, it felt good not to think about monsters with fangs for a second.

Ash was the first to speak. "We thought you were a goner, Joss. Thought the damn things had tackled you in the woods and swallowed every last bit of you. But then we heard that explosion and tracked you down."

Morgan gave Joss a wink. "A word of advice, if I may? Explosions are an excellent way to kill the undead. But you should probably take a few steps back first, kid. But we can talk about that when I teach you more about explosives next summer. Of course, something tells me you might even teach me a few things."

Roaring laughter filled the room and Joss sat up in his bed a little, enjoying their company, and so, so glad that he was still alive . . . and a hero, apparently. Even if he hadn't technically killed all those vampires on purpose. Who needed to know? Dead was dead, as far as Joss was concerned.

With awe in her voice, Paty said, "You must have killed twenty vampires with that blast."

"Twenty-four." Joss's voice came out sounding weak, and a bit like someone had scraped his entire windpipe with low-grit sandpaper. It felt that way, too.

The Slayers all smiled proudly. All but one.

Abraham shot Joss a look that said that he knew that the blast was an accident, and that something about that didn't sit well with him. Then he turned and limped out of the room without as much as a single word of encouragement or dissent. Joss didn't know if he should feel berated or relieved, so he left it alone. He'd had enough unpleasantness today. The last thing he needed was another moment of heartache.

Slayers kept him company for most of the day. In fact, it wasn't until Paty had brought him a tray of dinner that evening that he realized they hadn't left him alone for more than a few precious minutes at a time. Were they watching him? Or did they just appreciate him and admire his efforts? He'd never know. But that evening, when he was lying in bed, waiting for sleep to come, Joss allowed his thoughts to drift through the pain medication's fog back to the explosion. With pained realization, he knew that something horrible had happened. Sirus had been in that cabin when the blast had occurred. He was dead. And it was Joss's fault.

Joss rolled onto his side and closed his eyes, willing sleep to come, willing the emptiness to take him away again, to take it all away. Because despite everything that had happened, he was mourning the loss of Sirus. And he didn't know which was more upsetting: that he'd killed a man he'd once counted as a friend, or that the man he'd counted as a trusted friend had betrayed him in the worst way possible. Joss focused on the betrayal, largely because it was easier to hate than to grieve. Sirus had lied to him. Sirus had turned his back on him. Joss vowed then and there that he'd never be duped by a vampire ever again. He would study them, memorize their characteristics. He'd know vampires better than any Slayer ever had. And he would kill them all.

After a long time spent lying in the darkness and fuming over things beyond his control, Joss's eyelids fluttered closed at last and sleep took him into its warm embrace.

It wouldn't last for long.

Sometime during the night—Joss couldn't be certain when—a noise woke him from his dreamless sleep. It was the sound of his door being opened and footsteps moving carefully around his bed. He opened his eyes to a familiar form, a shape he knew, in the dark of his bedroom.

She didn't speak at first. And when she finally did, her voice sounded hoarse, as if she'd been crying a lot recently. Joss would have bet that she had.

Kat straightened her shoulders, as if she were trying to retain some semblance of dignity. "You killed Sirus."

Joss sat quietly, allowing his eyes to adjust to the dark. When they did, he could see a sheen on her cheeks. She *had* been crying, might still be crying. After debating how to respond, he simply sat up in bed and said, "Yes."

She sat on the edge of his bed then and buried her face in her hands, her body racked with sobs. Joss wanted very much to comfort her in some small way. But he knew she'd never allow it. After all, he was the cause of this pain. So he waited, shifting his gaze awkwardly between his covers, the window, the door, the floor. Anywhere but Kat and the tears that he was causing. Several minutes later, when the worst of it was over, she dried her face on her sleeve and sniffled, her voice shaking. "They're not like you think they are."

A strange sort of panic gripped his chest then. What did she mean? That Slayers weren't the noble fighters, defenders of mankind that he believed them to be? The idea was both horrifying and preposterous. "Who?"

"Vampires." The panic in his chest subsided as she spoke, but was quickly replaced by a new feeling—one of dread. This wasn't a conversation that he wanted to have. He wouldn't be swayed, would never be convinced that vampires were anything other than the terrible, bloodthirsty monsters he knew them to be. But he owed Kat this moment. He owed her something, anyway. For having stolen her father away. She glanced down at her interlaced fingers. "Vampires aren't all evil. Just like humans aren't all evil. There are some good ones. Sirus was one of them."

Joss swallowed hard, uncertain how to respond. After a brief pause, he settled on, "How long did you know he was a vampire?"

"Since the day he changed into one."

Joss lost his voice in utter confusion for a moment. If that was true, then why did Sirus make a big deal over keeping all things Society-related secret from Kat?

"We kept up pretenses and I feigned ignorance whenever the Slayers were around, but I knew. Of course I knew. He's my father, Joss. Or was . . . now he's just a memory, thanks to you." She glared at him, her eyes welling over with tears once more. This time, she didn't bother to wipe them away. Maybe she knew that there would be more to come. Maybe the effort of keeping her face dry was completely futile with such immense sorrow. "The night after he was turned, he tried to feed from me, but managed to resist and promised to protect me forever. He also promised to turn me into a vampire when I got old enough. I've lost that, too, thanks to you."

Joss shook his head in disbelief. "You can't want that. They're . . . monsters."

The word fell off of his tongue in a disgusted whisper.

Kat stood, raising her voice angrily. "You murdered my father and his friends in such a cowardly way and have the audacity to say that *they're* the monsters? You sicken me, Joss. I wish I had never met you."

He shook his head, refusing to believe that she

wished their friendship had never been. "You don't mean that, Kat. You're just sad."

But even as the words fell from his tongue, he knew that she did mean it. The same way that he had meant it not so long ago.

"Because of you." With another glare at him, she turned back to the door. As she opened it, her hand still on the knob, more tears escaped her eyes. "Sirus didn't believe in vengeance. But Sirus isn't here anymore. I'll get you for this, Joss. I'll make you hurt twenty times more than you hurt Sirus, if it's the last thing I do."

She held his gaze for a moment before disappearing out the door, closing it quietly behind her. Joss stayed where he was, staring at the closed door, his heart heavy with the truth that had rang through in her words. He wondered, briefly, why she hadn't enacted her need for vengeance right then and there, but then he realized that the answer had been there in her eyes the entire time. Kat hadn't killed him because she wanted to take her time, wanted to make him suffer. Plus, at the moment, she was simply too sad to do so.

He sank into his pillow, his heart heavy, and wondered what the morning light would bring.

·29·

AN IMPORTANT HANDSHAKE

nd so it is with absolute pleasure that we officially induct you into the grandest and most noble of traditions and accept you as our brother in arms and fellow member of the Slayer Society." The old man tapped Joss lightly on each shoulder—the left, then the right—with a wooden stake, before smiling and congratulating him with applause. The room, high upstairs in the Old War Office building near the office of the Ministry of Defense in London, was full of Slayers from all around the globe. Hundreds of them, each more dedicated to the cause than the next. Their numbers were impressive when gathered in a single room, but not when you thought about the millions of vampires that were lurking around the world. They needed every Slayer they could get.

Joss hadn't been told they'd be flying to London, and the only bit of the city he'd seen so far was on the drive from Heathrow Airport to the Slayer Society Headquarters. But he was so glad that he'd come. He was a Slayer now. It was official.

Joss stood and shook several hands. But it was his uncle's hand that he was most looking forward to shaking. Turning around, Joss smiled to see Abraham crossing the room, leaning on his cane a bit as he approached his nephew, his face alight with pride. "A Slayer. What would your father think?"

Joss chuckled and shook Abraham's hand. "He'd think 'What's a Slayer?'"

Abraham chuckled and gestured around the room. "This isn't a place that many Slayers see often, Joss, so you should take it all in. This is where the Society was founded, and where important Slayers gather to debate exactly how we approach the vampire problem. You're standing among history—both the past and what is currently being made. It's quite an honor."

Joss looked around at the ornately carved wood, at the immaculate marble floors, at the arched windows overlooking the River Thames, and smiled. He was honored. To be in this room, among these people, yes. But more so, he was honored to be a part of their cause, to be an instrument in the driving force that would do all for the good of mankind.

Over the next few hours, Joss had his back pounded more than once and was handed drink after drink after drink until he thought his bladder might burst. Sneaking out into the hall in search of a restroom, the old man who'd overseen his induction stopped him briefly. "I forgot to mention, Joss. As your first station, you have a choice. Anywhere in the world. But have that location in mind by the end of next week. Abraham will contact you to finalize the details. Your father will receive an unexpected transfer, and a small raise in pay, which ought to alleviate any frustrations. Unless you'd rather travel alone."

Joss nodded as the man moved back into the main room. "I'll think about it."

"Joss." He turned to see his uncle, standing at the end of the hall. Joss glanced longingly at the restroom door, and moved back down the hall to see what Abraham wanted. Abraham's expression was serious. He kept his voice low. "There's something I want you to remember. Something that we will discuss later. Once the celebration has died down."

"What's that, Uncle?"

Abraham leaned closer, his voice in a near-whisper. "Accidents, while fruitful, do not a Slayer make."

A weight settled on Joss's chest. He opened his

mouth to speak, to explain, but Abraham shook his head adamantly. "Don't apologize or explain what really happened. Especially not here. I just want you to remember that."

Then Abraham turned and walked back into the room where Joss's indoctrination had taken place. It didn't take long for Joss's bladder to remind him what he'd been about to do before his uncle had interrupted.

Minutes later, Joss washed his hands in the sink and toweled them dry. As he was pushing the restroom door open, a hand, gloved in shiny black leather, closed over its edge. The owner of that hand was dressed in black from head to toe. Joss smiled. "Oh, sorry. I didn't know anyone was coming in."

"I was wondering if I might have a moment of your time, Mr. McMillan." The man stepped inside, a tone of urgency burning on the edges of his words.

Joss stepped back. "How do you know my name?"

The man nodded his head apologetically. "Forgive me. I haven't properly introduced myself. My name is D'Ablo. I learned of your induction through a friend of your uncle's and was hoping that you might be of assistance to me regarding a rather delicate matter."

Joss tilted his head to the side, curious. "If I can, I'll try. What is it?"

"I've recently learned that a small town in the United States is under siege by a vampire. A very powerful vampire. Something that vampires refer to as the Pravus."

The tiny hairs on the back of Joss's neck stood on end. There was that word again. Pravus. It seemed to hold so much meaning, but Joss was completely clueless about what that meaning might be. "I've heard that word before. Pravus. What is it? What does it mean?"

An intrigued glint shone in D'Ablo's eyes. "The Pravus is a vampire of prophecy. It's believed he will come to destroy us all and end our way of life."

Joss straightened his shoulders. "I'm too old to believe in fairy tales, mister."

"Ahh, yes. But no one is ever too old to stop fearing what lurks in the darkness."

Instantly, the image of Cecile's killer looming over her bed in the dark of night flashed through Joss's mind. So hard, so quick, that it made Joss gasp.

D'Ablo shook his head, looking positively distraught. "The trouble is, even after pleading with members of the Slayer Society, no one will take my concerns seriously. And this is a serious matter, I assure you."

It was a serious matter. A vicious vampire loose in an unsuspecting town of humans? Very serious, indeed. "How can I help? If you've been through the usual Society channels, I don't see what else I can do."

"The Slayer Society has placed this task on a list of items to investigate. A long list. But my insistence that this beast must be stopped sooner rather than later has fallen on deaf ears. I think it would be best if this vampire were taken out of commission, as it were." D'Ablo's eyes darkened, then immediately brightened once again. "Killed, to be clear on our terms."

Joss bit the inside of his cheek for a moment before responding. Even as he did, he already knew the answer to his query. He'd heard the town's name in that dark vampire cabin and hoped beyond reason that the creatures had been wrong. But he knew they weren't, even before he received the answer to the question poised on his tongue. "Where is it? What town?"

"A small, nowhere place by the name of Bathory." Joss's heart seized at D'Ablo's words. Bathory. Home to his cousin Henry. There was a powerful, evil vampire lurking in the town where his family lived. An almost-panic gripped him. D'Ablo sighed, as if all hope was lost. "I am willing to pay handsomely."

Joss shook his head, images of bloodstained vampire fangs poised over Cecile's pale face filling his thoughts. They were followed by images of his cousin Henry, who he loved more than any brother he ever might have had. "I don't need money. I'm a Slayer. Killing vampires is my job. My duty." Hesitating, he thought about his mother, about the thrice a week therapy sessions she'd been attending since Cecile's passing, about the stack of bills on the kitchen counter that continued to grow, adding to his parents' stress. Then he lowered his voice to a near-whisper, almost ashamed to ask the burning question. "But out of curiosity . . . how much?"

An eager glint crossed D'Ablo's eyes. "Twenty-thousand American dollars. Ten now. Ten when I have a body."

Though his thoughts focused very much on all of those zeros, Joss mindlessly uttered, "We're not supposed to take private jobs."

"Slayers do it all the time. They just don't talk about it." D'Ablo leaned closer, smiling. "It'll be our little secret."

At this, Joss felt his mouth open and words escape, though he wasn't certain why. He wasn't sure if he meant them, wasn't certain whether he intended to follow through at all, but he spoke, and D'Ablo smiled. Before Joss realized it, he extended his arm, shaking D'Ablo's hand. "Mister . . . you've got a deal."

▸ 30 ◂

A SLAYER'S GIFT

Joss tucked the last T-shirt into his already-full suit-case and zipped it closed. He'd been doing his best to keep a guilt-ridden expression on his face all week since he'd been back at home with his mom and dad. Abraham had written them a long letter explain-ing that Joss had been fighting with the neighbor boys all summer and needed some good old-fashioned dis-cipline to teach him a lesson. Abraham recommended that perhaps some time away would help and had ar-ranged for Joss to spend the next school year with his cousin Henry, in Bathory. Of course, Abraham and the rest of the Slayers thought he'd chosen that town simply because it was close to family, and he was interested in doing some reconnaissance. Little did they know that Joss was on his first actual solo hunt. For the vampire called the Pravus.

It had disturbed him how readily his parents had agreed to send him away for nine months, but he couldn't say it surprised him. Joss was a reminder of his sister, and neither of them could bear the thought of Cecile. Besides, it would be easier to ignore even the invisible boy if he wasn't around.

From his front pocket, Joss withdrew the pocket watch that had once belonged to his grandfather. He pushed the button on the top and the tiny door swung open, revealing the picture of Cecile that he'd placed inside. He'd carry her image with him always, the way he carried her memory inside his thoughts, inside his heart. Then, snapping it closed again, he returned the watch to his pocket and lifted his suitcase, carrying it down the stairs. Outside, the taxicab honked its horn. Joss opened the door.

A man was standing on the front porch, wearing a pleasant smile, but he wasn't the cabbie. The cabbie was still sitting in the drivers' seat, looking impatiently at his watch. Strangely, the man on the porch looked familiar to Joss, but even with some thought, Joss couldn't place him. The man's copper hair shined in the sun. Under his arm, he carried a small wooden box. "Joss."

The man nodded his greeting, as if they had met and spoken many times before. Joss was embarrassed to admit that he couldn't recall those meetings, so he simply smiled. "Yes? Can I help you?"

A sad shadow passed briefly over the man's bright eyes. "I'm afraid not. No one can."

Immediately, Joss had the undeniable urge to help the stranger in whatever way he could, but he wasn't certain how to convey that without sounding like a psycho.

Then the man's eyes brightened again, as if a breeze had carried the troubled clouds away. "I brought you something. Something from the Society. May I come inside?"

It might have been an odd thing to trust someone you cannot recall having met, but Joss opened the door and gestured for the man to come inside. Anything from the Society was welcome, of course. But as the man passed through the doorway, Joss withdrew his Slayer coin from inside his jeans pocket and held it out in his palm for the man to see.

The man's eyes lit up and he patted his shirt and pants pockets with his free hand before casting Joss an apologetic glance. "My apologies. I'm afraid I've misplaced mine. I do have one, though. I keep it for just such occasions as these."

Joss frowned, but nodded and put his coin away.

It was a believable excuse. Coins are small and easy to lose. Besides, the man knew about the Society. He had to be a fellow Slayer. When the man entered, he crossed the house to the den, as if he'd been here many times. Once Joss had entered the room, the man closed the French doors so that they'd have some privacy in his gift giving. Then he set the wooden box upon Joss's father's desk and smiled proudly at Joss. "For you, Joss McMillan. It's been a long time coming."

Joss hesitated before crossing the room to the desk, though he wasn't certain why. When he reached it, he opened the lid of the box and gasped aloud. The inside was lined completely in velvet, and though the box and its contents were clearly very old, they were in impeccable shape. In dedicated sections, Joss found a cross, hammer, various small bottles, and at last, the most beautiful wooden stake that he had ever seen. As his fingers danced lightly over the wood, he swore that the man who'd gifted him with the artifacts shivered, but couldn't be sure. "This is . . . wonderful. Thank you."

"It belonged to your great-great-great grandfather, Professor Ernst Blomberg." The man smiled proudly. "I brought it from London. It seems Headquarters over-looked giving it to you after your indoctrination."

Joss didn't know what to say, so he repeated himself, hoping that better words would come to him in a moment. "Thank you."

The stranger extended a hand then, shaking Joss's hand warmly. He smiled, his eyes so full of kindness that it almost hurt to see it. "The pleasure is all mine."

"But . . ." Joss looked from the stake back to the stranger. "I thought I wasn't supposed to get a stake until after I made my first solo kill."

The man's smile didn't even wane. "Let's just say an exception has been made, shall we?"

Nodding, not really understanding why an exception would be made in his case, Joss plucked the only empty bottle from the case and held it up. The worn label on the side read "Holy Water." Joss furrowed his brow. "What happened to the holy water?"

The man opened the French doors and shrugged back at Joss. "I'm afraid I got a bit thirsty on the way over."

As the man was leaving, it seemed in a hurry, Joss gathered up the box and its contents, and went after him in quick steps. He breathlessly caught the man just as he was stepping off the front porch. "Wait! You never told me your name."

At that, the man turned back to him, his smile friendly, the sun gleaming down on him from a crystalline sky, and said, "My name is Dorian."

Behind him, Joss heard his mom calling his name.

"Joss, that cab is going to leave without you. Do you have everything you need?"

Joss looked back at her and nodded. When he turned to Dorian, his mysterious gift bringer was nowhere to be found. But something told him he'd see Dorian again. And soon.

Turn the page for a sample

of the next novel in

THE SLAYER CHRONICLES series,

SECOND CHANCE

PROLOGUE

Kilian whipped around the corner of the building, his long hair flowing behind him, his coat billowing in the wind. His heart beat steadily in an unhurried pace. His breaths came even and smooth. But Kilian was terrified and didn't know where to go, or who could possibly help him. He was alone now but for his tormentors. His brother, Jasik, was nowhere to be found. Perhaps they'd killed him. Perhaps Kilian had no brother now. He pressed his back against the brick wall, sinking as deeply as he could into the shadows, hoping against all reason that the vampires who'd been hunting him would give up their chase.

His stomach rumbled, and inside Kilian's mouth, his fangs elongated. He was hungry. Famished. He hadn't had a drop of blood to eat for two days. He needed sustenance. Especially if he was going to be forced to face off with four vampires who were much older, much craftier, and much stronger than him. But the city streets were eerily quiet, and even though Kilian was straining his ears to listen, he couldn't hear any human heartbeats in the near vicinity.

But he did hear something. Something that made his breath catch in his throat, and his hands clench into nervous fists at his sides.

Laughter. And footsteps. He wasn't certain which scared him more. But he did know that both belonged to four different people. And those people, those vampires, were headed straight for him.

"Come out, come out, wherever you are," called a singsongy voice that he could only attribute to Boris. Kilian turned his head, peering down the street—at first in the direction that the voice had come from, and then the other way. There was no escaping them, that much he knew. He could run, but they would find him. They were relentless, and nothing he could do would stop their pursuit of him.

But that didn't mean he wasn't going to try.

With a deep breath, he darted down the street with vampiric speed. He came to a stop several alleys over.

His ears were greeted with only a moment's silence before the brothers found him once again. This time, it was Kaige who spoke. "You'd think a vampire would remember that a rush of adrenaline only makes the blood taste that much sweeter."

Laughter, cold and hollow, followed. Then a smaller, less-confident voice chimed in with marked hesitancy. "The Council's put a warrant out for us. Maybe it would be wise to stop killing humans in the open now, and beg for Em's forgiveness. She might be lenient."

"Lenient? When in Em's existence has she ever proven to be lenient when a vampire has broken the law?" Their voices put them just around the corner from Kilian. And even though there were a million places he could run, Kilian felt trapped. A thread of panic tickled its way up his spine.

"Curtis is right, Sven. Em will kill us for our crimes. That is, unless we give her reason not to." Kilian could hear the smirk on Boris's lips. "That little stunt pulled by Slayers in the Catskills last summer? I just got wind that the Slayer Society's calling that group in to deal with us. If we bring her the head of the Slayer responsible, she might find it in her stone-cold heart to forgive our crimes."

"What about our friend here?"

Kilian darted his eyes all around, but couldn't see them, couldn't even sense their presence anymore as the terror took hold of him at last. He couldn't breathe, could barely move, and the exhaustion of running from them was finally catching up to him.

"Taking the life of a fellow vampire would be breaking the highest law. Is handing over one Slayer really going to ease Em's temper after that?"

His fingers were trembling as he traced his hand along the brick wall, stepping back, deeper into the alley. He had to get away from them long enough to regroup his thoughts, to quell his panic. If he didn't regain control of himself . . .

"Over twenty died in that blast. I say we kill him."

"So do it already."

A hand reached out from the darkness.

Teeth followed.

▸ 1 ◂

THE SAD REALITY

J oss lifted his suitcase from the trunk of his dad's car and turned to say something to his dad—something light and conversational about how it was good to be home, even though it wasn't, not really—but the side door of the gray house that they now called home was already slamming closed. So much for his homecoming. The drive from the airport had been long and silent—a strange, indescribable tension hanging in the air between he and his dad. It was like riding in the car with a stranger who couldn't stand the sight of you. Worse, though. Far worse. Because the stranger was his father.

The silence had given Joss time to reflect on the

school year that he'd just spent away, however. Not that they were pleasant memories. In the beginning they had been. Joss had lived with his favorite cousin, Henry, and had befriended a boy named Vlad. Only Vlad turned out not to be a boy at all, but instead a vampire.

Just like Sirus.

Joss had been duped twice now by vampires, taunting him with the gift of friendship, only to have them rip it away again with their horrible, menacing fangs. He was done with friends. He was done with searching for companionship. He only had his want of vengeance now, and the sense of duty and honor that had been given to him by the Slayer Society.

And his stake, of course.

Inside his right front jeans pocket, his cell phone buzzed to life. He withdrew it and flipped it open to read the incoming text message. It was her. Again.

He wasn't exactly certain how Kat had gotten his cell number. But she'd been sending him messages for days now—each one more troubling than the last.

This one was brief: ARE YOU GOING HOME FOR THE SUMMER, JOSS? MUST BE NICE TO HAVE A FAMILY TO GO HOME TO. I'M COMING FOR YOU. DON'T FORGET IT.—K

He chewed the inside of his cheek briefly, considering a reply. But then thought better of it and flipped the phone closed again.

Kat would have to wait.

He shut the trunk and lugged his bag across the lawn to the door, remembering a time when he and his family had lived in a yellow house. A house that had been filled with sunshine and laughter and love. It felt like those memories had transpired over a million years ago, in a time that they'd all forgotten. For a brief moment, Joss wondered if that time—when Cecile had been alive and their family had been whole—had just been a dream. But then he shook his head. No. It couldn't have been a dream. Not one of Joss's, anyway. His dreams were dark. His dreams were awful, haunting images that never let the goose bumps on his flesh settle. His dreams were nightmares. Nightmares about Cecile.

As he moved toward the house, he thought about the dreams that had been tormenting him since his sister's demise, about how they usually featured flowers in some way, and he wondered if they would ever stop. But he also wondered if they were just dreams, or if—as crazy as it sounded—Cecile was reaching out from beyond the grave, hell-bent on revenge. He didn't like having those thoughts—so much so that he usually pretended that he never had them—but the fact was that he spent too much time worrying about his dream sister in ways that he had never worried about Cecile. The dream Cecile scared him more than anything, even vampires, and he always felt so powerless against her. She carried messages with her, messages of his impending doom, impending death, and he worried, as silly as it seemed, that his death would not come from his job as a Slayer. But from Cecile herself.

It was stupid to think those things. And if ever asked, Joss would have laughed off the notion that he believed his dreams could ever physically hurt him. But the truth was, he wasn't at all convinced that they couldn't.

As he pulled open the screen door and lifted his bag over the threshold, he spied his mother sitting at the dining room table, that faraway look in her eye. Joss knew that look well, as it had been growing steadily worse every day since Cecile had died. His mother was a fragile creature, in ways that she had never been fragile before. He kept his voice low, so as not to startle her. "Hi, Mom. How are you?"

She glanced up from her sad fog and nodded, forcing a small smile. It made Joss's heart break to see his mother acting as well. "Fine, Joss. I'm just fine. How was your trip, dear?"

Stepping inside, he closed the door behind him and set his suitcase beside the laundry cabinet. "It was interesting. A lady sitting beside me on the plane was very chatty."

"Nice chatty?"

In a moment of pure awkwardness, he simply nodded and smiled. They were both actors now, and he hoped against hope that his mother couldn't see through his facade the way that he could see through hers.

He pulled a chair out and sat down at the table, grateful for this time, this moment with his mother before his father started in on him about something he'd done wrong in the five seconds he'd been home. Their relationship—his and his dad's—had changed dramatically since Cecile's funeral. His father had pulled away into a protective cocoon, and no amount of hugs or talks or high fives could break through that barrier. It was as if, through Cecile dying, his entire family had perished as well. He would have done anything to change it, to turn back time and have his family again. But there was nothing, Joss was slowly realizing, that he could do to restore their happiness. So he was doing the next best thing: hunting down the vampire that had destroyed them all. And when he found the beast, he was going to make it suffer.

"Joss." The look on his father's face as he entered the room was one of irritation. "Take care of your luggage. I shouldn't have to tell you that. You're old enough to start taking some real responsibility around here."

Joss's ears burned slightly. If his dad only knew that he was incredibly responsible, that he'd been charged with saving humankind, that he was someone that the world was unknowingly relying on for support. . . .

But his dad didn't know that, would never know that. As Abraham had taught Joss, being a Slayer was a thankless job, and one that had to be kept in the strictest secrecy. Even from your parents.

"Sorry, Dad. I'll take care of it right away." Joss pushed his chair back and stood, reaching immediately for his suitcase.

As his father turned from the room, he grumbled, "And we still have to discuss that report card of yours, young man."

Joss wrapped his fingers around the handle of his suitcase and picked it up, letting his eyes follow his father out of the room. He missed his dad more than anything—maybe even more than he missed Cecile—but he knew, deep down, that the father he had known and loved was gone for good, forever changed by an experience that haunted them all like a shadow in the corner of every room. With a heavy heart, he moved up the stairs to his bedroom without another word.

He'd only been to the room once before, just long enough to move some boxes inside. Then he was in the car and on his way to the airport, his dad lecturing him on how to behave while he was living at Aunt

Matilda and Uncle Mike's house. He hadn't even had a chance to unpack before moving on to Bathory, to a life that would bring him in close contact with a vampire called Vladimir Tod. He clenched his fists at the thought before entering his room.

His bed was unmade, and lining the walls were piles of small boxes, containing most of Joss's insect collection and books. The room looked more like a temporary storage facility than a teenage boy's bedroom, and didn't exactly provide the "welcome home" feeling he'd been daydreaming about. He lifted the bag and set it on top of the trunk at the foot of his bed, then retrieved a set of sheets, blanket, and pillow from the linen closet in the hall. For now, anyway, this house was home to him, so it was time to settle in and remind his parents in whatever subtle way that he could manage that they hadn't lost both of their children that night. They still had a son.

After making his bed, he reached for a box on top of the nearest stack and pulled it down, setting it on the floor by his feet. He crouched and tore the lid free from the packaging tape that had held it closed. Inside, under a wad of newspaper, were a stack of carefully bubble-wrapped frames. At a glance, he recognized them as some of his favorite collected specimens. He lifted them out and set them gently on the bed, then returned his attention to the box. The remainder of it was filled with books. Looking around the room briefly, Joss located his bookcase and picked up an armful of books. It was time to get to work. Time to put things away.

An hour later, his bed was crisply made, his bookcase was full and neatly organized, and the shelves on the wall were home to his favorite specimens. On his nightstand sat a small silver frame, containing a photograph of Cecile. Not nightmare Cecile, but real Cecile. The sweet, blond cherub who had brightened his life the moment he'd seen her in the hospital nursery.

He broke down the boxes as he emptied them, stacking the cardboard neatly in the hall outside his door. It was another mindless task—one where he didn't have to think about his shattered family or his botched private job or the betrayal of his closest non-family friend to date—and he welcomed it. He had seen too much in the past year of his life that he couldn't forget, that he couldn't numb away with the aid of video games and mass quantities of caffeine. And now, with the betrayal of Vlad, he was in danger of losing his cousin Henry as well. It was unbearable, to be so alone, to know that he had no one who he could rely on, that—apart from the Slayer Society—he was on his own. And the idea that Henry could even consider siding with a vampire against him! It sickened Joss. It hurt him. In ways that Henry could never understand.

So Joss needed mindless tasks. He needed a void in which he could tumble and roll without a care in the world, so far away from the harsh bleakness of his reality.

As he peeled the bubble wrap back from the framed Black Corsair, Joss smiled. This time it wasn't an act. This time it was a real, honest, actual smile, brought on by the love of his grandfather and the framed gift he'd bestowed upon Joss before he'd died. The Black Corsair was a large insect, and at first glance, there didn't seem to be anything vicious about it at all. But just try explaining that to the May beetle, the preferred victim of the assassin Corsair. The Corsair would attack from behind and hold on to their prey with the spongy pads on their legs. They were sneaky, these assassin bugs. Deadly. And no one would know it by looking at them. Just like a Slayer.

He'd wished he'd known that his grandfather had been a Slayer, but it was probably for the best that he hadn't. It was important for a Slayer to keep his position secret, especially from his family. Having that secret revealed could endanger them, and that was inexcusable. Family was important. More important, maybe, than anything else in the world.

His smile slipped, fading away just as quickly as it had come, and Joss set his prized possession on the bed. Stepping over the pile of cardboard, he moved back down the stairs and rummaged in the junk drawer for a hammer and nail. The Black Corsair, as in every house they'd lived in since he was eight, would hang in its place of honor over his bed.

Digging through the drawer, Joss frowned. In this house, much like every house they'd lived in, the nails and screws and batteries and tools and flashlights and weird things that had no place found their home in the junk drawer. But not a single nail was in the drawer. Furrowing his brow, Joss said, "Hey, Mom, where's a nail? I want to hang up my Black Corsair."

His mother was still sitting at the table, but now a steaming cup of tea sat on the table in front of her. Her fingers curled around it, as if huddling for warmth. The tea-bag string dangled over the cup's edge. He was about to ask her again, when something in her eyes shifted, as if the fog had momentarily lifted. "There's a box of them in the garage. Your father can show you."

He hesitated before he moved, mostly because he knew what would happen if he asked his father for a nail. They'd discuss his grades, or the fact that Joss needed a haircut, or something else that had nothing to do with the fact that his dad was still grieving and had turned Joss into the Invisible Boy. He bit the inside of his cheek until he couldn't bear it anymore. Then, on his way back upstairs, said, "It's okay. It can wait until later."

"Oh. Joss? I forgot. This came for you earlier."

When he turned back, his mother was sliding a large white envelope across the table toward him. Joss moved back down the steps, retrieved it, and headed upstairs. He was in his bedroom before he ripped the end of the envelope open. When the small parchment bundle tumbled out, his heart picked up its pace some. It was wrapped in a burgundy ribbon, and held closed with a wax seal that bore the initials S.S., meaning that it could only be from the Slayer Society. He wagered they were simply requesting his final notes on the reconnaissance he'd convinced them he'd done in Bathory, but hoped it was his new assignment, and that it would take him far away from this house and the emotional ghosts that haunted it.

Joss,

Your presence is required in Manhattan in two days time. There is private business to attend to. Bring your supplies and pack enough clothing for the entire summer. All arrangements have been made.

—Abraham

Don't miss the series that started it all...

The Chronicles of (S)
Vladimir Tod
by Heather Brewer

Visit **www.VladTod.com**
for exclusive access to sneak peeks,
author appearances, and sweepstakes.

Visit HighSchoolBites.com
for exclusive Vlad Tod products